A LETTER TO PEACHTREE

Benedict Kiely is a native of Co. Tyrone but has spent much of his life in Dublin where he went, as a student, to University College, and where he now lives. He has worked as a journalist and broadcaster, and also a university lecturer, both in Dublin and in different parts of the USA where he is well known for his New Yorker pieces. His most recent books have been fiction, *Dogs Enjoy the Morning, A Ball of Malt and Madame Butterfly* (stories), a much-praised short novel, *Proxopera*, published in 1977, and, most recently of all, *Nothing Happens in Carmincross* (1985). His celebration of Ireland, *All the Way to Bantry Bay*, was published in 1978.

BENEDICT KIELY

A Letter to Peachtree

and nine other stories

A Methuen Paperback

A Methuen Paperback

A LETTER TO PEACHTREE

British Library Cataloguing in Publication Data

Kiely, Benedict
A Letter to peachtree and nine other stories.
I. Title
823′.914[F]   PR6061.I329

ISBN 0-413-16490-X

First published in Great Britain 1987
by Victor Gollancz Ltd
This edition published 1988
by Methuen London Ltd
11 New Fetter Lane, London EC4P 4EE
Copyright © Benedict Kiely 1987

Printed and bound in Great Britain
by Cox & Wyman Ltd, Reading

CONTENTS

ETON CROP

I HAD AN uncle once, a man of three score years and three, and when my reason's dawn began he'd take me on his knee, and often talk, whole winter nights, things that seemed strange to me. He was a man of gloomy mood and few his converse sought. But, it was said, in solitude his conscience with him wrought and, there, before his mental eye some hideous vision brought . . .

Here and now I see him in my mental eye. He is in evening dress. He is always in evening dress. Tails. White bow. Silver watchchain. He raises his right hand. He raises it higher. He puts the back of his right hand to his right temple and extends and stiffens his fingers. The hideous vision may at this moment be catching up on him.

The night the big boxer swung at the man who taunted him and missed and, quite by accident, grazed Belinda's beautiful right cheek, established the Eton Crop forever for me as a special sort of hairstyle. Say Eton Crop to anyone under thirty or, perhaps, under forty today and they'll think you mean a sort of a horse-whip in use at a famous public-school, or a haircut administered there as a discipline, something like a crewcut. Or a bit of Swinburnian diversion.

Belinda, though, is part of another story. And Anna belongs to Eugene who was simple and honest and brave, proved to be brave, moreover, in a bloody battle that shook the world. But Maruna of the songs and the elocutions, Maruna of the silken thigh and the disabled electric kettle, Maruna belongs to me. Or the memory of Maruna.

What the man who taunted the big boxer said was: You're better at the dancing than you are at the boxing. What else are you good at?

So the big boxer swung and, being a little boozed and, possibly, also intoxicated by his company, missed and grazed Belinda, and she was in the house for a fortnight until the shiner faded and she could step forth to tell the town her side of the story. She said that he was a perfect gentleman and that she would dance with him again any time he asked her. There were so many girls in the town who envied her even that glancing blow. She said that it would be something to tell her grandchildren about. That was Belinda for you. She was a girl who always looked ahead.

The big boxer was on tour from one town to the next, not boxing, not dancing except for recreation, but singing from the stage. About the dear little town in the old County Down and about his little grey home in the West, and the hills of Donegal, and the tumbledown shack in Athlone. And kindred matters. But that was the only time he ever came our way.

There was not one in all the house who did not fear his, my uncle's frown, save I, a little careless child who gambolled up and down. And often peeped into his room and plucked him by the gown.

No, he is not in a gown now. He is still in evening dress. His head is raised. There is a pained expression on his face. The pain must be in his chest. For the tips of the fingers of both hands are sensitively feeling his breastbone.

For I was an orphan and alone, my father was his brother. And all their lives I knew that they had fondly loved each other. And in my uncle's room there hung the picture of my mother.

My uncle's right hand is pressed strongly against his forehead. He has taken a step forward, leading with the left foot.

There was a curtain over it (that picture of my mother), 'twas in a darkened place, and few, or none, had ever looked upon my mother's face. Or seen her pale, expressive smile of melancholy grace.

One night I do remember well . . .

But hold on a moment, I hear you ask me, who is this uncle and what is he doing in here with Belinda and the big boxer, and Anna and Eugene and Maruna whom we have not yet met.

Later, later, as the sailor said.

*

8

Eugene was in love with Anna and kept, not her picture, but a picture of Ginger Rogers pinned underneath the lid of his desk in the last but one year of secondary school. Ginger Rogers for the one time, that I know of, in her lovely life was a proxy or a stand-in. He could not keep Anna pinned underneath the lid of his desk. And for two compelling reasons: she went to the secondary school in the Loreto Convent over the hill and on the other side of the parochial house; and her uncle was a parish priest in a mountainy village ten miles away. If her picture were to be discovered in Eugene's desk, and recognized, life might never be the same again for Anna in the convent or Anna in the village. But Ginger Rogers was just Ginger Rogers, and loved by a lot of people and did not have, as far as any of us knew, an uncle anywhere a parish priest.

Eugene loved long and deeply. No doubt at all about that. Somewhere in the Pennine Chain, or in the Lake District, or somewhere, there's an Inn at the tiptop of a high pass. In the visitor's book a fellow who had cycled or walked up all that way wrote, long ago, that if the girl he loved lived up there he would worship and cherish her, ever and ever, but climb up to visit her, never no never. That wasn't Eugene. At weekends, and all through the holidays, he cycled, or walked and wheeled the bike, five miles up steep roads, free-wheeled five miles down, then, having refreshed his love, pushed or walked up again five miles and, by God's mercy who made the world that way, was enabled to free-wheel home the rest of the road. He gave it up in the end and went to the wars which he may have found easier going. Anyway she was a flirt of a girl even if her uncle was a parish priest and she, an orphan, lived in the parochial house: and she styled her hair in the Eton Crop. As did Belinda. And Maruna. That and some other matters they had in common. Eugene's sister, Pauline, who was marvellous, had her hair in pigtails for a while but she switched to the Eton Crop and was even more marvellous. Eton Crop was the way to be. It was a style that went with youth and beauty and of necessity, you might say, with a well-shaped head. The only comparable thing today might be a sort of Pageboy style, if that's what you call it. Except that Pageboy has a tame, even servile connotation while the Eton Crop had about it the suggestion of daring, you might almost say: Fast. If the word was any longer comprehensible. We have so accelerated. And it also seems to me, conscious as I am of *tempora mutantur et nos mutamur in illis*, and all the rest of it, that the Crop was easier on the eye, male and sexist, than the coloured contemporary Papuan.

One night I do remember well. As I said. Or somebody said.

My uncle is still in evening dress. He has raised his right arm just as if he were a policeman on point duty. Stopped the whole street with one wave of his hand. His left arm is extended, rigid, pointing downwards to the ground at an angle of about thirty degrees.

One night I do remember well, the wind was howling high. And through the ancient corridors it sounded drearily. I sat and read in that old hall. My uncle sat close by.

I read, but little understood, the words upon that book. For with a sidelong glance I marked my uncle's fearful look. And saw how all his quivering frame in strong convulsions shook.

A silent terror o'er me stole, a strange, unusual dread. His lips were white as bone, his eyes sunk far down in his head. He gazed on me, but 'twas the gaze of the unconscious dead.

Then suddenly he turned him round and drew aside the veil which hung before my mother's face. Perchance, my eyes might fail.

Gesture: Be careful not to allow the hands to move apart before the word, face, is uttered. The words in italic indicate where the hands may begin to come together. A slight startled movement is appropriate at: Perchance, my eyes might fail.

And indeed and indeed. I quite agree.

But ne'er before that face to me had seemed so ghastly pale.

— Come hither, boy, my uncle said.

I started at the sound. 'Twas choked and stifled in his throat and hardly utterance found.

— Come hither boy.

Then fearfully he cast his eyes around.

My uncle is sitting down. But on an ordinary kitchen chair, which is odd in that old hall, my uncle's room. The choking is getting the better of him. Again he raises his right arm. Touches his right temple with the back of his right hand. Extends his left leg to a painful rigidity. Leans back in the chair. Will he topple over? But no, by a miracle of cantilevership he is still in the saddle, and still talking.

That lady was thy mother once. Thou wert her only child . . .

Maruna had a pert, birdlike face, a style most attractive to me at that time. She was a very senior girl, all of nineteen, and was not compelled, when off parade and out of the convent-grounds, to wear school uniform. No more than was Belinda who had left school for two years and was as far away from me and my contemporaries as Uranus, or Venus, from the earth. But Maruna was still within reach, or sight, or desire, and because she could wear real clothes was an inspiriting vision of things to come. Out there somewhere was the World and Ginger Rogers and Life. Maruna was the symbol. She also sang like an angel. She sang at school concerts. She sang in the choir in the village she came from. One Christmas morning, it was said, people travelled miles to hear her *Adeste*. She sang at parochial concerts in the village and in the town. She sang at concerts all over the place. And she recited. That was what first brought us together: recitation. And at the same concert in the town hall. She was asking the townspeople about what was he doing, the Great God, Pan, down in the reeds by the river.

As for me: I was telling them, in the words of Patrick Pearse, that the beauty of the world hath made me sad, this beauty that will pass, that sometimes my heart hath shaken with great joy to see a leaping squirrel in a tree or a red ladybird upon a stalk.

At that time I had never seen a squirrel, brown or grey, except in Bostock and Wombell's travelling menagerie, and thought a ladybird was a bird.

Not a word of the whole thing did I believe. And the hell was frightened out of me. My first public appearance. She was two years older than me and as confident as Gracie Fields and had appeared on every stage within a forty-mile radius and she was as lovely as the doves in the grounds of the parish church. She was on the bill before me and for some reason, unknown to God or man or woman, she kissed me in the darkness of the wings before she stepped into the radiance and the applause. Afterwards she told me that the kiss was to give me confidence. But I doubt if it did. Even in the dark she was as daunting as Cleopatra. Then she was out there before the world and not a bother on her, and there was I, Caliban in the Stygian shades of gloom.

Now there were dirty-minded fellows who went to school with me who had their own notions about what he was doing, the Great God, Pan, down in the reeds by the river: and who were nasty enough to imply that it was nothing for a decent girl to be asking about, or miming on the stage, or anywhere else . . .

That lady was thy mother once, thou wert her only child.

Well, once is enough to be anybody's mother.

My uncle is still balancing perilously on that kitchen chair, his right hand raised high but both feet firmly planted. Pray God he shall not fall.

— Oh boy, I've seen her when she looked on thee and smiled. She smiled upon thy father, boy. 'Twas that which drove me wild.

He may topple.

It must be remembered it is an old man who speaks.

— He was my brother but his form was fairer far than mine. I grudged not that. He was the prop of our ancestral line . . .

Lansdowne Road and Twickenham and all that. Prop? The line?

. . . and manly beauty was of him a token and a sign.

— Boy, I had loved her too. Nay more. 'Twas I that loved her first. For months, for years, the golden thoughts within my soul I nursed. He came. He conquered. They were wed. My airblown bubble burst.

He is still in evening dress. He is still on that chair. But his hands are raised to heaven or the roof.

— Then on my mind a shadow fell and evil hopes grew rife. The damning thought struck in my heart and cut me like a knife: that she, whom all my days I loved, should be another's wife.

—I left my home. I left the land. I crossed the stormy sea. In vain, in vain, where'er I turned my memory went with me . . .

But my uncle has not gone anywhere. He is still before my eyes. He is leaning sideways on that chair, perhaps to indicate the rolling motion of a ship at sea.

And he is still in evening dress.

*

Can you hazard a guess now as to what was he doing, the Great God, Pan, down in the reeds by the river? He was spreading ruin and scattering ban, and breaking the golden lilies afloat with the dragonfly, and splashing and paddling with hooves of a goat.

She stamped on the stage. Her dainty feet were transformed. She was a marvel as a mimic.

He was tearing out a reed was the Great God, Pan, from the deep cool bed of the river.

Gently, coaxingly she drew it out from the footlights. It was clearly visible.

He was high on the shore was the Great God, Pan, whittling away what leaves the reed had: and from her sleeveless sleeve, or from somewhere sacredly invisible, she had produced a short, shining knife.

He was drawing out the pith of a reed like the heart of a man, and my heart most painfully followed her fingers. He was notching holes was the Great God, Pan, and dropping his mouth to a hole in the reed and blowing in power by the river, and the sun on the hill forgot to die, and the lilies revived, and the dragonfly came back to dream on the river: and the whole town thundered its appreciation and there was I in the darkness paralysed with love or something for that wonder of a girl, and with fear of the ordeal before me.

For when she had disposed of the Great God, Pan, there was nothing or nobody could save me from having to stand out there in the blinding brightness to grapple with Patrick Pearse and the melancholy beauty of the world. If she had not kissed me again, somewhere in the region of the back of the neck, and gently propelled me forward, I'd never have made it: and then there I was, stiff as a post, raising my right arm and then lowering it for the leaping squirrel and the red ladybird, raising my left arm, lowering it, like a bloody railway signal, for little rabbits in a field at evening lit by a slanting sun. The bit about children with bare feet upon the sands of some ebbed sea or playing on the streets of little towns in Connacht, I actually liked and believed in. That, my elder brother said, was the only bit in which I did not sound totally lugubrious, and all honour to the glorious dead and Patrick Pearse. But from the streets of the little towns the road wound downhill all the way and when the poet said that, between one thing and another, he had gone upon his way sorrowful, everybody believed me.

Yet I had a few friends at the back of the hall who contrived to set a cheer going.

On the chaste and protective stairs between the two dressing rooms, one male, one female, she kissed me once, she kissed me twice. And didn't give a damn if the world was watching. As some of it was. She said I was good for a beginner and not to worry, that I could be heard all over the hall. She allowed me to walk hand-in-hand with her to the place where her relatives were waiting to drive her home.

So there sits my uncle, pursued by his memory and roaming the wide world, but still in evening dress, still balanced precariously on that creaking chair. Although I cannot hear it, I know that it must creak.

—My whole existence, he says, night and day in memory seemed to be. I came again, I found them here . . .

The strain of all this is proving too much for him. His mouth is agape. He raises both hands as if somebody were pointing a pistol at him.

— Thou'rt like thy father, boy . . .

Well, why not, nuncle?

His rhyming for the moment has tripped over its feet. Thou'rt, for God sake. Did anybody ever say: Thou'rt?

— Thou'rt like thy father, boy. They doated on that pale face.

Whose pale face?

— I've seen them kiss and toy. I've seen her locked in his strong arms, wrapt in delirious joy.

He simply should not have been peeping.

The tone of his voice now is vindictive to begin with, weakening to the mildly sarcastic. His hands are clenched for a moment and allowed to rest on his knees.

— By heaven it was a fearful sight to see my brother now and mark the placid calm which sat forever on his brow, which seemed in bitter scorn to say: I am more loved than thou.

— He disappeared. Draw nearer, child. He died. No one knew how. The murdered body ne'er was found. The tale is hushed up now. But there was one who rightly guessed the hand that struck the blow. It drove her mad — yet not his death, no, not his death alone, for she had clung to hope when all knew well that there was none.

He is up, with a half-jump, on his feet.

— No boy, it was a sight she saw that froze her into stone.

My uncle makes a long pause in his speaking. He looks fearfully around as if seeking to discover the cause of my, evidently growing, alarm, by following the direction of my glances. Then he's off again:

— I am thy uncle, child, why stare so fearfully aghast?

But, nuncle, why not?

— The arras waves, he says, but know'st thou not 'tis nothing but the blast. I too, have had my fears like these, but such vain fears are past.

But not the rheumatics from sitting in the draughts.

— I'll show you what thy mother saw . . .

Now we're for it.

Eugene really must have been in love with Anna or he never would have cycled over all those mountains. Yet when the impulse, whatever it was, ended, he forgot about it very rapidly. Or so it appeared to us. One night I asked him about it. We were playing football in the dark. That may seem an odd caper to be at. But let me explain. Since Eugene's father was an officer in the British army we had easy access, day or night, to the great river-surrounded halfmoon of playing fields below the greystone barracks. Except to the hockey-pitch which was a sort of sanctuary. The smoothness of it was a wonder to behold and it felt like silk to the fingers, or to the bare feet when on summer nights a few of us would sneak out there, bootless, to play football with a ball painted white. That was away before 1939 and the world was easy. No warning bugles were blown, no rallentandos unloosed over our heads. That was the first white football we ever saw. Footballs in those days were mostly brown.

When, under the protection of darkness, I asked Eugene if he were still in love with Anna, he said he supposed he was but that you couldn't be sure about those things. It took me years to realize that what he meant was that he couldn't be sure about Anna. As for Maruna and myself. Well, I felt her leg once, also in the dark or the half-dark of one of the town's two cinemas. Felt rather her stocking, and that was the height of it. And had a notion for a long time afterwards, and without reasoning about it, that women, or their thighs, were, like the grass on the hockey-pitch, made of silk. Which is not so.

Thomas Moore, now that I think of it, felt the foot of Pauline Bonaparte. Left or right we are not told, but it was then reputed to be the daintiest or something foot in Europe. How did anybody contrive to work that one out? A foot-judging beauty parade? Sponsored by whom? And who felt all the feet?

Did the big boxer, I wonder, remember Belinda for any length of time. Insofar as we knew he had felt only her right cheek and that, and so to speak, only in passing.

— I'll show you what thy mother saw, my uncle repeats.

His tone is hesitating and fearful.

He says: I feel 'twill ease my breast. And this wild tempest-laden night suits with my purpose best.

He raises his arms as if he were about to take off. But instead he goes down on one knee.

— Come hither! Thou hast often sought to open this old chest. It has a secret spring. The touch is known to me alone.

Try as I may, I can see no chest. But my uncle is moving his hands back and forwards over something that clearly isn't there.

— Slowly, he says, the lid is raised and now what see you that you groan so heavily. That Thing . . .

He heavily emphasizes and repeats those two words.

— That Thing is but a bare-ribbed skeleton . . .

He has thrown his hat (metaphorical), at rhyme and/or what the poet called rhythmical animation.

— A sudden crash. The lid fell down. Three strides he backward gave.

He, or the voice of One Invisible, is telling me what is happening, what he is doing. But no crash do I hear. Nor has he stepped backward. He is again standing up but his feet are quite steady in the one place. This you may feel, and I must admit, is most confusing and it also now seems that my uncle is about to throw a fit.

— Oh God, he cries, it is my brother's self returning from the grave. His clutch of lead is on my throat. Will no one help or save.

He clutches his own throat. He collapses backwards on to that unshakeable cane-chair.

Sometime during the summer that followed Pan's invention of the flute and the lamentations of Patrick Pearse on the sadness and transiency of beauty, Maruna came into town one Saturday and in her hand, naked and unashamed, an electric kettle that wouldn't work. It was early days then for electric kettles. Real specialists and diagnosticians in their elemental ailments may have been few. How many elements anyway, in an electric kettle when it is alive and well? Air? Fire? Water? And Earth, if you consider the metal as earth, the bowels of the earth?

We were good friends, but just friends, by that time, Maruna and myself. So I carried the kettle and was proud to, and proud to be seen walking with her. She carried a cord shopping-bag with a handbag in it and, as I recall, three thin books. We walked the town from place to place, hardware stores, building-yards, and one motor-garage, and nowhere found a man to mend the kettle. Until we met Alec who was wise beyond his generation and who had first suggested playing football in the dark, preferably in mixed doubles which we never did achieve: and who told us that Ernie Murdoch, the photographer, could fix electric kettles.

— And he can fix more than electric kettles.

— What else can he fix, Maruna asked.

She seemed a little nervous of Alec. He had a grey, level glance and a well-chiselled, handsome face and a name with the girls, of all sorts.

— Your kettle-carrier, he said, will tell you. The slave of the kettle. Ali Baba.

But the kettle-carrier pretended ignorance, or innocence, and we left Alec smiling and Ernie fixed the kettle: and afterwards Maruna and myself went to the pictures. How could I tell her that Ernie sold rubber goods and allied products, down in the reeds by the river? She might not have known what they were about. Explication at the time would have been beyond me.

Ali Baba and the forty thieves were hard at it in one of the two cinemas. But after that gibe about the slave of the kettle I preferred the other palace. It had Virginia Bruce and John Boles and Douglas Montgomery, and others, and the Swiss Alps and balconies and flowers, and everybody singing that I've told every little star just how sweet I think you are, why haven't I told you. I've told the ripples in the brook, made my heart an open book . . .

She sang with them. She was a bird.

And down in the reeds by the river I once, just once and only for a moment, touched her silken thigh. That was as far as I ever got or perhaps, then, had the courage to try to go. There be mysteries. No golden lilies were trampled on. It was an innocent sort of a world.

Anyway, that was the end of it. She went one way and I went another, not with conscious deliberation, just went. Early days can be like that.

— Will no one help or save?

No one does.

This you may be glad to hear is positively my uncle's last appearance on this or any other stage. It might even seem that he has no more to say. That third person unseen, unknown, sums up for the unfortunate man who murdered his brother and locked him in a box, and drove his sister-in-law to lunacy.

— That night they laid him on his bed in raving madness tossed. He gnashed his teeth and with wild oaths blasphemed the Holy Ghost.

On the page before me the man in evening dress raises his right hand, bows his head reverently to atone for the blasphemy, and places his left hand round about where his heart may be presumed to beat.

— And ere the light of morning broke, a sinner's soul was lost.

And here and now, as I turn the last page in this little book, the man in evening dress covers his face with his hands. The instructions or directions in the text that accompanies the verse and the illustrations say that the eyes may be raised at the beginning of this passage and that the attitude given in the accompanying illustration must not be adopted until the final word, and that the reciter may then stand with his face covered for a few seconds, and with great effect.

Then beside that, and in the margin of the page, and in small neat birdlike script, someone has long ago written: Bring electric kettle to town. See musical picture with John Boles and Virginia Bruce.

So this curious little book is all that is left to me of Maruna and her singing and reciting, and of football in the dark and of Eugene who came to be a hero, and of Anna from over the mountains, and Belinda and the big boxer, and Pauline who was marvellous. Was it one of the three thin books that I saw in Maruna's shopping-bag on the day of the electric kettle? Did that gesticulating uncle go round and round the town with us and even into the studio of Ernie Murdoch who had power over life and electric kettles? Did he crouch in the dark when I touched silk and heard Virginia Bruce sing and Maruna sing with her: Friends ask me am I in love, I always answer yes . . .

As for the book. I open it again, for the hundredth time since, the day before yesterday, it came into my possession. A young man stopped me on a road in Donnybrook and handed it to me. He said: You knew my mother. She talked a lot about you. She said to me once that if ever I ran across you I was to pass this little book on to you.

And later, when we had talked for a while: She died a year ago. Singing to the end.

Humming the other day I was, about I've told every little star when a young person said to me that I knew the latest. And genuinely meant it. For a haunting song may return but a lost beauty never. Yet I can seldom look at or use an electric kettle without remembering Maruna. Away back in those days I wrote a poem to her: or about her, for I never had the nerve to show it to her. Here it is. It looks better in prose as most poems would nowadays. It was jampacked with extravagant statements. As that: On a dew-drenched April morning, the sky-assaulting lark, with his rising paean of gladness, to which mortal ears must hark, did never sing so sweetly nor ever praise so meetly as her voice, with full throat vibrant on the starless scented dark.

And wilder still: Never from the lofty steeple did the swinging bells chime down with a note so soul-exalting o'er the morning-misted town, as her voice in trilling rushes, from her lips the soft sound gushes on the air that heaves and dances like a bed of wind-stirred down . . .

Wonderwoman. Up and away.

There was a third verse, pointing a moral.

Sed satis.

Here followeth an exact description of the book.

Five inches by seven. Forty-seven pages, approx.

Cloth, now very much off-white, with green binding. One of a series of Illustrated Recitations by R. C. Buchanan: *The Uncle* by Henry Glassford Bell. Elocution taught by the aid of photography.

That is: Mr Bell wrote the horrendous poem and Mr Buchanan illustrated it with thirty-six photographic reproductions of a man in evening dress elocuting like bedamned. And added an appendix telling you how you also could elocute that poem. There was even a special edition of the poem, with musical background by Sir Julius Benedict and for the especial benefit of Sir Henry Irving when he felt the need to elocute.

How carefully and how often, I wonder, had Maruna studied that book? What secret life did she lead that I knew nothing about? To think that the movements of her body should have been monitored by Henry Glassford Bell who wrote that woeful poem, and by R. C. Buchanan who worked out the gestures, he said, to foster the love of elocution which, he said, was pre-eminently the art whose principles require to be imparted by oral demonstration. That's what the man said. Kissing in the dark wings, kissing on the stairway. Even then, said R. C. Buchanan, this instruction demands ceaseless repetition before it begins to bear fruit.

Should I have simply kissed back? Not felt in the dark for the smoothness of a silk stocking, while everyone suddenly burst out singing about I've told every little star?

But why did the sailor say: Later, later.

Please.

BLOODLESS BYRNE OF A MONDAY

THREE TALL MEN excuse themselves politely, close the door gently behind them, hope he doesn't mind. But they are exhausted putting fractious Connemara ponies on a boat for a show and sale in Britain. Odd caper to be at so early on a Monday morning, they admit. And, as well, they're all Dublinmen by accent, and may never have seen the Twelve Bens or Clifden or the plains of Glenbricken.

— Fair enough, they admit.

They are most courteous.

The tallest of the three says he knows the West of Ireland well, and knows the song about Derrylee and the greyhounds and the plains of Glenbricken and about the man who emigrated from Clifden to the other West, the Wild West, to hunt the red man, the panther and the beaver, and to gaze back with pride on the bogs of Shanaheever.

The tallest man also says that from an early age he has been into horses, the big ones, his father drove a four-wheeled dray. Then into hunters with a man on the Curragh of Kildare. Then, on his own and by a lucky break, into ponies. A bleeding goldmine. He is not boasting. The colour of his money is evident in three large whiskeys for himself and his colleagues, and a brandy and ginger for the stranger up from . . .

— Sligo, he says.

— On a bit of a blinder, he adds.

To be civil and companionable. They are three very, civil, companionable men. And he craves company. The need of a world of men for me. And round the corner came the sun.

To the tallest man the fat redheaded man says: Bloodless Byrne was a friend of your father.

The smallest of the three, the man with the peaked cloth-cap,

21

says: Bloodless Byrne of a Monday morning. The brooding terror of the Naas Road. Very vengeful. Bloodless drove a dray for the brewery.

— Bloodless Byrne of a Monday morning, the tallest man repeats.

He wears strong nailed boots and black, well-polished leather leggings.

— It became a sort of a proverb, he explains. Like: Out of the question, as Ronnie Donnegan said. Bloodless. A face on him like Dracula without the teeth. They tried calling him Dracula Byrne. But it didn't stick. He didn't fancy it. He was vengeful. Vindictive. He'd wait a generation to get his own back. He didn't mind being called Bloodless. They say he wrote it when he filled in forms.

— Mad about pigeons, says the stout redheaded man.

— Bloodless Byrne of a Monday. My father told me how that came about.

Carefully the tallest man closes the other door that opens into the public bar, cuts off the morning voices of dockers on the way to work, printers on the way home.

— Bloodless, you see, is backing his horse and dray of a Monday into a gateway in a lane back of the fruit and fish markets in Moore Street. Backs and backs, again and again. Often as he tries, one or other of the back wheels catches on the brick wall. So finally he takes his cap off, throws it down, puts his foot on it, stares the unfortunate horse full in the face, and says: You're always the same of a fuckin' Monday.

— Deep voice he had too. Paul Robeson.

The shortest man removes his cloth cap to reveal utter baldness. A startling transformation, forcing the strange gentleman from Sligo to blink tired eyelids upon tired eyes. The shortest man says: Bloodless Byrne of a Monday.

— Pigeons, says the stout redheaded man.

Bangers, the barman, belying his nickname, steps in most politely, making no din, to gather up empties and hear requests: so the gentleman from Sligo places the relevant order. These men are true companions. And prepared to talk. And what he needs most at the moment is the vibration of the voices of men. And he wants to hear more about those pigeons. And Bloodless Byrne. And why Ronnie

Donnegan said it was out of the question, and what it was that was. Drinks paid for, he has five single pound notes to survive on until the banks open and he can acquire a new chequebook.

— Out of the question, he says tentatively.

But the emphasis is on pigeons and the tallest man is talking.

— Fellow in America, Bloodless says to me, wrote a play about a cat on a hot tin roof. Bloodless never saw it. The play. He saw the poster on a wall. Could you imagine Bloodless at a play? Up above in the Gaiety with all the grandees. A play. Bloodless tells me the neighbour has three cats on a black tin roof, hot or cold, and says he wouldn't like to tell me what they're at, night and day. Bloodless has no time for cats.

— Pigeons, says the stout redheaded man.

— No time for the neighbour either. No love lost. No compatability. No good fences. So one day . . .

— Cats and pigeons, says the stout redheaded man.

— One day the neighbour knocks on the door and says very sorry there's your pigeons, and throws in a potato sack, wet and heavy. Dead birds.

It is difficult not to join in the chant when the stout redheaded man says again: Cats and pigeons.

— What does the bold Bloodless do? Nothing. Simply nothing. He bides his time. He waits and watches. June goes by, July and August and the horse-show, and one day in September he throws a plastic sack, very sanitary, in at the neighbour's door and says sorry mate, them's your cats. Just like that. Them's your cats. In a plastic sack.

There is nobody in the snug, nobody even in the packed and noisy public bar but Bloodless Byrne, nothing to be seriously considered but his vengeance: Sorry mate, them's your cats.

Face like Dracula without the teeth, he broods over the place for the duration of several more drinks which must have been bought by the ponymen: for the five pound notes are still intact and the ponymen are gone, and never in this life may he know what it was that was out of the question. His clothes are creased and rumpled. He needs a bath and a shave and a long rest. The noise outside is of water relaxing from shelving shingle. The snug is silent. The old boozy Belfast lady fell asleep in the confessional and when the priest pulled across the slide, said: Another bottle, Peter, and turn on the light in the snug.

His eyes are moist at the memory of that schoolboy joke.

June, July, August, and then in September: Sorry, mate, them's your cats.

He should telephone his wife and say he is well and happy and sober. Anyway he wouldn't be here and like this if she hadn't been pregnant so that, to some extent, she is at fault: and he laughs aloud at the idea, and rests his head back on old smoke-browned panelling, and dozes for five minutes.

How many years now have we been meeting once a year: Niall and Robert, Eamonn and little Kevin, Anthony and John and Sean and big Kevin, and Arthur, that's me? Count us. Nine in all. Since two years after secondary school ended in good old St Kieran's where nobody, not even the clerical professors, ever talked about anything but hurling and gaelic football, safe topics, no heresies possible although at times you'd wonder a bit about that, only a little blasphemy and/or obscenity might creep in when Kilkenny had lost a game: but no sex, right or wrong, sex did not enter in. No sex, either, on this meditative morning. As you were. That wash of waves retreating in the public bar is now as far away as the high cliffs of Moher on the far western shore of the county Clare.

Day of a big game in Dublin, Kilkenny versus Tipperary who have the hay saved and Cork bet, the nine of us come together by happy accident: a journalist and a banker, a student of law, a civil servant, a student of art and theatre, another journalist, a student of history, an auctioneer and valuer, that's me. There's one missing there somewhere. Count us, as they do with the elephants at bedtime in Duffy's circus. *N'importe*. Bangers looks in and pleasantly smiles, but the glass is still brimming and the five pound notes must be held in reserve until Blucher gets to the bank. Nine old school-friends meet by happy accident and vow to make the meeting annual. Tipperary lost. How many years ago? Ten? More than ten. Twenty? No, not twenty. Then wives crept in. Crept in? Came in battalions, all in one year, mass madness, Gadarene swine, lemmings swarming to the sea: and college reunions and laughter and the love of friends became cocktails and wives who don't much like each other: and dinner dances. So nothing to worry about when this year Marie is expecting, and all I have to do is meet the men and make excuses and slip away, odd man out: which seemed a good idea at the time, late in the afternoon yesterday, or early in the evening, for in this untidy town afternoon melts un-noted into evening and, regrettably and returning as the wheel returns, it is now in a day as we say in the Irish when we say it in the Irish: and here I am, here I am, here I'm alone and the ponymen are gone, and five pound notes is all between now and the opening of the banks . . .

Outside, the translucent stream, as he once heard some wit call it, slithers, green and spitting with pollution, eastwards to the sea. The sun is bright without mercy. His eyes water. His knees wobble. Where had he got to after he left the lads to get with their good, unco guid, wives to the dinner dance? The sequence of events, after their last brandy and backslapping, is a bit befogged.

This town is changing. For the worse. Nothing to lean on any more. Where, said Ulysses, where in hell are the pillars of Hercules. The Scotch House is gone. Called that, I suppose, when a boat went all the way from the North Wall to Glasgow, and came back again, carrying Scotsmen who would look across the river and see the sign and feel they were at home. Scotsmen were great men for feeling at home anywhere, westering home with a song in the air, at home with my ain folk in Islay, home no more home to me whither must I wander, and the Red Bank Restaurant gone, it's a church now, and the brewery barges that used to bring the booze downstream to the cross-channel cargo boats gone forever and for a long time. He's just old enough to remember when he first made a trip to Dublin and saw the frantic puffs of the barges when they broke funnels to clear the low arch, and the children leaning over the parapet, just here, and yelling: Hey mister, bring us back a parrot. A monkey for me, mister. A monkey for me.

And slowly answered Arthur from the barge the old order changeth yielding place to new. That went with a drawing in a comic magazine at the time: a man in frock-coat and top-hat standing among the beerbarrels on a barge, Arthur Guinness of course, immortal father of the brewery bring me back a monkey, bring me back a parrot. And God fulfills himself in many ways, over from barges to motor-trucks.

Sorry, mate, them's your cats.

There in that small hotel the nine of us met the day Tipperary lost the match, and met there every year until the hotel wasn't grand enough for the assembled ladies. Then it descended lower still to include a discotheque: and that was that. Nine of us? Dear God, that was why this morning I counted only eight the second time round, for Eamonn who discovered that little hotel and liked it, even to the ultimate of the discotheque, Eamonn up and died on us and that's the worst change of all.

Somewhere last night I was talking mournfully to somebody about Eamonn, mournfully remembering him: and God fulfills himself in many ways.

Out all night, and cannot exactly remember where I was, and did not get home to my own hotel which, and this is another sign of the times, is away out somewhere in the suburbs. Once upon a time the best hotels were always in the centre. Like America now, the automobile rules okay, the centre of the city dies, and far away in ideal homes all are happy, and witness a drive-in movie from the comfort and security of your own automobile: and the gossip and the fevers of the middle-ages, middle between which and what, fore and aft, I never knew, are no more: and I am dirty and tired now, and want a bath and a shave and sleep. Samuel Taylor Coleridge emptied the po out of a first-floor window. While admiring the lakeland scenery.

But this other hotel outside which he now stands is still, and in spite of the changing times and the shifting pattern of urban concentrations, one of the best hotels in town. At this moment he loves it because he knows it will be clean, as he certainly is not. In the pubs of Dublin the loos can often be an upset to the delicate in health.

So up the steps here and in through the porch. There is a long porch. Jack Doyle, the boxer, used to sit here with an Alsatian dog, and read the papers and be photographed. That was away back in

Jack's good days. As a boy he used to study those newspaper photos of handsome Jack and the big dog, and envy Jack because it was said that all the girls in Dublin and elsewhere, were mad about him.

He has heard that a new proprietor of this hotel has napoleonic delusions: and, to prove the point, *l'empereur* in a detail reproduced from David and blown up to monstrosity, is there on the wall on a horse rearing on the hindlegs, pawing with the forelegs. The French must fancy that pose or position: Louis the Sun King on a charger similarly performing is frozen forever in the Place des Victoires.

Tread carefully now, long steps, across the foyer for if that horse should forget himself, I founder.

A porter salutes him, a thin sandy man, going bald. He nods in return.

Were we here last night? Could have been, for the nine of us used to meet here: and the eighteen of us, until that changing city pattern swept the dinner dance away somewhere to the south.

This morning anything is possible. He raises his left hand to reinforce his nod, and passes on. Upstairs or downstairs or to my lady's chamber? Destiny guides him. So he walks upstairs, soft carpets, long corridors, perhaps an open, detached bathroom even if he has no razor to shave with. Afterwards, a barber's shave, oh bliss, oh bliss. He finds the bathroom and washes his face and those tired eyelids and tired eyes, and combs his hair and shakes himself a bit and shakes his crumpled suit, and polishes his shoes with a dampish handtowel. A bit too risky to chance a bath and total exposure, although he has heard and read the oddest stories about deeds performed in hotel bathrooms by people who had no right in the world to be there. Bravely he steps out again. A brandy in the bar, and the road to the bank and his own hotel and sobriety, and home: Bright sun before whose glorious rays.

Sorry, mate, them's your pigeons.

Before him in the corridor a door opens and a man steps out.

This man who steps out is in one hell of a hurry. He swings left so fast that his face has been nothing more than a blur. A black back to be seen as he hares off down the corridor to the stairhead. Hat in one hand, briefcase in the other. Off with quick short steps and down the

27

stairs and away, leaving the door of the room open behind him. His haste rattles me with guilt. That man has somewhere to go and something to do.

To sleep, to die, to sleep, to sleep perchance to dream, and his eyes are half-closed and a mist rolling at him, tumbling tumbleweed, up the corridor from the spot where the man has vanished: and the door is open and the devil dancing ahead of him. There is no luggage in the room, not in wardrobe nor on tables, racks nor floors, no papers except yesterday's evening papers discarded in the waste-basket, no shaving-kit in the bathroom: and the towels, all except one handtowel, all folded as if they have not been used. No empty cups nor glasses nor anything to prove that the robin goodfellows or goodgirls of roomservice have ever passed this way. That's odd. The blackbacked hurrying man must carry all his luggage in that briefcase: but, now that he remembers, it was a big bulging briefcase, brown leather to clash badly with the black suit, big enough to hold pyjamas but scarcely big enough to accommodate anything more bulky than a light silk dressing-gown. Woollen would not fit. *N'importe.* There are two single beds, one pillowless and unused, all the pillows on the other, which is tossed and tumbled. That man must have had a restless night. But who in hell am I supposed to be or what am I playing at? Sherlock Holmes?

The phone on the table on the far side of the rumpled bed would do very well for his expiatory call to Sligo. He reaches across first for it and then, the most natural thing in the world it seems for him to subside, not just to subside but to allow himself to subside, gravity and all that: and to close his eyes. The bed is quite cold even to a man with his clothes on, and that's also odd because the man with the brown briefcase had moved so fast that his couch should not yet have had time to cool. Perhaps he had genuinely passed such a restless night that he had tumbled on the bed for a while, then sat up or walked the floor until dawn. To hell with Holmes and Dr Watson or Nigel Bruce and Basil, Basil, the second name eludes me. Pigeons fly high over a black roof that is crawling with spitting cats.

Opening his eyes again he reads seventeen in the centre of the dial and, with the phone in his hand, says not Sligo but: Room seventeen

28

speaking, room service could I have, please, a glass of brandy and a baby ginger, not too well this morning, a slight dyspepsia, nervous dyspepsia, something I'm liable to.

The explanation perhaps was an error, too long, too apologetic, never apologize, like Sergius in the Shaw play, just barge ahead and hope for the best. Not too late yet to cut and run but, to hell with poverty we'll kill a duck, here's a pound note for a tip on the table between the beds, charge the brandy to the blackbacked man's bill, any man who moves so fast would need a brandy: now down, well down under the bedclothes, nothing to be seen but the crown of my head: and your brandy, sir, the ginger sir, will I pour it sir, do please, mumble but be firm, and thank you, that's for yourself and have one on me, and thank you, sir. It was a man's voice. A porter, not a chambermaid. You can't have everything. And where is the chambermaid, as the commercial traveller said in the Metropole in Cork when his tea was carried to him in the randy morning by, alas, the nightporter. Can't say, sir, about the chamber but the cup and saucer are the best Arklow pottery. Oh God, hoary old jokes: but then my mind is weakening or I wouldn't be here.

The door closes. This is the sweetest brandy he has ever tasted and cheap at a pound. Four notes left. Let me outa here. But gravity strikes again and, eyes closing, he is drifting into dreams when the phone rings and, before he can stop himself, he picks it up and the voice of the female switch says: Call for you, sir.

— Thanking you.

— That you, Mulqueen? Where the hell are you?

A rough, a very rough, male voice.

— Room seventeen.

— Balls. What I mean is what the hell are you up to?

That would by no means be easy to explain to a man I've never seen and on behalf of a man I've never really met.

Mumble: Up to nothing.

— Can't hear you too well. You sound odd. Are you drinking? A bloody pussyfoot like you might get drunk in a crisis.

That's the first time, the reely-reely first time, I was ever called a pussyfoot. Say something. Mumble something. What to say? What to mumble? Have another slow meditative sip. Never gulp brandy, my uncle always told me, it's bad for your brain and an insult to a great nation.

— Mulqueen, are you there? Are you bloody well listening?

— Everything's fine. Not to worry.

— Never heard you say that before, Mulqueen. You that worried the life out of yourself and everybody else. But I should bloodywell hope everything is fine. Although I may as well tell you that's not what the bossman thinks out here in the bloody suburbs. He's called a meeting. You'd better be here. And have the old alibis in order.

— I'll be there. When the roll is called up yonder I'll be there. I'll be . . .

Perhaps he shouldn't have said that, but the brandy, brandy for heroes, is making a new man out of Pussyfoot Mulqueen or whoever he is. Anyway, and God be praised, it put an end to that conversation for the phone at the far end goes down with a dangerous crash that echoes in his ears, if not even in the bedroom. He finishes the brandy, beats time with his left hand and chants: I'll be there, I'll be there, when the roll is called up yonder I'll be there, oh I wonder, yes I wonder do the angels fart like thunder, when the roll is called up yonder I'll be there!

Sips at the empty glass and draws his breath and continues: At the cross, at the cross, where the jockey lost 'is 'oss: send down sal, send down sal, send down salvation from the lord catch my flea, catch my flea, catch my fleeting soul.

And orders another brandy and ginger, and plants another pound, and submerges, and all goes well, and surfaces and drinks the brandy, and realizes that he must not fall asleep, must out and away while the going is good and the great winds westward blow, and is about to get on his feet when the phone is at it again. Here now is a dilemma, emma, emma, emma, to answer or not to answer, dangerous to answer, more dangerous not to answer, the ringing may attract attention, the not answering may bring searchers up. It is a woman's voice.

— Is that you, Arthur.

Arthur is my name.

— Who else?

— You sound odd.

— The line is bad.

— Your hives are flourishing.

My hives? I don't have hives. Good God, the man's a beekeeper, an apywhatisit.

— But Arthur, I'm worried sick about you. What is it? What is wrong?

She is crying.

— O'Leary rang looking for you. I told him where you might be.

— That was unwise.

— I had to. He said things were in a bad way.

— He would.

— Arthur. You sound very peculiar.

— I feel very peculiar.

— What were you up to?

He still doesn't know what he was up to. He says: these things happen. So does Hiroshima. So does the end of the world.

— Arthur, how can you talk like that? You don't sound in the least like yourself. And there is something wrong with your voice.

Best put the phone down gently and run. But she will only ring again before he can get out the door and away.

— Laryngitis. Hoarse as a drake.

He coughs.

— Don't do anything desperate. Promise me.

— Promise.

— In the long run it will be better to face the music. Think of the children.

— I always do.

— You have been a good father. You were never unkind.

She is crying again and he feels like the ruffian he is for bursting in on the sorrows of a woman he has never seen, may never see, pray God. Then his self-respect is restored and his finer feelings dissipated by a male voice, sharp and clear and oh so nasty: You blackguard. Mary is much too soft with you. She always has been.

Nothing better to say than: Who's speaking?

— Very well you know who is speaking, you dishonest automaton, this is your brother-in-law speaking, and a sorry day it was that you ever saw Mary or she ever saw you, or that you brought a black stain,

31

the only one ever, on the name of this family, get over to your office this minute and face the music, it will make a man of you, a term in jail . . .

Christ save the hastening man who has this faceless monster for a brother-in-law. I am shent, or somebody is, Pussyfoot the automaton is shent as in Shakespeare. But what to say? So unable to think of anything better he says: Bugger off.

Somebody must stand up for Mulqueen who is not here to stand up for himself.

— Filthy language now to make a bad job worse, your father and mother were decent people who never used words like that . . .

— They never had to listen to the like of you.

— I'll offer up my mass for you, as a Catholic priest I can think of nothing else.

And slam goes the phone and the gates of hell shall not prevail, and the Lord hath but spoken and chariots and horsemen are sunk in the wave: sound the loud timbrel o'er Egypt's dark sea: and he is halfway to the door when the loud timbrel sounds again. Let it sound. Divide the dark waves and let me outa here. And the bedroom door opens and in steps the thin sandy porter, going bald, with a third brandy and ginger on a tray, and puts the tray down carefully, and picks up the phone and says hello and listens, and cups his hand carefully over the mouthpiece and says: It's for Mr Mulqueen, sir. It might be as well to answer it. Just for the sake of appearances at the switch below.

Sounds, he means. Appearances do not enter into this caper. It's a wonderful world. As the song assures us.

A woman's voice, husky, says: Arthur, this is Emma.

Emma, dilemma, dilemma, dilemma.

He says: Emma.

— Arthur love, don't bother about what they say. Come over here to me.

Which at the moment he feels he might almost do, if he knew where she was. Or who. That voice.

— Arthur, do you read me?

— Loud and clear.

— Are you coming?

— Pronto.

And puts down the phone, and turns to face the porter and the music.

So the porter pours the ginger into the brandy and hands it to him and says: You sat here for a while last night, sir. After the others had gone.

Remembering Eamonn. Now he begins to remember something of the night.

— Nine of you used to meet here.

— Eamonn Murray and the rest of us.

— Poor Mr Murray, God be good to him. One decent man. He thought the world and all of you.

A silence. The phone also is mercifully silent.

— About Mr Mulqueen, sir.

— Who?

— Mulqueen, sir. His room, you know.

— Of course. Face the music, Mulqueen.

— You know him, sir?

— Not too well. A sort of passing acquaintance.

— You'll be glad to hear he's well, sir. They fished him safely out of the river. Nobody here knows a thing about it yet. An errand boy came in the back and told me. I sent him about his business. No harm done.

Another silence. He puts the last three notes on the table between the beds, flattens them down under an ashtray: That's for your trouble, Peter Callanan.

Memory, fond memory brings the light.

— How much do I owe you for the brandy?

— It came out of the dispense, sir.

— The name's Arthur.

— They won't miss it for a while.

— But we can't have that. I'll be back as soon as the banks open.

— No panic. No panic at all. You're old stock. Nine of you. And Mr Murray. The flower of the flock.

— What did he do that for? Jump?

— God knows, sir. He seemed such a quiet orderly man. Never

33

touched a drop. And in broad daylight. Stood up on the wall and jumped with the city watching. He couldn't have meant it. Missed a moored dinghy by inches. But he did miss it.

— He had luck, the dog, 'twas a merry chance.

— What's that, sir?

— Oh, nothing. A bit of an old poem. How they kept the bridge of Athlone.

— Athlone. It's a fine town. I worked there for a summer in the Duke of York. Mr Murray was a great man for the poetry. He could recite all night. Under yonder beechtree. And to sing the parting glass.

He leads the way along the corridor and down the backstairs to the basement, then along a tunnel with store-rooms like treasure-caves to right and left. They shake hands.

— Many thanks, Peter.

— Good luck, sir.

— Them's your cats.

Two cats are wooing in the carpark across the laneway.

— What's that, sir?

— Oh, nothing. Just a sort of a proverb where I come from.

— Like out of the question as Ronnie Donnegan said.

— Something like that.

Bloodless Byrne to the right, Ronnie Donnegan to the left, he walks away along the laneway. He hasn't had the heart to ask Peter Callanan what it was that was out of the question. Ahead of him Eamonn walks, forever reciting: Under yonder beechtree, single on the greensward, couched with her arms beneath her golden head, blank a blank a blanky, blank a blank a blanky, lies my young love sleeping in the shade.

He must ring Sligo and tell her that all is well. All is well. Somewhere poor Pussyfoot Mulqueen is being dried out through the mangle. All may not be well. The music is waiting.

There is a group of seven or eight people by the river-wall. One young fellow points. As if Mulqueen had made a permanent mark on the dark water.

He has never seen the man's face. Shared his life for a bit. Shared it? Lived it.

And he goes on over the bridge to the bank.

34

MOCK BATTLE

HE SINGS A few lines of the song about blue birds over the white cliffs of Dover. He looks through the downpour at the black face of the stone quarry. It leans like doom over the tiny station. The Belfast-bound train moves on to give them a clear view of the quarry's brute ugliness. Nobody working there today, no bewildered rooks fluttering before that formidable face. No sensible bird would be out of the house in such weather.

He says that all his life he seems to have been looking at that quarry, in all weathers: going south, going north, ever since he first went to Dublin when he was ten, on an excursion train and that was twenty-one years ago.

She says: If the photographer doesn't fish why does he always carry a fishing-rod in the back of the car?

— Only when he's travelling in the country.

— But why? Even in the country. If he doesn't fish. You wouldn't expect him to drive round and round Belfast with a fishing-rod.

— It's quite simple.

He is, and he knows it, painfully flippant. He knows that she also knows. The air is gelid in the wooden shelter. Although outside, even in the downpour, it must be hot and sticky. It is the middle of July.

— You didn't explain how simple.

— He has good contacts with that sort of magazine, in London and in the States, *Field and Stream, Over the Hills and Faraway, Up the Aery Mountain and down the Rushy Glen, Beyond the East the Sunrise beyond the West the Sea, Come Hear the Woodland Linnet, Wander Lust, Stand and Stare*, and all that sort of thing. You can imagine.

— I can quite easily imagine.

35

Twenty-one years ago, going south, he had passed along here, not more than twenty paces from where he now sits sheltering. Not another soul now to be seen on the drenched pitiable platforms (only two) of the junction or station or halt or what you will. The brutal quarry over all. The few people who have disembarked with them from the northbound train have departed in automobiles, leaving them to wait in that wooden box of a shelter for the cameraman driving from Belfast with his fishing-rod and, it is to be assumed, his camera. But twenty-one years ago the sun had been shining. He sat beside his father, a travelled man and proud of it. Jamie Kyle, the town-crier from his own home-town, sat across from them. Now, as a much-travelled journalist, he knows that there are only two town-criers left in Ireland, one in Listowel in Kerry, one somewhere in Connacht. He has told her about that journey: how Jamie, looking out the window, had misnamed every landmark they passed, and been patiently corrected by his father. The town-crier was not a travelled man. His duties did not demand it. That was the first time he himself had seen the Mourne mountains, the Carlingford hills, the Irish Sea.

She takes one step into the rain, stands shivering for a moment, steps back again. She says that it's a great day for a battle or a pageant or whatever. She says that she can quite easily imagine but she still can't understand about the fishing-rod. If he doesn't fish.

— A day like this, she says, will destroy Alison's service. She'll rust.

He ignores that one. He tells her about the fishing-rod.

— He likes to take photographs of people fishing. Preferably with an old humpy stone bridge in the background. So wherever and whenever he sees a fine old stream and a pleasant bridge . . .

— A railway bridge wouldn't do.

. . . he ambushes the first passing stranger, what George Moore would have called a chance shepherd . . .

— The apt literary reference.

. . . . and mounts the rod, puts it in the stranger's hand, asks him to stand on the bank and be photographed. He's made some masterly pictures that way. The *Observer* once used a whole page of them. He's a first-class man.

She has lost interest. She touches, with those elegant hands, her slightly-hollow cheeks. Those hands were the first things he had noticed, at rest, swans on a lake, on a desk at a German class in college. A sideways kick of the wind scatters rain around them. In such a place, on such a day, the white Parisian net, binding or ornamenting her dark hair, is to him aggravatingly absurd. She says: Weather like this must be bad for the guts, I mean of tennis racquets. Alison will wilt.

Coatless he stands in the rain and looks south towards Dublin: and there on the platform, and praised be to Jesus, is the photographer proudly advancing, stepping in through a gateway in the white wooden railings, normally a tall greyheaded, bespectacled, professorial sort of a man, but now, with an overcoat and a pacamac over it, an enormous egg, or an elongated, bloated french-letter: Princely O'Neill, and that isn't his name, to my aid is advancing with many a chieftain and warrior clan: he carries no rod, he carries no tripod, he carries no cross and he carries no stone but he stops when he comes to the grave of Wolfe Tone.

The rain has eased somewhat. One solitary stupid rook is peering and picking around the face of the quarry. The ghosts of twenty-one years ago go south down the line.

The fishing-rod, the camera and more besides are in the boot of the car. In their company he places his briefcase and overnight bag. He explains to the photographer that, after the mock-battle, they will leave his wife, Dublin-bound, back to the station. Then the two of them will go on to Belfast to cover the opening of that new theatre. She explains that she must go back to Dublin to relieve the baby-sitter and look after the children. There is one child. She says that Anthony's favourite sport is tennis, not fishing: You couldn't keep him away from Fitzwilliam. Even when he's supposed to be working.

Innocently the photographer responds: I played there once myself. In a club competition. I have relations in Donnybrook, quite close to Fitzwilliam.

— Then you'd understand perfectly.

They pass over a canal bridge, old and narrow, with a high arch. Nobody around to be conscripted or pressed into fishing. Then through a village where the sun is shining and the photographer says

37

that it may be a good day after all. She is in the back seat, half-reclining, her hands locked around her knees, gracefully raised. She says: Anthony says that life begins every day you waken up. Isn't that a beautiful thought?

From a rise in the road they see to the east a small handsome pear-shaped lake. It glistens under a brightening sky. Beyond the lake a broad slope of parkland. On the crest of the slope a great house with a backdrop of high trees.

— That's the field, the photographer says.

With a childish curiosity, subtly planned, and in a most gentle voice, she asks: What field, Mr Lockhart?

— Where the mock battle's held. What else? The two armies get ready in the yards behind the house.

— That must be fascinating. Two armies. They have to be very big yards.

He is a simple man and notices nothing, Anthony hopes, in the style of her talk, slightly elevated, carefully picking and pronouncing the words, a missionary lady speaking English to a black baby. When he was a boy the missionary propaganda urged you to buy a black baby. Somewhere in Africa he now must own six or seven, grown-up and bouncing. Male or female? He laughs at the idea.

— Anthony, she says, is amused. He has secret jokes.

— It's good fun, Lockhart says. And, unlike a lot of what goes on here in Ulster, it's harmless. Just a pageant. Orange and Green. King James and King William. Year after year. Celebrating the battle of the Boyne in 1690, you know. Not a shot fired in anger. You crossed the Boyne today on the way up from Dublin. Over the big viaduct at Drogheda.

She has lost interest: a trick she has. She says: There's a chap Anthony knows, a printer, a rather coarse fellow. He goes to all the tournaments in Fitzwilliam. He says tennis brings out the woman in a woman. I wonder what he means.

— Pageants, says Lockhart.

He is speaking into a long silence. Outside the sun is making a brave effort.

— Pageants, he says, have a way of going aft agley.

— Ah, she says, like the best-laid plans of mice and men. Burns sounds so much better in an Ulster accent. Anthony reads Burns so well.

It doesn't seem necessary to acknowledge the compliment.

— There was a chronic pageant at Carrickfergus in County Antrim. I got a good picture of the actual incident. Right under the big Norman castle. It must be the biggest castle in Ireland.

— Trim, Anthony says. I mean Trim Castle. In County Meath. Or perhaps Liscarrol by Buttevant in North Cork. Except that Liscarrol's only a shell now. Goats depredating within the empty walls.

— Anthony, she says, is very good on castles.

— I was lucky to get that picture. The actual incident. Chronic. It made a holy laugh out of the whole business. You see it was meant to be the landing of King William of Orange. That actually was where he landed. Carrickfergus. Before 1690 and the battle of the Boyne. The sea was choppy that day. And at the very moment when the king was to step on to the quayside the boat bucked and King William landed on his backside in the briny.

— The real King William.

She asks so innocently.

— No, of course not. The man in the pageant.

Lockhart seems, for the moment, taken aback. Anthony is annoyed. All very well to play this game with or on your familiars, meaning your erring if suffering husband, but not with or on strangers. So with great determination, and knowing that she feels she may have gone too far, he caps the story of what happened at Carrickfergus with the story of what happened on the Boyne at Drogheda. The great resonant Shakespearean actor, Anew McMaster, was involved: playing St Patrick in a pageant for a Patrician jubilee year. That, they say, was where St Patrick landed. Drogheda. McMaster dressed in a long white linen robe. Stepped out on what he thought was solid ground and went up to the hips in mud. Floundered out, cursing blue, went into a riverside pub, squelching and dripping, and proclaimed: *Ego Patricius, filius diaconi Calpurnii, servus servorum Dei*, and in the name of Christ crucified who rose again even for the redemption of the citizens of Drogheda, serve me a large glass of Irish whiskey.

Lockhart thinks that is a very funny story and goes to prove what he always thought about pageants. The Dutch King goes forever, and seat first, into the salt water. The Britoroman Saint resurrects, orating and cursing, out of the mud of the sacred river, Boyne. The brave effort of the sun is weakening. The woman is silent. Anthony hums a tune. They drive on towards the mock-up of an ancient battle.

In a barn behind the Big House and gathered all around a silent resting tractor, the young fellows are dressing for the mock battle. King William sits high on a tractor studying the style of both armies. He is the only one to wear a crown. He has a grey moustache. King James wears a bowler. Anthony thinks of Oberammergau. He has never been there.

Back in the village the one hilly street has been crowded. This is a rural festival, a market-day as well as a pageant. Stalls on the streets and the rain beginning again. Loud singing from public houses. Men wearing orange sashes and blue sashes and black sashes all glittering with metal insignia. And bowler hats by the billion. Like London stockbrokers. Men staggering two by two and three by three out of one pub and into another, defying the weather, friends greeting friends. On one market stall a splendid display of delph chamber-pots, brightly beflowered.

— Twenty yards long if it's an inch, Lockhart says. Sixty feet of Charleys.

He is lost in wonder. He is a tall grey, gentle, inoffensive man. He takes several photographs. He asks the man who owns the stock and the stall to hold two of the bright objects aloft and takes two more photographs.

— No happy home, the man says, should be without at least one.

— All rural comforts, Lockhart says. And repeats: All rural comforts.

She walks on through the mizzling rain. Anthony follows. From the boot of the parked car Lockhart takes one of those large coloured umbrellas you see at racecourses. All along the avenue from the village to the field of battle patient people shelter under dripping trees. Steam rises from a tea-tent. Three pipers, all in Stuart tartan, drone in meditative preparation in a corner of the barn. They have to be brothers. They look like bloody-well triplets. They disregard the bucolic warriors. They greet Lockhart as an old friend.

— Brothers from Belfast, he says. In Scotland once they piped for the queen.

He takes their picture: for the twentieth time, he says. But this is special. They will lead two kings and two armies to the watery field. They stand and pipe under a picture of the queen on the wall of the barn. She sits on her horse. She wears a busby and a crimson jacket and looks very well. The warriors, some of them, cheer. For Lockhart or the pipers or the queen in the saddle? Does she know that if it hadn't been for what's going to happen today she mightn't be sitting there? Anthony opens his notebook and begins to ask questions. She says: Record it all for posterity. A day to remember. Another day out of our lives. I'll go to the tea-tent and the loo if there is one.

She walks away, swaying with style, stepping well in black, glittering, well-fitting kneeboots. No sodden wrinkles or furrows there. She knows how to wear those things. The warriors show some interest and for a moment Anthony is, nostalgically, compelled to admire. But why, oh why, had she ever said that she wished to come?

It isn't all that easy to distinguish one army from the other. Berets, and cocked hats plumed with esparto grass, brown corduroy breeches and white canvas breeches, and wellingtons, and hobnails and leggings are all over the place. And braided jackets, some red, some blue, some green, whimsically distributed it would seem. More greens than reds or blues, which is odd. No orange jackets. Which is odder.

— Collect our swords, King James says, and we'll fight you in front of the house.

Asking around so as to fill his notebook Anthony discovers that every man is a bit vague about the exact origins of the battle. Nothing in that to wonder at. Three hundred years ago did the poor bloody footsloggers who marched down to the Boyne water at Oldbridge, or defended the last ditch at the defile of Duleek, know what in hell it was all about? King William himself, a stout cheerful purple-faced

41

man and well able to handle his unhistoric but traditional off-white horse, is non-committal: It's a day out, you see. It's a day out for the local people. The weather's seldom as bad as it is today. We should have held it over by Poyntzpass.

— Why so?

— When it rains in Scarva the sun shines in Poyntzpass. That's what you'd call a proverb.

A young man who admits to being a Jacobite says cheerily as he gathers up his blanks: We'll riddle ye.

Another voice says: Where's Morrison till I get a rattle at him.

King James says: No shouting, boys. No language. Remember there are ladies on the platform. Real ladies.

Over a loudspeaker, and away round at the front of the house, somebody is making a speech: but a gusty wind and the strengthening rain make mockery of all oratory. Croaking rattles, minor explosions, a few scrambled words get as far as the farmyard, words you'd expect anyway and readily recognize: loyal, the Queen, the Union and the United Kingdom, No Surrender, Derry, Aughrim and the Boyne, No Popery, the Pious and Immortal Memory.

With a hey-ho, the wind and the rain.

A Williamite, also self-confessed, says: Put all your bullets in at wance and you'll have a machine-gun.

And another voice and another and another: How many bullets do we get? Do they let a bang? They wouldn't be much good if they didn't . . .

Babel of voices and several bangs and somebody shouts: Save your bullets for the battle.

And a voice that most certainly belongs to a horsetrooper ignores the regal veto on language and wants to know what hoorin' bastard stole his gun.

King William commands: Boys, no firing in the farmyard.

King James in the hayshed retreats up a haystack to get out of the rain and, after a while, calls down, voice muffled by warm hay, to know if the service is over. From outside, rising and falling with the wind and the rain, comes the sound of the singing of hymns: the human voice, unlike the crackles of the loudspeaker, riding easily on the elements. Lockhart sings along: Awake, sweet harp of Judah, wake, retune thy strings for Jesus sake. When God's right arm is bared for war, the thunders clothe his cloudy car, where, where, oh, where shall man retire to escape the horrors of his ire?

Lockhart reckons that that's a good question. He suggests the tea-tent. He says he has enough pictures of idiots to fill a *Mad* comic. A Jacobite whose gun won't work holds up for a while the march to Armageddon and King William takes him behind the lines, into the hayshed, to make the weapon battleworthy. King James descends from the haystack and slowly and stiffly mounts a bay cart-horse, a tank of a horse. He is a cadaverous Quixote of a man. One voice cries: Foward March.

Another voice responds: We can't be out there galloping around in the middle of God Save the Queen.

One young man tells Anthony that he's dying for a drink but the rule is no booze before the battle. Another, more academic, tells him that in former times they used to take the royal prisoner, meaning King James, back to the barn with his hands bound behind him. Anthony is about to say that King James wasn't captured at the Boyne, that he was halfways to Cork or Waterford or somewhere on the road to gallant France before the bloody day was well begun. But who cares and what's the point? The hymn-singing is ended. On distant brass the anthem has been played. King James in his stirrups stands up and cries: Follow on, boys, follow on.

Anthony notes: If he had only been so forward at the original battle history might have been altered.

So they march to the field and their banners, they have several, are so gay, defying even the brutal downpour: the Jacobites in the lead: but before and foremost of all the three famous pipers, the three McCoys, all splendid in the battle-plaid of the royal Stuarts. They play the piobaireacht of Domhnall Dhu and Lord Mansfield's march, and the Munster battle-song (Rosc Catha na Mhumhan) to which, depending on your politics, you can also sing the words of the Boyne Water: July the first in Oldbridge town there was a grievous battle, where many a man lay on the ground by the canons that did rattle. King James he pitched his tents between the lines for to retire. But King William threw his bomballs in and set them all on fire.

The dating is old-style in the old verse. Anthony is writing like mad. He notes: Today, unlike in the past, it is an ecumenical sort of a battle.

And: If the only guns ever heard in the north of Ireland were the guns of Scarva then the north of Ireland would be a happy place.

In her absence his genius is unrebuked.

With Lockhart beside him, or half a pace ahead, he brings up the rear leaving a desolate dripping farmyard behind them. Oddly enough no animals are to be seen. Hidden in an upland booley while the marauding soldiery passes? Lockhart's pacamac glistens with a thousand jewels. Somewhere out in the rain, on the sodden slope going down to the pearl-shaped lake, the battle is joined.

— There was a fellow there, says Lockhart, who told me that one year King James won the battle.

— Kidding. You must be.

— No. The same King James is here today. The gloomy fellow. Settled and sober now. He took religion. But a wild one when he was young. Got roaring drunk and cleared the field.

Anthony has his lead par: Here on the historic field of Scarva, where year after year the battle of the Boyne is replayed in pageant, the course of history was, on one celebrated occasion, dramatically reversed . . .

Lockhart is laughing. He has a helpless silent laugh that shakes his body and contorts his lined, amiable face and, just at the moment, showers raindrops all around him: That's pageants for you. Essentially ridiculous. All end up in mockery. Pageants are preposterous. The pipers told me that if they played all the Roman hymns and Irish rebel songs ever heard of these rustics wouldn't know the difference. Still it's a day out. A day out for the country people. Pos and all.

Anthony writes: In days to come a man from these places may proudly hold up a delph domestic utensil and say to his son: My great greatgrandfather brought that home from the mock battle of Scarva.

Heirlooms. Tradition. The meaning of history.

All the way to the tea-tent Lockhart is singing in the rain: Then pure, immortal, sinless, freed, we, through the Lamb, shall be decreed: Shall meet the Father face to face and need no more a dwelling-place.

All Anthony can think of saying is: And all day long the noise of battle rolled.

In the tea-tent she is seated, legs elegantly crossed: and it's not all that easy for a lady in long boots to sit cross-legged with elegance. She sips tea and talks with two women in blue overall coats. They are the supervisors of the six girls who serve the tea and they have suspended their own serving and supervising to talk with the handsome stranger. She is very gracious. She is always gracious to other women, even to Alison when they meet. Which hasn't been often. She says she admires young girls who play tennis well: such fine leg-muscles so well displayed by those short white skirts, gorgeous Gussie, frills on her panties. Or is that passé: and do they, perhaps, go to tennis in dungarees, like the young ones you see on the streets nowadays, all dressed up for the shipyards?

One of the blue ladies brings tea to Lockhart and Anthony. Then the two of them excuse themselves and go back to their work. She says: Anthony, they're so polite. One of them told me she saw the Queen speaking to Roman Catholics. At an army parade in London. She says the Queen doesn't mind Roman Catholics. That's the way she put it. The Queen doesn't mind Roman Catholics.

Lockhart says that in his local in Belfast there's a little Orangeman in a bright-check cloth cap who sits on his own in a corner of the snug and laughs into his pint and at intervals says to himself: Roman Catholics make me laugh.

— You have strange ways up here, Mr Lockhart. Anthony comes from up here. He often tells me so. Even if the Queen never spoke to him. But then he's only a lapsed Roman Catholic.

Passing with a tray of steaming cups of tea, one of the blue women says: The wasps would worry you. There must be a nest of them here where we planted the tent. They're thick around the sandwiches.

But she seems quite cheerful about it. Even more cheerful when Lockhart tells her that the wasps are half-Orange and have every right to be there: and then he demonstrates to her that a few spoonfuls of strawberry jam dissolved in a big jar of boiling water, and cunningly placed in a corner of the tent where she suspects the

45

nest may be, will draw the wasps from the sandwiches to a warm, sweet doom.

Wasps and tents. Wasps in a tent. Even a single wasp in a tent. Anthony first met Alison in a tent. At night when you're asleep into your tent I'll creep, bleep-bleep-bleep, for I'm the Shake of Awrabee and your love belongs to me. That was at a charity tennis-tournament in a village in the Wicklow mountains, and how he found his way there or what he was doing there he cannot exactly remember. It was a warm day and the trestle-table holding the teacups and sandwiches was out in the open air. But the honey-coloured, blonde, young girl, short white skirt, legs well-made yet by no means trunks of trees, had withdrawn to the tent to sip tea in the shade. They sat beside each other on an upturned, wooden packing-case. They laughed a lot. Her forehead perspired from the tennis and the tea, and bore the faint thin line left behind by the green eye-shade. Nobody in the tent except the two of them and a single wasp buzzing somewhere unseen. So he told her about another tent and time, and even about another wasp: when he was ten or thereabouts, on a bright day at a sports-meeting just outside his home-town. A pileup on the track in a cycle-race and one of the cyclists, a big golden haired man, had an injured leg.

— He was helped into this bell-tent, you see, and I peeped in and there he was, sitting on the ground, dribbling whiskey into tea and sipping it. He saw me peeping and called me in. He had sandwiches, too, the thinnest sandwiches I've ever seen. He offered me a sandwich. But this one wasp kept buzzing around it. His hair was nearly the colour of the yellow or golden bits of the wasp. There was a smell of whiskey from the tea. But it was nothing to the smell of embrocation, so thick in the tent you could nearly see it. It put me off. I didn't know what it was. At that time. So I refused the sandwich and I can still see the look of hurt and puzzlement on his face. He seemed to be a gentle sort of fellow. And all the time that one bloody wasp kept buzzing.

Alison listened to all that and seemed to take him seriously. Not the brightest girl in the world, perhaps, and with none of the style of somebody with a French mother. But she listened to that story as if it meant something to her. Then they searched for that one wasp but, although they could hear it buzzing as merrily as a bird sings, they never did find out where it was.

From the field where fame is lost and/or won, wet people come in, really dripping, to be warmed by cups of tea. The tent is filling.

— Anthony, she says, is at his dreams again. He's smiling to himself.

Yet he feels that he detects, just for an instant, the echo of affection in her voice.

At Poyntzpass, as Lockhart puts it, the sun is splitting the stones. But she points out that while the sun is shining and no rain falling the stones are unperturbed. Nobody, just or unjust, to be seen. They're all back at the battle, or the aftermath of the battle, and the rain, most likely, lashing merrily down.

— It was always assumed by me, Anthony says.

— A statement, Mr Lockhart. Anthony is about to make a statement.

— That when my decent Orange neighbours had a day out they were blessed with good weather. Nobody ever heard that it rained on the great day, the twelfth of July. So why should it rain all day in Scarva on the thirteenth.

She suggests that the reason may be that the sun shone on Scarva all day yesterday.

Sharp and clear the quarry stands up like a monstrous desert fortress on the rim of the ridge ahead of them. A long freight train goes South.

— It's a mystery, Lockhart says, that we may never understand.

— Don't bother to wait with me, she says. You must get to Belfast. You have a play to cover. It might be a scoop. It might be a hot story.

The rooks have left the quarry-face and flown off homeward to join their own chapel.

— Won't you come with me?

He is doing his best, he thinks, to settle the row that blew up on the train from Dublin. But she doesn't answer him. She says to

Lockhart: I've things to do in Dublin. More or less urgently. And early in the morning. And there are the children.

One child. And a housemaid. There was one miscarriage.

Lockhart says that he knows, he knows. That children are a problem. She raises her right hand and opens and closes it in farewell to Lockhart, and walks away from them along the empty platform.

For the people of this new theatre a local poet has written a fine celebratory poem. To players everywhere, he says, he owes much thanks. Such circumstances, he says, they have set before his mind that he has shed his momentary care. Anthony's care seems more than momentary. She's in Dublin now, finding a taxi to take her home. At the first interval Lockhart and himself slip out for a whiskey. It has been a long, wet, disheartening day. To the mad King and his fool the poet sends his thanks, to the broken man who sees flame make a saint, to the peevish pair who wait beside the tree, to the harridan who urges her cracking wheels beyond despair, to all who have given him rapt occasion of a richer kind, O'Casey's humours, Lorca's sultry rage, the Theban monarch's terror, gouged and blind. A fine poet, but at the moment doing nothing for Anthony. She is opening the hall-door now, entering the house they had once entered so happily. At the second interval Lockhart and himself go out for another whiskey. During the third act he dozes for a while. Grotesque yokels march out to do mock battle. Alison and himself fail again and again to find that wasp.

In the foyer when all is quiet a few of the theatre people are drowsily chatting. He sits by the telephone in the manager's office which opens off the foyer. He sips a third and very large whiskey, courtesy of the house. Lockhart, similarly sipping and quite content, stands in the doorway. In Dublin the telephone rings for a long time: is answered at last by a sleepy housemaid. She isn't home yet. But he can hear her voice out there in the foyer, talking to and being welcomed by a tall actress, an old friend: But you're so late. I should be in Dublin. It's so lovely to see you. The Dublin train I missed. Nothing for it but to come to Belfast. But we didn't know you were coming. Anthony didn't tell us. Anthony didn't know. He will be so surprised to see me.

48

She is in the doorway beside Lockhart. He replaces the telephone. She says: Surprise, surprise, surprise.

She says: Is Alison not here? Or there?

Then: There may be a dance in the club. The mirth may be so high that none of them can hear the phone.

Lockhart is trying not to listen, trying to shuffle away.

— Or is she not there, where and when you expected her to be. An awful thought. She may be fickle. La donna etcetera.

Lockhart has moved out of sight, far enough away to meet and briefly prevent the tall actress and the manager's wife.

— You were phoning her.

— Who's her?

— Bouncing little Alison, playing bat and ball. You were phoning her.

— No I wasn't. I wasn't phoning Alison, bat or ball or bouncing.

— Who then were you phoning?

Nobody could better answer that question than herself, but she's not in Dublin to answer it. Which is absurd. He is very tired. He gulps his whiskey: hot but tasteless. The tall actress, the manager and his wife, and Lockhart playing a hopeless delaying game, are at the doorway. The manager wears a crimson shirt. He says: A most unexpected pleasure. You must kip with us. We'll have a ball.

— We wouldn't dream. Would we Anthony? Anthony has had a most tiring and disappointing day.

He picks up the telephone. He says: My wife missed the Dublin train and came on here.

Lockhart smiles at everybody in turn. All over Ireland and the neighbouring island and France and Germany and Spain, all over the bloody world, there are wonderful rivers and bridges and passing strangers who will readily pose as anglers. Anthony fingers the dial: There's the Royal Avenue hotel and the Grand Central and the Union.

— The Union let it be. You could call it symbolic. Anthony sees symbolism all over the place.

— I stayed there when I was a boy.

— What happy associations it will have. For Anthony.

The tall actress has felt the cool wind and is talking and acting as

49

she never did on the stage. The doorway is suddenly crowded with people. The manager pours drink for all, large glasses and a steady hand: it's a solution of a sort. The ball is on. So from memory he dials the number and says: Is that the Union hotel?

And, as it so happens, it is.

THROUGH THE FIELDS IN GLOVES

He never will forget the face of the first of the sixteen girls he
assaulted. Of the lot of them perhaps she appealed to him most.
Light on her feet. Bouncing. Miniskirted. Minnehaha. Auburn hair
in little kinky curls that looked as if you strummed them they'd play a
tune. She was so surprised she couldn't say a sound. Her mouth
opened in a perfect O. A perfect pink O, and little teeth showed and a
flickering tongue, but no sound came out. Blue jacket with brass
buttons. White silk flouncey scarf. White skirt, and so little of it that
he had free play with her fragile legs. She raised her arms, hands
drooping, as if she was about to fly. Her white small handbag fell to
the ground and he was sorely tempted to grab it as a souvenir: there's
nothing left for me of days that used to be, there's just a memory
among my souvenirs. She wore no gloves. She was up on tiptoe for a
while, really about to take off. But he flew instead, his work well
done, her white skirt splashed with red. He could run like a hare,
quick round the corner past the big, rich red-brick houses, high
spiked iron railings, high privet hedges, a road on which you seldom
met moving people. Then across the park by the lakeside walk, high
hedges again, God himself can scarcely see what's going on down
here. Out on the bank of the river, across the bridge by the bakery,
down along the riverwalk: on the opposite side of the roadway a chain
of small, poor cottages, a different world. No one would ever expect
to find you in two such different places on the same day: then sit on a
bench and watch the river widening towards the sea. A pity about the
white handbag. The wife woulda loved it, even if she couldn't show it
off. But perhaps it was safer that way. No evidence of his deed. No
souvenirs. There's nothing left for me when Mama's had her tea, she
eats as much in hours as I could do in years. He doesn't like that

51

song. Some fellow who thought he was funny made up the words all over again and all wrong, just as if he knew about what wasn't his business.

As quiet here as in a church when there's nothing going on. There's a bit of a green park and a few benches. The river's very wide and slow now. Brown and green blobs of scum floating on it. A few ducks. A man said to him one day do you ever go up to evening devotions in that church in that convent in Drumcondra, you should you know, all the nuts in Dublin go there, who's a nut, but he meant no offence, all the nuts do go there, why he doesn't know, hopping from one foot to the other, sticking their thumbs in their mouths, but very quiet most of the time, that's the way to keep them: quiet. If the river and the city were not so dirty you could smell the salt from the sea.

The second girl was beautiful, but beauties can sometimes have no character, nothing you'd talk about or remember. Perfect complexion. Oh, a lot of bottles went into the making of that. Nose, a bit long. Long blonde hair. Light brown costume, a sort of fluffy hairy material. And nursing in her arms a packed plastic shopping-bag. So that she couldn't defend herself or her costume. She didn't scream. She said: Fuck you. You shit. Fuck you.

She was no lady. But he was gone like a flash before she could do fuck all about anything. It was oil that time.

The third girl: but how could you expect any man to remember everyone of sixteen girls. Or who would want to hear about them. But the fifth girl now was odd because she had a lame leg and ran after him and almost caught him. She could run like the black streak or the brown bomber or whoever it was. Something very abnormal about that and she lame. He felt sorry for her. In a sort of a way. She wasn't as well-dressed and fancypants and slim as the others.

Nobody to be seen in any direction but a few children playing by the edge of the water, and a wisp of a girl wheeling a pram, somebody else's pram, not her fault. A jet roars up from Collinstown, roars over the city, roars off to the south, roars and roars like a madman: at home, when they fly over, he can't hear his ears, or Martha whispering and sighing in her big chair, or Julia, who has goitre, rattling on forever about the Children of the Atom. They have a bloody nerve making that much noise. What he'd like to know is who gave them the right; packed full of slim bitches, that one still roaring, off south to Paris or Turkey or Torremolinos. He sweats at the thought of it, and shivers with the cold even though the sun is shining on the dirty water. The roar dies away. It's over Wexford by now: and he can again hear the children, little voices like birds. One of the Fatima ones was called Jacinta, but you don't say it like that, but with a hawk and a ha as if you were clearing phlegm. Julia and the goitre and the Children of the Atom. She can pronounce nothing. Some people were born with no brains.

Carefully he picks up his blue airlines zipper-bag: and walks home, thinking it's the funniest way to get to know people, women especially. You see them before. You see them during. You see them after: and sometimes you can even read what they say about you. He keeps the clippings, carefully hidden away. Poor Martha can't move and never would find them, but Julia's a curious hawk. And women get things wrong. And they tell lies. That one with the thin spike-heels, and pink pyjamas on her, out in the bright light of day: and a bundle of black hair, fuzzed out and blowing, and a face all painted, a bit of a tart and no better than she might be. When she saw the weapon she tried to run, but the left spike broke and down she went, and was at his mercy, covering her face with her hands and crying to the ground: and she was purple, hair and all, not pink, when he was finished with her. But the liar, she told the guards she fought like a tiger and might have marked his face. You couldn't trust their bible oath. Moreover she should have said tigress.

His cottage is number four in the last block of seven brown-brick cottages. Across the narrow roadway and over the low wall the tidal flow has held the greasy river to a standstill. Beyond number seven there's an acre of sparse salty grass, then sand and the flat sea. The sea-wind and sometimes even the spray or a flooding high-tide burn the grass. He turns to the right at number one, then left up the back laneway to the collapsing old garage at the rear of number four: his happy home. You could hide a corpse here, let alone a blue zipper bag: and if it didn't stink nobody would ever find it: old mattresses and old tea chests, the chassis of a dismantled motor, two broken lawnmowers, a discarded dresser. The landlord, who has houses out at rent all over the place, dumps everything here and removes nothing. But we can't complain, can we, he doesn't push for the rent, and he was always most considerate about Martha's misery, and he never minds us running the bit of a shop on the premises?

Here in an old wooden meat-safe that got woodworm is the perfect place for the bag of tricks, as secure as in the Bank of Ireland in College Green: Julia calls it the Bank of the Island, she can pronounce nothing. Nothing. Then out again and around the front of the cottages, approaching this time from the side of the sea: and down two stone steps and into the shop, alarm-bell ringing, and through the shop, Julia gulping with the goitre behind the scales and the counter: and into the kitchen behind the shop, and Martha in her chair, God help us all.

He lives on eggs most of the time, henfood out of their own shop. Julia isn't much of a cook and Martha can't rise out of the chair, a big rocking-chair that because of her weight won't rock. So he cooks his own eggs, boiled, fried, poached, scrambled, but not omelettes, he was never any good at omelettes, it's just as well that he doesn't like them: and the bin on the day before the dustbinmen call is always so full of eggshells that he fears that when he lifts the lid to put in more eggshells there'll be nothing more or less to be heard but chirping chickens. Martha lives on slops and milkfoods, stuff for toothless children, that Julia cooks for her, if you could call anything that Julia does cookery: and the bell rings from above the shopdoor, and Julia runs in and out, gobbling like a turkey, between the scullery and kitchen and the shop: mostly children sent out on messages by lazy parents, small orders, eggs, loaves, bottles of milk, tins of stuff, on and on long after the big shops have closed, the thin ones in white coats won't work after six, out walking with idlers who'll get them all in the family way and that'll fatten them. That's the advantage we have, charging high when the other shops are closed and the public can't get it anywhere else. He'd spoil their whiteness for them, only you couldn't very well go into a crowded shop in broad daylight on a commando: he had thought, off and on, of wearing white, white overalls like a painter, when he was out on a raid, but then you'd be too easily seen from a long distance, either advancing to attack or retreating, mission accomplished, in good order.

No, the best disguise was the old cloth cap, the old reliable: although he had thought of blackening his face like a paratrooper. The trouble was how would you get it washed again in time: in the lake in the park with the ducks quacking at you and the water thick as treacle from those Muscovy monsters? Too pass-remarkable. Once when he was a young fellow and sneaking out at night to try to pick up the dirty young ones that hung around a certain chipshop on the Northside, Martha had always been a decent girl and hadn't hung around like that and look at the thanks the goodness of God gave her, he had walked right under the nose of his own father, and a fine long nose he had, he takes after his father in that, who didn't know him from Adam because he was wearing a cloth cap he always kept hidden in a secret place of his own in the house: nobody at home knew he had it and it wasn't much of a cap but it was as good as a mask. In Belfast, a plumber's mate once told him, they called cloth caps dunchers, neither he nor the plumber's mate who worked for a while for his own father with the nose, knew why: and in Glasgow, hookerdoons, because you hooked them doon over one eye. He often laughed to himself at that joke, Scotchmen were funny like Harry Lauder, when he was a boy he had seen Harry Lauder in the old Royal, laughed his sides sore.

Julia is sitting there as she always sits on the very rim of a round-bottomed cane chair, the sort you see in bootshops, always on the rim as if she hadn't enough backside to fill a chair: and reading out of the evening paper and saying Peter the Painter strikes again. Every time she reads out about Peter the Painter she tells over and over again what the Raid Indian did to the girl in Summerhill on the Northside, she means Red Indian, she never gets anything right. She says she knew the girl and the Raid Indian but with Julia, who's as thin as a broomstick except for the goitre God pity her, you never can credit a word.

The Raid Indian, she says, wasn't a proper Indian at all but a fellow from Ballybough on his way to a Francy Dress Ball in the Mansion House, and in Summerhill he stabbed a young one with a knife.

55

And Martha stirs and the chair strains and she says what did he want to do that for.

As if she hadn't heard it all before.

Julia says that the young one was sixteen and as bold as brass.

But why, Martha goes on, did he stab her.

He pays no attention. Julia's slim, fairenough, but it doesn't do her much good, she's able to walk but she's not out there on the streets, dressed to the ninetynines.

Julia says that the fellow was all dressed up you see for the francy dress, feathers on his head and things hanging out of him of all colours like the bend of the rainbow, and a knife in a bag, like the pictures, and two more with him, and a crowd after them, jeering, and the young one caught and pulled out a handful of his feathers and the next thing she knows a stab in the back.

Martha says the dirty brute.

Little she knows: but how would she know anything and she too heavy to get out of the chair and too afraid of choking to lie down. He could weep. And all those others free to come and go as they please.

But Julia says the judge said the fellow didn't mean it, and he was carried away and thought he was a real Raid Indian and the young one was tormenting and jeering and pulling his feathers. The cut was an inch and a half long and on the left side of her back bleeding and the fellow said he was doing a wardance and waving the knife and the young one hit against him and he didn't know he cut her until somebody told him, case dismissed. She had only two stitches.

Martha says that wonders never cease. She always says that.

Julia says pray, pray to Our Lady and the Children of the Atom, Russia will be converted and the sun started to roll from one place to another and changed colours, blue and yellow and everything, and came down nearly to the ground, and the people all crying and telling their sins out loud and there wasn't a priest anywhere, and then it jumped up again into the sky as cute as a coolcumber.

Julia's crazy: Julia says but this Peter the Painter must know he's doing it, he's done it before and he'll do it again.

Martha asks who was it this time, and points to the evening paper; and two of them, Julia says, photographs and all, they look as if they're pregnant: and the shopbell rings and Julia is up and out like a greyhound, so fast that he hasn't time even to ask her to bring him back a handful of eggs, all that running and excitement is good for the appetite, jogging.

Right well he knew but nearly too late that they were not pregnant. It was the funny clothes they were wearing. Julia never walks about on those swanky streets and roads, and knows nothing about the latest fashions. They looked like twins, short, bright, blonde hair, rimless glasses, little turneduppity noses: dressed like twins in blue-and-white smocks that made him make his mistake and use the spray, women who were up the pole couldn't run, spray one, spray two, red white and blue for England's glory, he mightn't have bothered about them only for that, red, white and blue like the Union Jack: and the way they looked at him as if he was of no account. But light white runner-shoes and bobbysox like John McEnroe and that should have warned him: took after him with the speed of light, saying nothing, just racing quiet like bad dogs, bitches, but no brains, no teamwork, no co-ordination. Tripped over each other and came down with a crash like a house falling, glasses flying east and west, and one of them was so winded that she couldn't get up or see where she was and the other stopped to help her, twins. The holy show of tangled legs and petticoats he saw when he looked back tempted him to give it another go and spray their legs so well that they'd be stuck together for a month of Sundays. But they might be only foxing, so he outfoxed them and vanished in the bushes.

But the lies they told. When Martha was asleep in the chair and Julia was busy in the shop with the late customers he cutely slipped the evening paper under his jacket so that later he could clip the clipping. Said he struck them and knocked them down, and that was a bloody lie because it was completely against his principles to touch a woman, slim or thin or fat or obese the doctors said, with his hands: and poor Martha, Julia says, has a gross of obesity. But, just like Julia, there never was a woman who could get anything right, except about the cap, in every clipping it said that Peter the Painter wore a cloth cap, but could never tell the colour, they didn't know he had three hookerdoons, that was as funny as Harry Lauder's red kilt, all three of different colours: and he'd buy a few more only it might be dangerous now to be seen in a shop looking for cloth caps: and they didn't know how easy it was to slip a cloth cap into a zipper bag and walk away, as cute as a coolcumber as Julia says, a tall bald man with a long nose. No woman or no clipping ever noticed that he had his father's nose but how could they since they had never known his father.

As he had known him when his father took him with him to help on jobs, and paid him a helper's wage, and he only a boy in short pants: his father was a decent man and fond of poetry. On the northside the father was a plumber, was no more, was long gone and resting in the faraway end of Glasnevin cemetery where all the patriots are buried. In the middle of the meadows, his father used to say, beside or behind Glasnevin or something, the corncrakes cry or creak all night long, or something like that, it was part of a poem: and his mother was a thin, quickwalking, brownfaced woman, hat pinned on one side, sixpence each way, never more and you couldn't have less, up and down the street all day long to the bookies, she could run like a hare: whatever happened to poor Martha to be there night and day like that in the chair: and the place that as a boy he liked best with his father was up on the roofs of the houses between the Strand Road and the northern railway, low houses and low roofs but with great gullies like mountain valleys and all sorts of treasures there that the kids would throw up from below, tennis balls, glassy marbles, yoyos, toys and once, believe it or not, a full-blown football: he had a world of his own up on those roofs and could think of all sorts of things: and the big black engine would go north on the same level as the roofs, and the people waving, and his father saying they'll be in Derry or Belfast before we're home for tea, and that you could write poetry and books about trains, the big wheels and the stories of all the people passing. Up on the lead of those gullies he learned to use the blowlamp, dead easy and the paintspray on the same principle, change the nozzle, one for paint, one for oil, and easy to come by for any man in the trade, and any God's amount of paint, he doesn't need much. As for poetry he was never much for that: but once in a pub, he could remember exactly when, because it wasn't often he darkened the door of a pub, redfaced bastards on whiskey and overdressed bitches drinking gins and tonics that cost the moon and sixpence, and a fat woman walked past to the loo as they called it nowadays and a drunk at the counter said why do you walk through the fields in gloves fat white woman whom nobody loves: and then said to the barman that that was a poem, as if anybody wouldn't have known, even if it wasn't much of a poem.

Misery Martha can't walk through the fields but she loves nice gloves. She has lovely small hands, not too pudgy about the knuckles and how did that drunk know that nobody loved the fat woman who walked out to the loo?

Julia doesn't like Peter the Painter. Julia says that if a girl works hard and saves up to buy good clothes, she ought to be allowed to wear them in peace and not to have some madman spraying her with paint and easel oil. How does Julia know they work hard: and the worst thing is that Martha agrees with her, creaking in her chair and saying yes, wonders will never cease, to everything Julia says: and Martha says the dirty brute where does he get all the paint, and he thinks that's all the thanks he gets.

Julia's a sort of a farout cousin to Martha and not too clean, and, sitting with the two of them in the kitchen, he often thinks that she could make a better fist of keeping Martha comfortable in her chair: and if it hadn't been for Julia and her tongue going like a hambell Martha would lie down at night, much better than sitting all the time except for the usual, and he always leaves the house then, and the two of them to work it out between them. He would never have shown Martha in the paper about the case of the woman choking, but Julia, no, nothing, nothing could stop her, a forty-stone woman crushed to her death by her own bulk while firemen, all in the evening paper, tried to widen the doors of her home to take her to the hospital: and the doctor said that she had recently developed influenza and began lying down in bed, and that that wasn't good for her and the fat around her chest crushed her to death: and for years before that she had slept sitting up, and that way, the weight didn't press on her. Eight men carried her on mattress-covered plywood boards and a whole other slew of men sawing the doors wider but she died before she could be put in the pickup truck that was waiting in front of the house: and all that, faraway in sunny California, full of slim stars dressed to kill and married forty times. But one girl, now that he thinks of it or that the clippings remind him, and the only thing she said she noticed was that Peter the Painter had a long nose: but he can remember nothing at all about her.

Does Julia ever wonder why the evening paper vanishes every time there's a piece in it about Peter the Painter: you'd never know with Julia, and thin people are hell for curiosity, and he must remember to take the evening paper away all the time, and not just now and then.

This particular morning the first one he notices is a girl in red tights and a long red thing halfways between a jacket and a proper coat: not much sense in spraying her with red paint. That was a sort of funny, and he should have said miss, can you wait here for a while and I'll run home and change to white or green: the green above the red as the song says. The evening before that Martha was watching teevee and Julia getting ready to go out to her sodality and rattling on about the Children of the Atom: and about how Lucia, Looseyah Julia says, had asked the lady about two girls who had died recently, from some place with a funny name, and how the lady said that one of them was already in heaven but that the other one would be in purgatory until the end of the world: and that was a long time to be in purgatory or anywhere else: Looseyah mustn't have liked the other one: and the little boy, Francisco, said that he saw God and God looked so sad that Francisco said that he would like to console him, and Lucia said that many many would be lost: not much point in being God and lord of all if you have to lose so many and to look so mournful about it, although to have to listen to the like of Julia and to look at poor Martha like a mountain in the chair would put a long face on Harry Lauder, keep right on to the end of the road, keep right on to the end: and Jesus wept and would weep again if he saw the way Julia washes herself, a dip to the tips of her fingers and a stab of the comb to her hair, and the hat cocked on her head and trotting off to her prayers with a regiment of pious ones the like of herself. For himself he washes long and hard, not that he needs it but his father was a clean man and he likes to take after his father: as fancy as those slim ones are they mightn't be any better at the washing than Julia, and a spray of paint might do them a good turn by forcing them into the bathtub. He had worked in bathrooms in swanky houses and it wouldn't do you good to look at some of them: and working by night in the cellarage of some fancy lounge bars, you couldn't work there by day because you and the staff would be falling over each other, the rats were as big as cats or calves, if people only knew what they were drinking or where it was stored: and a man once told him that nuns never washed below the navel, it was the rule, but he supposes it would be a sort of a sacrilege to go in for spraying nuns with paint, or even oil.

But keep right on to the end of the road, keep right on to the end, though the way be long let your heart be strong, keep right on round the bend: and round the bend is bloody well right and you can say that again or sing it, and plenty more where that came from, and you're breaking my heart all over again oh why should we part all over again, and poor Martha used to love that song: and perhaps this is the day that he should pack it: for that one in the red tights gives him a very hard look but he goes on his way and pays her no attention. How can she know what he has in his mind or·what he has in the zipper: and the next girl is a tall one with canary-yellow trousers and a blue sleeveless sweater, and the half-sleeves of a white blouse: all crying out for a splash of red. Thinfaced, redheaded, chewing, tightly pulled-in at the waist: her backside, though, when she falls and it's looking up at him, is fat and flabby and he feels that he may have made a mistake, and then he goes and makes a mistake for he stoops and hesitates and with one wipe she claws the cap off his head and nearly takes the head with it: and there he is, bald as a hoot as Julia says, and to make a bad job worse he isn't near the park that day but in a long quiet road at the back of the football grandstand and not a bush within miles: if you're tired and weary still journey on till you've come to your happy abode, and as he runs his feet hammer out the tune, and the road quiet and nobody to be seen: with a big stout heart to a long steep hill you may get there with a smile: freedom to run to the sound of your own hoofbeats like the bighorn sheep on the wild prairie and springtime in the Rockies on the teevee. Nobody to be seen but that one with the red tights fifty yards away along a side-road and waving her red arms at somebody in an upstairs window and shouting out allahakbar: he should have let her have it in the first place.

After that mishap he wears a hat: but some bloody burglar breaks into the old garage and breaks this and that and all round them, and steals the old mattress he keeps the clippings in. Julia says there are people around this place who would steal the grace out of the Hail Mary but, leaving all sides ajoke as she puts it, time it is and more than time that somebody put a stop to that Peter the Painter: and that one girl got a good look at him and that she had seen him before when he poured paint all over her, and that he was a bald man with a long nose. Martha says that wonders will never cease, it could be you, but he says I'm not the only one in the world: but, anyway, caution from now on and a nod's as good as a wink.

But the glooms and the restlessness when he looks at Martha in the chair and listens to Julia talking about Martha and Mary, and the Lord himself sitting in his chair, but well able to rise up out of it when he takes the notion, and ascend into heaven when the day comes round: and the Lord's Martha was able to move, not that she got much thanks for it, killing herself cleaning the house and Mary sitting on her ass at the Lord's feet getting all the kudos: a hell of a house it would be for the Lord or anybody else if Martha sat down and refused to get up and left the dishes in the sink.

On top of the hollum oak, says Julia to Martha, and Julia is always busy about many things and Martha, like Mary, sits and sits but not at the Lord's feet and, God of Almighty, she has not chosen the better part: on top of the hollum oak, the lady came from where the sun rises and places herself on top of the hollum oaktree, like the big trees in the park, that's what Francisco said when the Canon asked him: does she come slowly or quickly, she always comes quickly, do you hear what she says to Looseyah, no, do you ever speak to the lady, no, does the lady on the hollum oak ever speak to you, no I never asked her anything and she only speaks to Looseyah: and who does she look at, says the Canon, you and Jack Hinta or does she only look at Looseyah: no she looks at the three of us but she looks longer at Looseyah.

Whoever it was that robbed the old garage they wouldn't be able to make head or tail out of the clippings in the thin cardboard box in the old mattress, if they ever found them, or even, if they did find them, they'd just throw them away and never know that they were of any importance to anybody.

Martha says to Julia that the lady was very beautiful as if Martha was asking Julia a question and as if Martha hadn't heard this rigmarole twenty times over.

A hat isn't as good as a duncher or a hookerdoon: it doesn't sit so steady on the head.

Julia says that Francisco said that the lady on the tree was very beautiful, more beautiful than anybody Francisco had ever seen, with a long dress and over it a veil which covers her head and falls down to the edge of her dress which is all white except for gold lines, and she stands like somebody praying, her hands joined up to the height of her chin, and a rosary around the back of the palm of her right hand and hanging down over her dress, and the rosary as white as the dress: and if she had the misfortune to meet that Peter the Painter fellow she'd regret it.

He says before he can stop himself that Francisco never heard of Peter the Painter, and regrets that he said anything: but Julia, rattling on, has noticed nothing and is scattering the evening paper all around her, sheets all over the floor, and reading out about this man who owned a restaurant somewhere in England: and come from the east like the majors, Julia says, who came to King Herald who killed all the babies: or like the lady in white herself coming from the east to roost like a white bird on the hollum oaktree. But the wife of that man from the east could no more get out of the chair than Martha here, says Julia, and the poor man got depressed and made up his mind to burn the whole place down, and all in it: he went beresk, Julia says, and put the torch to the house and poured so much paraffin that he might have wiped out half the town except that it didn't catch right, and the floor was so slippy that when the eggspector of police walked in he slipped and measured his length and ruined his good uniform, and was so mad he hit the man: and the woman in the chair threw a bowl at the eggspector and cut his face, and it's all up in court, a holy show.

Oh lady, mother of Christ, on the hollum oaktree, get me out of here, away from the rattling-on of Julia, and Martha saying that wonders will never cease: and keep my head in the state of grace, that's what my mother used to say when the ways of the world were too much for her: and I'll say nothing lest I offend the Lord with my tongue. Then she would curse like a trooper and my father would laugh.

Great white gulls drift in the windy day, or strut like boxers on the seawall, like the white lady on what Julia calls the hollum oaktree. The hat does not sit easy, but it looks well and it looks different, and that's important, it isn't so easy to change your nose, that's funny: and he carries the machinery now in a white plastic shopping-bag with the name of the shop written on it: and he crosses the street if he sees a woman wearing anything red, a stitch in time saves nine. The playing children on the flat place by the widening river do not so much madden him as halt him, with not a pain exactly but a cold weakness, and memories of the happy days spent on the gullies of the roofs, treasure island, with his father: and the train with all the people puffing off to the north.

Sometimes he thinks as he walks across that flat place that burning the whole caboodle up or down might not be such a bad idea: the shop and Julia, and Martha in her chair, the garage and mattresses and all, and himself as well.

The park this day seems to have more children in it than he ever saw in one place in his life before. Where do they all come from? Not that he doesn't know. They congregate mostly in one corner around seesaws and swings and chutes and the like: and the big joke is that at that corner and just outside the red park-railings some cute builder has put up a block of fancy expensive flats, or apartments as they call them, or service flats who do they serve and with what, every modern this, that and the other, view of the park and the river and the mountains away faraway, alone all alone by the wavewashed shore, and not a bloody word about the view of the playground, and the children squalling all day long Maryanne outside your wide solar window. Crowd of crooks today in the building business, as much as a tradesman can do to get his money out of them: it wasn't that way in my father's time: but nothing now is on the mend: and Martha will never move out of that chair except to be carried, and crazy Julia can rattle on forever about the white lady and the Children of the Atom, and pray, pray, pray and Russia will be converted, and the sun jumped out of the sky, and the cow jumped over the moon, a likely story, if it jumped out there in Portugal it would have jumped out everywhere else, even here.

He does not come this way often: small streets of redbrick houses around the corner from the block of francy flats, he is beginning to talk like crazy Julia, and the sun jumped out of the sky: he doesn't like these streets, narrow, no gardens before the houses, the little windows too close to you, every Tom, Dick and Harry, and Biddy and Bridget, and Jack, Sam and Pete, and Sexton Blake, and Buffalo Bill, and Laurel and Hardy, can see you little old lady passing-by: and there she is in a blue sweater with a Mickey Mouse on each breast, and black hair pulled back in a bun and parted distinctly up the middle, and tight blue levis as thin as sticks, and her little backside bouncing out, and as quick on her feet as a sparrow in a bush of bridesblossom or mock-orange: and he goes for the glasses and the dromedary Mickey Mice, for those bloody skintight levis would be no loss, one way or the other: and his hat blows off and the bloody street is full of Children of the Atom, and there he is as bald as a hoot, as Julia says, and dropping the shopping-bag and no time to pick it up, nor his hat even wherever it may be: and keep right on to the end of the road, keep right on to the end, though you're tired and weary, still journey on till you've come to your happy abode: and racing for the park and the bushes: and the children after him shouting, and he clips one of them on the ear: and across the grass of the soccer pitches, and a car in the park against all regulations, a bloody squadcar across the grass and no park-keeper to stop them: and the children around him like bluebottles, jeering: and he goes beresk, as Julia says, and kicks three of them and knocks another down with his fist: and so here we have you in the heel of the hunt, me bold Peter the Painter, says the fat man with the moustache as he leaps out of the squadcar, and two guards with him, and your painting days are over as the tattooed lady said when she killed her husband: and beyond the bushes there is Julia, darting like a rabbit.

For a minute he thinks it is his mother, hat cocked and pinned-on, and up and down the street, sixpence each way, never more and you couldn't have less: but no, it is Julia, and the children cheering, and the squadcar going back across the park and, swear to God, driving clean through a flowerbed: nothing these days is on the mend.

YOUR LEFT FOOT IS CRAZY

THE STOUT MAN whose wife and two daughters run the school of ballroom-dancing doesn't sleep with his wife and tells me so almost every Monday and Thursday. Can I be the only man he confides in? He wears an expensive dark-brown suit with a darker stripe. And wide-toed, handsewn brown shoes. He is bald but with dark tufts at the ears. He has thick blackrimmed spectacles with golden arms, three rectangular perforations in each arm. All this gives him a scholarly appearance. He doesn't dance. He's the business manager. Or perhaps the clerk. His wife, stout and motherly but in an authoritative sort of way, doesn't dance but she supervises the dancing while he seldom or never puts a foot on the dancing-floor. He sits behind a desk in a sort of ante-room but it isn't too easy to see what exactly he does beyond just sitting behind the desk: he smokes, he reads, he shuffles sheets of paper with lists of names but the fees are paid in advance at the beginning of a season and paid to his wife on the dancing-floor after a brusque lecture about the rules of the Academy; the rules are brief, no booze, no big boots or hobnails, proper dancing pumps and formal clothes, no sweaters, no denims, this is a dancing academy not a shipyard, not tails exactly, although they're not prohibited, nor tuxedos nor claw-hammer coats or what you will, but respectable suits, preferably dark-brown or navy-blue and, for the ladies, long dresses not all the way to the waxed floor but well-below the knee, no slacks, no summer shorts, no mini-skirts, no disorderly behaviour. This is a very civilized dancing-school.

Who is the maid on the dancing-floor, he hums to himself, and since I know that song, which Sydney McEwan has sung so well, I can go on with the words in my mind and wonder what he's really thinking of and why he doesn't sleep with his wife. He never tells me why. Like foam on the wavetop, foam on the wavetop, who is the maid on the dancing-floor, who but the bride who came sailing. Is that what's in his mind as he hums?

The two daughters demonstrate and teach, God of the dance do they demonstrate, and their two young men in impeccable tails to help them. The ante-room glitters with the cups the four of them have won in competitions in Ireland, England, Scotland, Wales and the Isle of Man. One of the daughters is a brunette who mostly wears whites and greens, the other, a blonde, favours pinks and mauves. Mostly they demonstrate tangoes because most of the cups are tributes to their undeniable ability to tango, but tangoes are very advanced stuff for students and far beyond the powers of Peter who dances as if he had two wooden legs or was a little snubnosed bear doing his paces on a hot plate: and it is Peter's plight and his falling in love that have me in a dancing academy for the first and, I promise myself, the last time in my life. Tangoes are not for me, so I sit in the ante-room with the father of those female dervishes and he tells me that he doesn't sleep with his wife, but never tells me why or why not, and I tell him about Buckramback who taught dancing in South Tyrone in the early part of the nineteenth century. We also talk about football and fishing and women. We are at the back part of the fourth floor of a corner-house on the quays above the Liffey. At the front the music plays and the dancers dance, and who are the maids on the dancing-floor? Nobody pays the least attention to us: nobody ever pays any attention, that I notice, to him, and my fees are paid for the term or season and nobody gives a fiddler's flute whether I tango or trot or fly through the air with the greatest of ease.

It was the time in the history of Europe when American troops in large numbers and in uniform appeared on the streets of Dublin for the first and, so far, the only time. British soldiers did not so appear. Even, or especially, Irishmen in British uniform. Because of history? Because of the hardness of our hearts? But American troops were different. General Mark Clark was Irish, wasn't he? Most American troops were Irish, weren't they? This was Spencer Tracy and the Fighting 69th alive and well and walking about in Dublin. So they were to be seen all over the place and everybody was very glad to see them, and glad they were to be there to be seen, and glad that the war was over. Peter and myself used to watch them out of the high corner-window at which we spent a lot of our time. We were minor civil-servants, which is a nice way of putting it, and had an easy-going boss who spent a lot of his time in a pub across the street, the door of which was visible from the high window, so we sat and smoked and watched the door and the street and the traffic and the people, and the American troops because there were so many of them about, and one day Peter said: I want to dance. I must dance.

And I said: Dance and be damned and enjoy yourself. He's over in the pub.

And he said: But I can't put a foot under me.

Which in a way wasn't to be wondered at.

Peter was just out of a seminary, having made up his mind that he wasn't fit for martyrdom, red or white, on the foreign missions. Or had his mind made up for him: he was hesitant in speech and action. There are priests and nuns, postulants, neophytes and novices who can dance like David. Peter wasn't one of them. He had entered the seminary from a strict home where dancing had been discouraged. Dancing meant drink and women and dark corners. As well as which he wasn't made for dancing. To glide was not in his nature. He hopped. In a later style of dancing, if you could call it that, he might have managed. He was also shy: the strict home and the seminary had made their marks. A small snub-nosed man with close-cropped hair and a tight jacket.

The brass-ornamented swing-doors of the pub across the street opened and our boss stepped out. A poet I know wrote that ancient Celtic monks prayed in dark stone cells so that when they came out into the sunlight they really knew whether God was. He blinked. Rubbed his eyes. Stretched himself, actually stretched himself, a senior civil servant, on the public street, and yawned, then placed his right hand round or about his navel and, I'd say, belched. We stubbed our cigarettes, buttoned our jackets. Peter always had some difficulty with that operation. Not because of corpulence but because the jacket, brown tweed, must have predated the black, now discarded, jacket or jackets he had worn in the seminary. We prepared ourselves for our desks. But wait. He's not making a move to cross the street towards the office. He's facing right, staring with interest. Seeing God? He was a very stout man.

— Running on oil, Peter said.

Then into our field of vision, as they call it, came the tall, strong, blackhaired whore, one of two wild-eyed sisters from the County Roscommon who had taken off for town when they heard of, or sensed, the passing of a part of the great army. By her side and with his arm around her waist (a man may allow himself a few liberties when away from his own home town: that's a quotation) walked a tall, thin, blond, American soldier. He looked shaken. Drink, perhaps, and a wild night with that wild woman in one of the lodging-houses opposite the railway station up the street. He could have been embracing her just to keep himself from collapsing. Harder on him, I thought, than the Battle of the Bulge. But, because of Peter, I didn't say that out loud. She smiled at the boss. She and her sister were friendly girls and had a wide acquaintance. He stood to attention and gave a fair imitation of a military salute. Which the soldier courteously returned. That must have cost him an effort. They walked on out of our field of vision. He looked after them and smiled at nothing and rubbed the back of his head, then disappeared again through the swinging doors. We lit two more cigarettes.

— Peter, I said, beware of the women.

— That's it. That's the trouble. The way it is I'm walking out with one of a set of twins and she dances.

— Let her dance with her twin.

— She's a girl, too.

— It has been known to happen. I'm told you see them at it in all the dance-halls.

— It's no joke. You've no notion how awkward I feel.

— I'll give your condition deep thought.

— If I take Brenda out Joan comes too. They link each other and smile sideways at me. Like meeting yourself twice in a mirror. If I was able to dance I'd get one of them on her own.

— Which is which?

— Brenda is which.

— You've no complaint. Two for the price of one.

— If you would help out.

— Anything for a friend.

— And if you'd come with me to a school of ballroom dancing, on the quiet like, not telling the twins, I want to surprise Brenda some night by taking her to a ballroom.

— And I'll surprise Joan.

— You're a friend indeed.

— Is a friend in need.

The boss resurfaced, looked east and west expecting another vision. Not finding one he began to cross the street. We went back to work.

From the far side of the river Liffey the Room or School of Ballroom Dancing, high in a fine red-brick building and with wide windows looks, in the dusk or the dark, like a garden of delights; coloured paper lampshades like kingsize concertinas, swaying, undulating shadow-shapes that must be something nobler than men and women, and, on warm evenings, the sound of music on the waters.

— An oriental garden, I say.

We are very young. We lean with our backs against the parapet of the bridge and look up at the coloured windows, the dancing shadows, and he sings, a daring song for a modest man: There's a soldier in the garden and with him I will run for my heart's filled with pleasure and I won't be a nun, I won't be a nun and I shan't be a nun . . .

— They wouldn't have you, one of the girls says. You're the wrong shape.

They have come up beside us, crossing the bridge on their way to the tango which they are quite capable of performing in a robust, rural fashion. They are not the twins nor yet the wild sisters, the courtesans from Roscommon. They most certainly do not look like twins, they are not even sisters and one of them comes from Ballyvourney in West Cork, and the other from Nenagh in Tipperary. They dance together when they feel like it, although not quite with the approval of the lady of the house. But they'll dance with anybody and they dance well, would even dare to match their style with the two elegant boyfriends of the beautiful dervishes: and why they bother coming to the school at all we cannot well make out.

One is small and dark and round as a pudding, a very tasty pudding. The other tall and redheaded and you'd see her if you closed your eyes and for a long time after, and that evening on the bridge she says to me: Why don't you dance? I'd like to dance with you. I fancy you.

Admittedly, that's flattering. But somewhat to the amazement of Peter, who has never heard the story before, I tell her about the broken ankle that has never properly set; limp a little to prove it too as we climb the stairs and the beat of the music grows louder. It's a lie, not the music but the spiel about the ankle. Because even from Peter I have to conceal that I know as much about the theory of dancing as he does, and as for the practice . . . Well in that as in other things I may be a disgrace to my family, for while they are all elegant dancers I'm no better at it than the renowned Clarence McFadden who, in a song my mother used to sing, went to a dancing-academy to study the waltz: One, two, three, come balance like me, you're a fairy but you have your faults. When your right-foot is lazy your left one is crazy, but don't be unaisy I'll larn you to waltz.

And in the summer Gaelic College in the Rosses of Donegal the whirls and thuds of the dusty stampedes of the Irish dances, the Walls of Limerick, the Siege of Ennis, the High Caul Cap, have simply made me dizzy, when I had the nerve to join them at all: so that my talks with the good man who never tells me why he doesn't sleep with his wife are for me a refuge and a haven. They keep me from being out on that there waxy floor making a bloody fool of myself. On which dangerous floor the daughters and the boy friends go round and round like seraphim on the wing and sway backward and forward like the saplings bent double by the gale when the wood is in trouble on Wenlock Edge.

We get on splendidly together. He seems to be happy when we talk and, because of that, his wife who is kindly, if authoritative, leaves both of us at peace and, as Dr Johnson might have put it, compels me to no gyrations. That is, doesn't force me to dance nor try to, and I am at ease. Or was until the tall redhead told me she fancied me. Her company would be most desirable. But, oh God, at what a price: and inside the dance goes on and outside the two of us sit, heads together, cigarette smoke rising, two veterans in an ingle talking of lost wars.

— I'm going to write a book, I tell him, about William Carleton. He wrote novels in the nineteenth century.

To write that book is my honest intention.

— Bully for you, he says. I look forward to reading it. Why Carleton, more than anybody else?

— Well for one thing he was a novelist and so am I. I mean I will be.

— 'Tis in reversion that you do possess.

The quotation takes the harm out of it. We roar laughter into our cloud of smoke. It is an odd place for Shakespeare, or perhaps it isn't. Beatrice was born under a dancing star. The tall redhead who fancies me comes out from the music and movement of the inner room, stands in the doorway and looks at us for a while, then says to us that some people have all the fun.

— Join us, he says, and make the fun better.

She does. That doesn't make me teetotally happy. She has told me that she fancies me and she's lovely to look at: it's the sort of thing that sooner or later affects a young fellow. But to respond to her may mean that I'll end up in agony out there on the slippery floor and, unlike Peter, I am not as yet goaded on by the desperation of love.

— For another thing, he came from Tyrone and so do I.

She asks me who I'm talking about but with the din from the dancing-floor I can pretend not to hear her and still be polite.

— For a third thing, I was as good as reared on him. I'm deeply devoted to him and his people. They're my own people, not much changed over a century.

Looking at his most professorial, he says that that's the best reason yet: and again she asks me who I'm talking about. This time I allow myself to hear her. The flattery of her open-mouthed interest is pleasant. Not open-mouthed exactly. She's too beautiful to gape. Just lips a little moist and slightly parted. Othello felt the way I feel, in the early stages that is, when he charmed her ears and all with tales of antres vast and deserts idle, and cannibals that eat each other, the Anthropophagi, and men whose heads do grow beneath their shoulders. But look, oh Lord, where the flattery of an open mouthed attention led Othello.

— And one of the great experiences of my early boyhood was to read his novel *Fardorougha the Miser* in serial form in the *Ulster Herald*. It was more exciting to read it that way. You had to wait a week for the next movement. As people used to wait for the next of Dickens.

She blinks a little: well, I am talking to impress. A civil servant can be as learned and literary as any professor and, moreover, it is my intention, when I have enough money stashed, to get out of that job and back to college.

— And one of the funniest characters he ever wrote about was a teacher of ballroom-dancing. Buckramback. That was his name.

— Buckramback, he says. Fancy that.

He laughs until he chokes and coughs and has to take off his glasses to wipe his eyes.

What, I wonder, is he thinking of.

— But Buckramback, she says, that's a comical name.

Thereafter there's a fourth person with us while, with the help of William Carleton, I try to explain to them about Buckramback, to set him curtseying and prancing on the floor before us: while inside the music sounds and the tango goes round and round and Peter hops and hops towards the wild moment when he will have Brenda cut off from the herd and all on his very own.

— They called him Buckramback because he had been for a time a drummer in the British Army. He didn't like soldiering. He deserted so often and was caught so often and flogged so often that his back was cartaliginous. As hard as buckram, that is.

But they know what I mean.

— He was a dapper light little fellow with a Tipperary accent crossed by a lofty strain of illegitimate English he had picked up in the army.

— Tipperary, she hums, never more will I roam from my dear native home, Tipperary, so far away.

He compliments her on her singing voice and she is obviously pleased: he has such a way of humouring the ladies that it's a continual wonder to me why he doesn't sleep with his wife: she's not as young as she used to be but she goes out and round in all the right places. And is well perfumed.

— He wore tight secondhand clothes, shabby-genteel, and his face was as secondhand and tight-skinned and wrinkled as his clothes. And tight breeches, and high, brightly-polished high boots, also cracked, and white stockings, and a tall hat and coloured gloves: and small as he was he would take on to fight any man. But he was also and always a gentleman to the ladies.

— The image of yourself, she says.

And sounds as if she means it, the bit, that is, about being a gentleman to the ladies, and I try not too well to pretend that I haven't heard.

— He kept his dancing-school in a roadside cabin, and the country-girls around him in all their frocks and ribbons, and the young fellows in knee-breeches and green-tailed coats.

— Like a postcard for St Patrick's Day, she says, Paddy and the pig, and the pig running wild and twisting the rope round Paddy's legs.

— But dancing was the least part of what Buckramback had to teach. He could teach the country boys and girls how to enter a drawingroom in the most fashionable manner alive. They that never saw or would see a drawingroom.

— You never know, she says. You should see me at work. Even if it's not my own drawingroom.

— He taught the whole art of courtship with all politeness and success as it was practised in Paris during the last season.

She says that she would give her heart and soul to see Paris and Gene Kelly and Leslie Caron and all the dancing. And singing.

— And how to write valentines and love-letters as Napoleon wrote them to his wife or his two wives.

He says that Buckramback would be a useful little man to have about any well-ordered house: and, if I hadn't been swept away by my own eloquence and learning and the elation of owning an audience, I would have known that the mention of valentines would set her humming: I'll be your sweetheart if you will be mine.

— And teach the ladies how to curchy and the young gentlemen how to shiloote the ladies.

Curchy, she knew, was curtsey.

— But shiloote, she says. Did he mean salute? I've heard old countrymen say shiloote.

— He meant salute.

75

— Like soldiers in the army. All present and correct.

She stands up, our four eyes fixed on her, and performs in a way to warm the heart of any sergeant-major, or any other man.

— No, he meant kissing. To shiloote was to kiss.

— Amo, amas, amat he says. Followed by osculo, osculas, osculat. Or perhaps osculo comes before amo.

— Amo I know, she says. L'amour.

Her eyes glow. This is perilous country. This could lead me out there, and in the company of this maid, to the dancing-floor where she, but not her spavindy partner, would move like foam on the wavetop, foam on the wavetop.

In my secret and poltroon's heart I knew that I wanted to be her partner. But not out there under coloured lights, in jostling crowds and perpetual motion, and contrasting comically with the prizewinning boyfriends. Or even with Peter who must by now be picking up something. The shadows I craved, green secrecy and silence: and I didn't need a man who didn't sleep with his wife to tell me (which he did politely when she had left us for a while to do a routine tango with her tasty pudding of a friend), didn't need him to tell me, I repeat, that it was an odd way to make love to a girl, to talk on and on about a character from an author dead and at rest in Mount Jerome cemetery for the better part of a century. And what young fellow in love was ever afraid to go dancing with the loved one? The primitive country-boys in caubeens, knee-breeches and green-tailed coats, were more daring. Clarence MacFadden, awkward and all, was a better man than I was: he tried. Peter was a better man: he was trying. And this was the middle of the twentieth century and the streets full of heroes returning from an ended war: and faint heart never won, and all the rest of it. My friend and confidant was kindly and fatherly. It wasn't in him to be otherwise. But in the cloud of smoke that bound us together he was concerned and critical. It would have been no satisfaction to me, even if I had had the gall to do it, to *tu quoque* him and tell him that he didn't even sleep etc. For my own good he was talking, I knew. He was telling the truth. At every stage of development or decline, love, it occurred to me, had its special problems.

*

But I want to tell you about the twins, Peter's twins. Brenda and Joan.

They lived in Donnybrook in a quiet side-street of bay-windowed houses built at the turn of the century out of good red brick from Somerset. The Joycean ship that came into Dublin out of Bridgewater with bricks carried across the Irish Sea the walls of most of those houses. The side-street led to, still leads to, the beauty of Herbert Park. So on a bright Sunday morning after Mass the four of us met for the first time between the lake and the bandstand in the corner of the park by the Ballsbridge bakery wall. All very pure and proper, and shaded and pleasantly fanned by noble trees: the faint odour of fresh bread an added intimacy. The band would not be out until the afternoon.

It was the season in which the ducks walked the grass, parading their ducklings. Two Muscovy ducks, like boozed geese with the whiskey-drinker's crimson horse's-collar round their necks, stood on the concrete rim of a small leafy island and scowled at the water and the world. They always kept the same place and everybody, the other ducks I mean, left them alone. They looked both dirty and dangerous.

One of them affected, as we'd have said in another century, bright colours. I'm talking now about the twins. The other went abroad in more demure shades. Brenda was the bright one. They were handsome girls, both of them: if one was the other almost had to be. They spoke well, the good, clear, unaccented (almost) English of the Dublin middle-class: as in Bernard Shaw. They had dark-blue berets and brown eyes that were always smiling. They were good-humoured but never laughed out loud, not, at any rate, while we were with them. They were self-assured, capable I'd say, good managers, good housekeepers, the pride and joy of their parents, and rightaway I could see how they had Peter rattled. One of them would have rattled a veteran. Two was, or were, by much too much or too many.

Twice round the entire park we walked slowly. That, roughly, would be three miles.

First we headed north across the lime-lined road that cuts the park into two portions. By the happy corner where there's a toy railway for children, seesaws, a long-armed tree that God grew to

77

pleasure pygmy climbers. By the back of the tennis-courts: where, out of respect for Peter's pure passion, I looked ahead, keeping my eyes from the strong thighs of the girls leaping about in short skirts. Brenda went on Peter's arm, Joan went on mine, and with such military force and precision that those who met with us were forced unto the grass. By the bowling-green where stout ladies and elderly gentlemen in white peaked caps were doing the Francis Drake. Where do they come from, the good people who join bowling-clubs? Four-deep, we looked at them over the precisely-clipped hedge and I made the inevitable remark about my bias running against the bowl, then had to explain what the hell I was talking about.

Diagonalwise across grass that was half-white with fluff from the maples. Back again across the dividing roadway and along a pillared walk that showed us the splendid planned vista of the lake. All around the sporting-grounds where roaring youths were engaged at soccer, Gaelic football and hurling. In another happy corner there was a whirligig for children, and chutes, and twenty little girls on twenty swings were rising and falling in rhythm and singing the same chirping song. To our right was the river Dodder, then high trees and big houses and, a few miles away, the blue Dublin-Wicklow mountains to which, Peter wildly proposed, we would some Sunday go cycling. But also cunningly: it isn't so easy to maintain on bicycles the four-deep flying formation. Somewhere in Wicklow heather he meant to have his will, whatever it was.

But back for now to the empty bandstand and the corner by the Ballsbridge bakery wall. Then round the course once again, clockwise, except that the second time round we didn't stop to look over the hedge at the bowlers and I did peep sideways at the stout thighs of the girls playing tennis: as I was riding on the outside, if you follow me, and could pretend to be looking at Peter who was hugging the rails. Four deep all the time. Four at a table we had poisonous coffee at a lounge-bar in Ballsbridge. Then Peter and myself took a bus into town. The two young ladies walked home across the park. Because their parents mightn't like to see them escorted home so early on a Sunday morning. Better, I savagely thought, than late and drunk on a Saturday night. Not one word can I now remember that anybody said on the walk or at the coffee-table. Nor could remember even on the very next day. Apart from that bit about the bias and the bowl.

Only pity kept me from telling Peter what I thought. Only sheer force of friendship brought me out again on safari: second-time to a cinema where we sat four abreast and no scuffling took place. Chocolates were consumed. The twins didn't smoke and didn't fancy the smell of smoke. There was much whispering and crinkling of tinfoil. An elderly gentleman in the row in front asked us, loudly, to be quiet, and the usherette shone her lamp on the elderly gentleman and asked him to be quiet, and voices all over the place asked everybody else to be quiet: this was long before the days when cinemas became so infested with riotous ten-year-olds that you couldn't even hear the uproar of Star Wars.

Afterwards, we had coffee and sweet-cakes in a green-walled green-carpeted restaurant where I knew all the waitresses: principally Josie who was tall, wide-mouthed, most affable always to me; and Marie who was only gorgeous and had a married lover who wore a fur-coat and walked the streets leading a big dog on a silver chain. Something odd about chaps who wear fur-coats and lead big dogs on silver chains. He and the dog came in that evening and were introduced to Peter and the twins. Who liked style and dogs. Who were so impressed that on the way home we walked two-by-two at a distance of almost twenty paces. And hand-in-hand. Peter held Brenda's hand. Joan held my hand. My heart, I now knew, was elsewhere. Off the bus at Ballsbridge. Along the river-walk to Donnybrook. The Dodder, ten feet below us, whispered of all sorts of things.

To Joan I told how somewhere in the mountains and along the upper waters of that river, perhaps in Glenasmole or the Glen of the Thrushes, might be the spot where, in mythology, had stood the hostelry of Da Derga. How the King, Conaire the good, had been murdered there by Irish outlaws and marauding sea-rovers: and the hostelry burnt. How the murdering marauders or the marauding murderers had camped on Lambay island and sailed in, under darkness, to Merrion or Sandymount strand where James Joyce had set Stephen Dedalus walking between the markings of high and low tide. How Conaire went to his doom because he had had the ill-luck on the way to the hostelry to break all his geasa or taboos. How one of those geasa was: Do not let two reds [redheads] go before you to the house of a red.

She listened with exemplary, if obvious, patience. Somewhere else, I said to myself, and to the sound of music and dancing, I would find a livelier, more loveable listener for one of the greatest of all stories. Yet that thing about the taboo got to wherever her head was. She repeated it over and over again: Do not let two reds go before you to the house of a red.

We leaned against the park railings, the park closed and the dark behind us. Across the narrow water great trees stood up like clouds: the lights of the mansions on Anglesea Road shone through them. Music came to us over the water from the dance-pavilion in the grounds of the rugby-football club. We whispered and kissed. Peter kissed Brenda: believe it or not, but I saw him at it. Joan kissed me and I kissed her in return: fair's fair. The thin red line had been broken by the symbolism of a man in a fur-coat, with a gorgeous, only gorgeous, mistress, and a big dog on a silver chain.

On the Dodder bridge at Donnybrook Peter stood as proud as a turkey-cock, and said: Have the rothar [bicycle] oiled for next Sunday. We're off for the mountains. Brenda wants to see the Devil's Glen.

Looking out of high city-windows any more you don't see as much as you used to, for the odd reason that the streets and sidewalks are more crowded. More people, in Dublin at any rate, more cars, too much wood, fewer distinctive trees. People I saw then from our spy-window and smoking-room I can see quite clearly to this day. As well as that there was a darkhaired young woman who worked in our office: lonely, hollow-cheeked, slightly sallow but lovely, who sometimes when the boss was across in the pub used to stand with us at the window and, while we smoked, sip tea. A cup held delicately between finger and thumb, never a saucer, and we never saw her brew the tea nor knew where. She brooded. She was mysterious. She went away to be a nun and it pains me a little still to think that, in her presence and all unwittingly, Peter used to sing his daring song: There's a soldier in the garden, etc.

80

His daring song! Far below us the soldiers from the war returning walked up and down. She sipped her tea and talked little and was one of those people I can see as clearly now as I did then.

Gobnait, the red, comes out to us. She is flushed from the dance. Through rings of smoke like the rings round Saturn we contemplate her beauty. She is, I am now convinced, the most beautiful woman I have ever seen. She is called Gobnait because, as I've said, she comes from Ballyvourney and that odd name (say it with a vee) is the name of the patron saint of that place: a consecrated virgin, Gobnait of the Bees, who cooled the ardour of a chieftain, who would have explored her virginity, by unleashing at him a hive of honeybees: sweets to the sweet, farewell. She stands in stone, cut by the great sculptor Seamus Murphy, above the holy well at that place, and bees, cut in stone, circle forever around her chaste feet.

Gobnait knows all about Gobnait and can stand still and mime the statue and with pursed lips make a noise so like swarming bees that you'd run for cover. Nobody but a born actress could compress such a mouth to a thin colourless line. Through the smoke two sour chieftains look at her and, speaking for myself, lust and wonder: foam on the wavetop, foam on the wavetop. Her tasty plump little pudding of a friend sits at a distance and is clearly very happy. She's a jolly girl, would be most attractive if Gobnait were not standing there and the bees buzzing around her. They are very fond of each other, Gobnait and the jolly girl.

Gobnait has absorbed every word I've said about Buckramback. One evening she mimes him. It's uncanny, even a little alarming, how a tall redhead with so much about her that you can't take your eyes off even when your eyes are shut, can become a dapper light little fellow with secondhand clothes, shabby-genteel, tight bree-ches, brightly-polished high boots, white stockings, a tall hat, coloured gloves. She bows and scrapes to the ladies and in a roadside cabin, long-gone, kisses laughing rural beauties, long-dead. He lilts: One, two, three, come balance like me.

She, or Buckramback or Clarence McFadden, waltzes to the lilting. Marcel Marceau himself couldn't do better. The music in the inner room has ceased. Peter is standing in the doorway wiping his brow. Behind him the crowd is gathering, even the motherly lady herself and the dervishes and their boyfriends, tails and all: and when the lilting and miming stop, the applause and laughter begin, and one of the boyfriends waltzes Gobnait round the room, her red hair flying. For the only time in my life I feel weak and sick because I'm a disgrace to a family who are all good dancers.

Peter and myself walk Gobnait and her friend to the last Enniskerry bus. They work in a big house there and that's twelve miles away. There's no time for coffee in the green restaurant. She takes my arm, holds it close to her, she is very warm and my knees are weak. She says: I'd love to have seen him. Buckramback. I'd love to have gone to those dancing classes.

So I tell her that while I'm not able to enable her to see Buckramback I can bring her and her friend some Thursday afternoon, which is afternoon-off for domestics, to the national gallery to show her the portrait of the man who created or remembered Buckramback. The friend's name is Pauline which I don't know until that moment. She is one of those amiable girls who don't seem to need a name: I ask her also to come to the gallery because through sudden fright I crave the safety of numbers. In contrast to Peter.

It is the first time that I have looked real love in the face.

When the last bus has gone off towards Enniskerry and the dark mountains Peter says to me: Tonight I danced my first tango.

Christ keep Brenda when he gets her in the mountains, and if he finds her in the glen her blood will stain the heather.

No, we never did get as far as the Devil's Glen. It was a windy day with showers blowing up all the way from Ballyvourney, a place I now thought of all the time. No matter in what direction you faced, that wind was against you. Cycling was slavery. The best we could do was make the secrecy of Calary lake to the right of the high road from Enniskerry to Roundwood. To the east the Sugarloaf stood up sharply over the moor. To the west, and high above us, the gloom of the woods and Djouce mountain into which, about that time, a French plane had crashed because the pilot hadn't been speaking to the navigator. Down there in the woods the long lake hugged itself, arms tightly folded.

We walked along the west of it, then across at the dam and sluice-gate, then along the east of it and back again, and across again and back along the west of it: you could sing that. Joan and myself in the lead and hand-in-hand, Brenda and Peter ten paces in the rear and stepping well. On a carpet of damp pine-needles we picnicked. Neither God nor St Patrick intended Ireland for picnics. Murderous midges came around us in the damp and fed on us. We fed on ham sandwiches and lukewarm tea. Then halfway up Djouce mountain, searching for and not finding the wreck of the French plane: and talking about nothing else. Those girls were dull and so was Peter. Not their fault that day, perhaps. For as we walked I kept repeating: Bosomed high in tufted trees, bosomed high in tufted trees.

To the wonderment of all.

Because on the far side of Enniskerry, where the road falls steeply to the bridge over the Dargle, was the mansion in which Gobnait worked. And Joan. Just like that: bosomed high in tufted trees.

To the dripping woods I proclaimed: Where perhaps some beauty lies, the cynosure of neighbouring eyes.

They were used to me now. They made no comment.

No bums disturbed, no blood stained the damp pine-needles. Segregation went only so far.

But the sun came out in the evening and, homeward bound, we could see, faint and faraway, the outline in Ulster of the Mourne mountains.

In Enniskerry I sneaked a secret half-whiskey and a pint. Badly needed. Those girls were deadly. Courage for the dreary walk, pushing bicycles up that hill.

Halfway up the wonder happened. Two on one bike they came down like the wind. A man's bike. Pauline on the bar, Gobnait in the saddle, hair flying. They called my name. And Peter's name. They didn't stop. Out of sight round a corner and down to the bridge and the village. Bosomed high in tufted trees.

Brenda asked what was that.

— Girls from the office, I told her.

For Peter's sake: to preserve the secret of the school of ballroom dancing. That first fine careless tango.

83

The mizzling rain came on again and kept us company all the way to Donnybrook.

Peter never could have been described as passionate and I had only gone with him to balance the boat, as I take care to explain to Gobnait on the following Thursday afternoon.

— Pushing up the hill, she says, you all looked so woebegone it was funny.

She laughs so happily, right before the portrait of the man who had created or remembered Buckramback. There he sits: a long, strong, heavy, northern face, hair going grey and thinning over the temples, a respectable black coat, a quill in the right hand, an elbow resting solidly on a copy of *The Traits and Stories of the Irish Peasantry*.

— And a fine man indeed, she says. Very like my father. A fine countryman. You might look like that when you're growing old. You might look distinguished. We'll wait and see.

She has come without Joan. We walk hand-in-hand on the polished slippery floor. We stand for a long time before the battle of the Boyne, and the merriment and mayhem and writhing limbs around the nuptials of Eva and Strongbow: my arm is around her waist; the gallery is as secret as the woods of Djouce mountain to which some day when the sun is shining we will go together. Her hair is on my shoulder.

The zoological museum is noisy with school-children.

— But, she says, children I love and all these things are better than just pictures.

Skeletons of whales, apes, male and female, with all found and every hair numbered: and the Rathcannon elk about which I am the greatest living authority as, on that day and being inspired, I am about many other things: no longer even has the dancing-floor any terrors for me, foam on the wavetop, foam on the wavetop, and I tell her that my father's father and the Rathcannon elk came from the same place. She says that there's a definite family resemblance. She stands back and studies me and the high proud skeleton.

— Your father's father wasn't so tall. What was he?

— A policeman.

— They made them bigger then.

— They found him in a marsh in 1824.

— Your father's father?

— And dug him up.

— Not a pick on his bones.

— From his toes to the tip of his antlers he's ten feet and four inches.

— Your father's father's people were a fine body of men. You take after them.

We kiss to clinch our happiness in the presence of the Rathcannon elk and his two skeletal companions, one female. Passing children giggle. The man at the turnstile bar scratches his old beard. We are past caring. We aren't laughing any more. Round the corner then to Stephen's Green to sit on a bench in the sun and look at the lake. We talk little, we don't need to. Then to tea in the Country Shop with all the delicacies a minor civil servant can afford. She laughs again when I tell her about the ham sandwiches and lukewarm tea in the wood under Djouce mountain. When we go there together the fare will be better. She promises.

Even to please Peter there was little point in pretending much longer with the twins: Joan or Brenda. For a while we went on parading in the park, cuddling mildly at the movies, sipping coffee in the all-green restaurant, chatting to the affable Josie and the gorgeous Marie who was having some trouble with the lover with the fur-coat and the big dog on a silver chain. We stood regularly in the shadows on the river-walk by the Dodder, and kissed a bit and whispered. Peter may have been well content. His ambitions went no further. Joan and myself stood here. Brenda and Peter stood there, twenty paces away, regulation distance. Or did they? For I had begun to suspect something peculiar. That the twins changed their clothes, swapped I mean, and their colours. Was it taste, was it touch, was it odour?

It couldn't have been sight. They looked alike. Or hearing. They talked alike. Poor Peter I thought: and tested and tricked them with the magic formula from the tale of the death of King Conaire the Good: Do not let two reds go before you to the house of a red.

Joan couldn't remember the words. It wasn't Joan. For three nights later she was word-perfect, and without prompting. That was Joan. Three nights later she hadn't a clue. That was Brenda. Poor Peter.

They tasted the same. And sounded and looked etc. They were playing a game and the stakes weren't high, they hadn't even bothered to do their homework, they stood to lose nothing and we, sure as God, had nothing to gain. Never knew if Peter ever knew and, as in two little girls in blue, we drifted apart: and Gobnait and Pauline made the newspapers, not the headlines exactly but not a brief paragraph neither.

They got two and a quarter inches, single-column, provincial papers please copy, and I kept the clipping for a long time. And that was that, the man's bicycle one in the saddle one on the bar, brakes that snapped and the stone bridge at the foot of that precipice of a hill: foam on the wavetop.

On my last visit to the dancing-academy we talked about it through the smoke.

Now and again I communed with the Rathcannon elk and thought of Buckramback and Clarence McFadden.

Peter and myself never did take Brenda and Joan to a dance: and four years later I met Brenda, or so she said, on a street near Ballsbridge. She was married and happy and wheeling a pram and halfways to filling another, and I wondered, but was too polite to ask, was her sister similarly situated. Of course it could have been Joan. How was I to know? They tell me there's only one sure way for a man to find out.

THE JEWELLER'S BOY

∾

THE FIRST DAY the boys from Gallows Hill paid any attention to Robbie, the barefooted son of Jamie the Jeweller, was the day Shorty Morgan's watch got broken in a wrestling match. It was an Ingersoll watch with a black face on it, and phosphorescent digits you could see in the dark, and a phosphorescent railway engine puffing across the centre of the black face. It had cost five shillings. It was Shorty's favourite Christmas present ever. The glass of it got broken when Lanty Cassidy fell on Shorty in this wrestling match in which we were supposed to be Finn MacCool and his Fenians. Lanty was Finn. He was a born leader.

Shorty picked himself up when he heard the crunch and reached frenziedly for a patch watch-pocket that a fond mother had stitched on to the front of his trousers. Then he sat down and began to cry. It was poor behaviour for a follower of the great Finn, captain of the warriors and hunters of ancient Erin. Yet we felt too deeply for him, and for the magnitude of the tragedy, to speak any word of reproof. Nobody else owned a watch. Shorty was a spoiled child. We sat in council in a circle around the Big Tree on the top of Gallows Hill. Just as the men of Finn might, according to the story-books, have sat in council, after a hunt or a foray, on the Hill of Allen in the County Kildare. The Big Tree was only the stump of a tree. Somebody with nothing better to do or, perhaps, to make a tethering base for straying cattle or goats, had once driven deep into the trunk two iron bars with hooked ends. That was enough to make us think that people had been hanged from that tree, thus giving the hill its grisly name, and the area around the tree-stump a special awe and sanctity suitable for our council meetings.

We assessed the damage. The glass was gone. The hands were

miraculously preserved, but paralysed. The back was dented and bent and refused to open. So it was no longer possible to view with fascination what was going on in the very soul of the machine. The railway engine that gleamed so splendidly by night was a sad thing in the harsh daylight of ruin. Pathetically, soundlessly it puffed on, going nowhere forever and forever.

Shorty ceased to sob. He was a blond, squinty, shortsighted little boy with thick, oval-shaped, silver-rimmed spectacles and close-cropped hair. He gulped and tried to be brave.

— There's nothing for it, said Finn McCool, but Jamie the Jeweller. They say he can bring the dead to life.

— That means, somebody said, going all the way down to John Street.

— The police are down there, said yet another Fenian.

— They're after the whip-fighters still.

— They're only after Tall John.

— They're after the jingbang lot of us.

— It's a big risk to take.

— Well, Finn MacCool said, if you're all feared to ride into town I'll go myself. Give me the watch, Shorty.

But we couldn't let our captain shame us. Nor could we let him go down on his own into the suspect world of orderly, police-patrolled society.

So, led by Lanty, we descended, crossed the Fair Green, clattered in nailed boots along the staid blue pavements of John Street, shops and offices all around us. Past the Methodist meeting house where the air was always fluttering with pigeons: and to Jamie the Jeweller's where John MacBride who was musical said he could stand all day listening to the ticking and the chimes.

Bearing the wounded watch Lanty entered. The rest of us, awe-struck, looked through the window at the dumb-show going on inside. Jamie was a short, grizzled gentle stump of a man and he had something like a miniature telescope stuck in his left eye. Expertly, he opened the watch as we had not been able to do. There was a sad saintly little smile on his face. It was also a giggle but we couldn't hear that part of it. He switched on a light that was under a green shade on the counter. He applied the light and the telescope to the watch. Then he ceased to smile. Or giggle. He shook his head sadly. He handed the wounded thing back to Lanty and with a cry of agony Shorty was in through the door to gather to himself his beloved engine. We followed like chief mourners.

— Not Tompion himself, said Jamie, and he was the greatest clockmaker that ever lived, could make that engine move again.

He groped under the counter, came up with a silvery pocket-watch, shook it, wound it, set it, held it to his ear and nodded with satisfaction.

— How about a swap, young Morgan, he said with great kindliness. Your watch for one that goes. I might get a spare part or two out of yours. Here, take this one.

He held it out towards Shorty who backed away suspiciously.

— Can you see it in the dark?

— Well no, said Jamie. But I reckon you could always strike a light.

— It's no good, said Shorty, if you can't see it in the dark. And there's no railway engine on it.

— No. But the works work.

— It's not a fair swap, Shorty said.

Jamie smiled sadly, accepting the stubborn obtuseness of the young.

Then a voice spoke from the shadowy, chiming, ticking sanctuary at the back of the shop. Since, for the moment and until the speaker stepped forward a little, we could see nobody, it almost seemed as if Jamie, the Magician, possessed a clock that could speak. The voice said: Give him his own watch too, dad. That way, at night, he can look at one and listen to the other.

— Son, said Jamie, that sounds like a mighty fine compromise.

Then the voice stepped forward. We looked in gratitude and awe at this Daniel come to judgement. We already knew him by sight but, for several reasons, he didn't belong in our world. The first of the many extraordinary things about him was that he had been born in America and, away back before jets and Lindberg, America was a long way from Gallows Hill. Jamie, a native of our town, had gone to Boston as a young man, married there and lived there until his wife died, then sadly and quietly came home bringing with him his one rare child, a boy about fourteen years of age. But what a boy. He went bootless and bare-legged, from the knees down, except in deep winter. Not from poverty, for Jamie the Jeweller made real money. But the mild little man with the telescope to his eye could never force that beloved son to wear shoes against his will: and in those days the police minded their own business, like murder, robbery, rebellion and poteen, and left social welfare to the few old ladies who cared. The wild boys from the Hill envied Robbie. They were never allowed to go barefoot. There was too much broken glass left over in that part of the town from the Saturday night homeward courses of drunken men. To add to their envy, Robbie, since his father brought him to the town twelve months previously, had successfully resisted any attempt to send him to school.

So the Hill boys, myself among them, assuaged their feelings by referring to Robbie as Girly Girly. He wore a velvet corduroy zipper jacket and knickerbockers, which looked to us like long bloomers, of the same material. He had a pale oval face, large liquid blue eyes, a wide forehead and brown curling hair: the sort of face that I saw long afterwards in an early portrait of Rupert Brooke. It was said that he was delicate and needed nine different colours of pills. Yet for the sake of Shorty we were grateful to him that day. Even if embarrassed by the necessity for being grateful.

He followed us as we went, shuffling and bumping against each other, into the street.

— Hillbillies, he said.

Not with contempt but with curiosity. He was rationally considering us.

— Do you still fight with whips up there on the Hill?

He spoke to us as if we came from some interesting place. Like the moon. And not from a suburb five hundred yards away. He was the urban man. We were a little in awe of him because he had crossed the Atlantic in a liner and seen buildings higher than the church steeple which was all of two hundred feet.

Shamefacedly we admitted that the whipfights were no more.

— Tall John and the razor fixed you, he said.

But with pride we said: The police fixed us.

It pleased us to consider ourselves as wanted men.

The whipfights had taken place between the boys of the Hill and the boys of Brook Street, another suburb at the far end of the town. Nobody paid much attention to these mass and manly conflicts until Tall John, a broad muscular dwarf of a Hill boy with a curious sense of humour, tied a cut-throat razor to the end of his whip and drove both armies before him into the staid streets where professional people and merchants worked and lived. Shop windows were broken. And old ladies knocked down. And the police appealed to. No arrests were made. But terror descended on Brook Street and the Hill. Whips were confiscated, or hidden as, in days of ancient rebellion, steel pikes were hidden in cornstacks in haggards or in the thatched roofs of mountain cabins.

— A pity, Robbie said to us, you had to stop. It was a fun thing. This town needs excitement. I'll give you some. As from tomorrow.

With patience and with scepticism we asked him how?

— I've got this job. Driving the van from the railroad to the post office. Look out for sparks. Always wanted to drive a horse and van.

Then he said that he hoped Shorty's new watch would go. Then left us with the feeling that we had been dismissed as soon as he had made his pronouncement. He went back into the ticking, chiming shop and, as we went, all the clocks began in chorus to tell us that it was teatime.

We didn't believe what he had told us. Yet the coincidence of his departure to all those chimes left us with an odd feeling that he might readily turn out to be a wonder. So we were only half-reassured when John MacBride who was musical said: That fellow's the greatest liar under heaven. Who'd ever trust him out of the house with a horse and van.

At that time the town possessed only one demon driver and he was a ghost. Few people had seen him. Those who claimed to have done so were not the most trustworthy of the community. Sam Mullan, for instance. Sam thought he was a Scotland Yard man. So he hid behind walls peeping at people. Or in Sunday dusk darted from lampost to lampost tailing people who generally ended up by turning into the cinema or into the Sacred Heart church for evening devotions. But Sam swore that he had seen the headless ghost of Adam Tait, an evil landlord of the past, flog his four spectral horses down from Gallows Hill where so many of his victims had gasped their last. The horses dragged a flaming coach down John Street and High Street and Market Street to vanish, still galloping but rising into the air, over the County Hospital. There were imaginative young people, Shorty Morgan was one of them, who swore that by night they heard the passing of headless Adam and his wheels and horses.

But when Robbie, a uniform cap on his head according to regulations, took over the mail van we forgot about ghosts and headless monsters.

Goaded by an ashplant and excited by shrill nasal cries the old bay horse that pulled the two-wheeled covered wagon was galvanized into a gallop. The top half of the van was of red wickerwork with the royal insignia done crudely in black. Twice a day like a crimson flash it swept from the post office to the railway station and back again. As green with envy as the van was red with paint, we sat on the top of a high wall by the Station Brae, and watched the wild fellow pass, and raised a cheer that we hoped was ironical. Then John MacBride who was musical would say: He'll kill himself. That's what he'll do.

— He'll wreck the town, said Lanty. But, God, you have to hand it to him. He has go in him. Wherever he's going.

On his return journey Robbie was merciful enough to allow the tavered horse to walk up the Station Brae. Then he'd wave his ashplant at us and call us hillbillies. But with a laugh and in a voice that nobody could resent. And when he came to John Street off he'd go with a slap of the plant and a wild drumming of hooves. In Jamie's chiming shop old ladies clutching ailing clocks under shawls shuddered as the demon driver went past. On one occasion Mrs Gormley's alarm-clock, a new-fangled effort that had stopped the week after she bought it, started again and rang at the reverberation. But Jamie, helpless before the uncanny wildness of the girl of a boy, never looked up. He simply smiled, or giggled, and peered more intently through his glass at the intestines of watches and clocks.

— In America, said Lanty, I'd say his mother's father drove a stagecoach. Or a runaway covered wagon.

We had seen the film about the covered wagon and the film about the thundering herd. It was Robbie's genius to bring them to three-dimensional life, off the screen, right in the heart of our town.

Once a month the shopkeepers barricaded themselves against cattle. Because, on the monthly fairday, buying and selling of cattle overflowed from the Fairgreen at the butt of Gallows Hill and all along the level of John Street: and even on to the High Street and the steep hill before the Court-house. The oldfashioned Irish fairday, driven out by orderly marts conducted in large concrete buildings, has gone nowadays. Except from towns like Drumshanbo in the County Leitrim where you can buy a good blackthorn for seventeen old pence or a small hairy donkey for five old shillings. Or from Killorglin in the County Kerry where once in a year the local people worship not God but a gentleman goat, raised up on a platform: and where tinkers and tourists flock to the fair of Puck, and where a tall fashion model from London once slipped on the steep street and measured her elegant length in liquid cowdung.

But in our youth and in our town the old ways still survived. Merchants were forced to put up wooden palisades to protect plateglass from the buttocks of bullocks. Cattle heaved, jostled and relieved themselves on the pavements. Dealers bargained and spat and slapped hands. Sheep stood in sad, terrified semi-circles, heads together and to the wall, trollopy tailends turned to the incomprehensible world. It could have been the crowds, or the smell of dung. Or the suggestion, brought with them by drovers and cattle, of wide pastures remote from the treadmill of post office to station and back again. Or it could have been the accumulation of torment he had already endured at the hands and ashplant of Robbie. Or all those things together. But this fairday the old bay horse transmogrified into a raging Bucephalus and went running wild through a herd of red bullocks on the Courthouse Hill. Foaming at the mouth he circled three times the black female figures on the Boer War monument. Bullocks went right and bullocks went left. One drunken drover climbed the monument for safety and hid, a child again, in the sheltering arms of the big-bosomed Victory who presided over her lesser sisters: Peace, Prosperity, Love and Industry.

93

Seated behind the glasscase counter in his shop of glass and glossy tiles Mick Jones, the deaf tobacconist, lifted his eyes from the morning paper to find himself confronted by a whitehead bullock who had wandered in to escape from the tumult. The counter had to be removed before the animal could be coaxed, tail first, out of a confined space in which one twist or sideways shuffle would have caused ruin.

Then, on the fourth time round the monument, the horse tired, slipped, came panting to rest on his belly. Robbie and the Royal Mail rolled out on to a street exactly like the one that had befouled the fair figure of the London model.

It was a miserable end to his first ambition.

— To drive a horsedrawn vehicle to the danger of the public is in itself a heinous offence.

That, in due process of law, was Captain Flower, the magistrate.

He had more to say: But to carry His Majesty's Mails is an honourable responsibility of which even the youngest should be aware. Or, if not already aware, they should be instantaneously and in no uncertain fashion made aware.

Shod for the occasion, and wearing a new cloth suit, spectacles, and a patch of sticking plaster on his wide forehead, Robbie stood at the bar of justice. No longer had he that fey appearance of a magic creature that he had when he emerged, barefooted and knickerbockered, from the melodious shadows at the back of his father's shop.

— But for your youth and extreme inexperience, said Captain Flower, and the respectable standing of your father in the community, I would impose on you a heavy fine or even commit you to prison or a reform school.

Then with a roar that rent the musty, scribbling silence of the courtroom: Attend to me, young man. What in the name of heaven are you staring at?

— Your honour, at the doodles Mr O'Neill is making in his little book. They fascinate me.

Captain Flower was a redfaced frog of a man who had fought both Boers and Germans.

Eddy O'Neill, one of the town's two reporters, made on his pad the doodles that meant: Laughter in Court.

Captain Flower was a renowned salmon-fisherman and the president of a rose-growers' association. He lived in a big countryhouse by a bridge over the Drumragh river at a place where, it was said, Red Hugh O'Donnell watered his horse when he was escaping back to his native Donegal from durance in Dublin Castle and the power of the first Elizabeth. In the gardens, ranked with roses of all colours, before the captain's house, were white marble statues of heathen goddesses, of vast interest to the growing boys of the town. But it was always risky to encounter the captain, who considered that even to peep over the hedge was a form of trespass. He was a man of the utmost wrath.

So Eddy O'Neill doodled his most vivid descriptive writing as the captain's gavel rapped the bench, and the captain's red face turned purple, and the laughter died away in the courtroom.

— What age are you, young man?

— Fifteen, your honour.

— Look at me, young man. Not at Mr O'Neill.

— Certainly, your honour.

But his eyes could not keep away from the point of the magic pencil touching the reporter's pad, scraping, twisting, darting, making curves, recording words and thoughts as a seismograph records the tremors of an earthquake. This was something more wonderful than horses and wagons or the insides of his father's clocks.

— You are an American citizen, young man.

— Yes, your honour.

— In that land of the free and the home of the brave they may never have told you about contempt of court.

— Never saw the inside of court before, your honour. It's mighty interesting.

Having narrowly missed apoplexy the captain was settling down, the purple slowly fading into the grey of the face of an ironic man who had been everywhere and seen everything.

— The court is overjoyed that you find something here to interest you. For the benefit of our young visitor you will, Mr O'Neill, doodle this on your paper: Bound to the peace for two years to be of orderly behaviour.

— It's not law.

Said the lawyer who had been engaged by Jamie to make a formal appearance on behalf of the son.

— In this Court my learned friend should be aware that what I say is law. With motor machines becoming a greater menace on the road every day. With tractors ousting from the land the beneficial horse. With all that and more, the public must be protected from speed maniacs. Doodle all that down, Mr O'Neill, for the instruction, edification and benefit of our young friend from the New World.

Eddy O'Neill doodled down a lot more than the words spoken or the sentence passed in that comic court. Comic: because the world knew that any decision made by Captain Flower would be, if challenged, automatically upset in any higher court.

Eddy's brown overcoat trailed its tails. It was never buttoned: was frayed at the cuffs and stained with porter. His black felt hat had once been walked on in a scuffle at a political meeting and retained concertina wrinkles. In the snug of Broderick's pub, halfways between the courthouse and his office, he reigned as lord of all discussions, did most of his work, a share of his sleeping: and sipped good malt and hollowed his cheeks as he rolled the first sip round and round his mouth giving, as he said, full benefit and blessing to the remotest cavern of every hollow tooth. He wrote with a pencil stub in a sweeping, curving long-hand: The only factor that has this latterday Jehu, born in Boston city, like the burglar renowned in song, still walking at liberty among us, is that it was not in the power of our esteemed magistrate, Captain Flower, to impose any more severe penalty.

Then raising his eyes as the door of the snug opened he saw Robbie before him, again barefooted and knickerbockered, wearing no spectacles but identifiable by the brown curls, broad forehead and the sticking plaster.

— Your pleasure, young man.

— Pardon me, sir.

— I would offer you a drink. But the law forbids. The law we must respect. As today you learned from our choleric captain.

— The redfaced gentleman, sir, who has all the statues in his rose garden.

— Young Uncle Sam, you are observant. You have a sense of style. What book are you in?

— Book, sir?

— Class, form, grade? Grade you call it.

— I don't go to school, sir.

— Why not?

— Never could see the point in it, sir. I wanted to drive horses.

— Your horse-driving days are over. Thanks to the ukase of Flower, the grower of roses. What do you aim to do now?

— Be a reporter, sir. Just like you.

— Just like me. Vaulting ambition. Have you looked closely at me?

— Yes, sir. Saw you making the signs. The doodles, sir. Cutest thing I ever saw.

— Young man, when I used to tell my mother that I wanted to be a reporter. Or a journalist. As I grandiloquently put it. Do you know what she used to do?

— No, sir.

— She would go to the dresser where she kept her prayerbook. A big Key of Heaven with coloured ribbons hanging out of it. Behind a willow pattern plate. And forthwith she would launch into the Thirty Days Prayer.

— Why, sir?

— You see, I thought being a journalist was something like being fat and rich like G. K. Chesterton. And taking part in debates with George Bernard Shaw and talking philosophy and whittling bits of stick and impressing the people. And writing essays once a week in the *Daily News* for princely sums, and collecting the essays later into little red books to be published by Methuen of London, with your signature done in gilt on the cover. And being honoured by the Pope and all.

— Yes, sir, Robbie said.

He rubbed his bare feet sensitively on the floor.

— But my mother thought that being a journalist was having nothing but dirty overcoats. And sitting most of the day in the snug of a pub. And reporting cases of serious offences by army recruiting

97

officers against young girls. That was why she made the Thirty Days Prayer. Not that it did her much goood. Except that the Lord spared her and she didn't live long enough to know how right she was.

— I still want to be a reporter, sir. I like the idea.

— O. Henry, a gentleman in your country, was of the opinion that a journalist was a man with dandruff on his coat collar and a whiskey bottle in his hip pocket. And not so far wrong. And Bernard Shaw, a fellow from Dublin, said he never met a journalist who owned a pencil or could spell. But then he was a perfectionist.

So Robbie said he owned several pencils.

— But my barefooted, brownheaded young man, do you put them to any use?

Shifting on his seat, surveying with a gleam in his eye the other inhabitants of the snug, his faithful audience, drawing his ancient brown coat around him as if it were a patrician toga, taking a longer than usual sip of the yellow malt, painstakingly blessing every hollow sucking tooth, then swallowing with one quick warming gulp, Eddy said: But Robbie, son of Jamie of the gems and jewels, you're a hero any man would take to. I'll make you a reporter if you do three things for me. I'll put you under three geasa or three taboos the way the daughter of a King did with an ancient hero. Do you understand?

— I reckon I do, sir.

— The first thing is you will go to school and study above all things the King's English. Which, at the moment, you speak with variagations. As Biddy Mulligan, the Pride of the Coombe, in the city of Dublin, would put it. Then to the technical school to study shorthand. The magic doodles, you know. The dots, strokes and curves that mean mouthfuls. That can record both Captain Flower and the thoughts of Socrates.

— Yes sir, said Robbie.

Obedience in his drooping shoulders he turned sadly away.

— And the third thing, Robbie, is to go home and put on your boots and keep them on. Because, while from here to Ludgate Circus and the Rose and Crown on Dorset Rise, I've seen gentlemen of the Press in many's the sore condition, I've never yet seen one in his bare feet. Then come to me in a year with your pencils sharpened.

— Yes, sir, said Robbie.

He went home, his naked soles kissing farewell forever to the smooth sidewalk, blue as the pigeons, of John Street.

Aleel, the swineherd, who was bid by Forgaill's daughter, Emer, go dwell among the seacliffs, vapour-hid, did as he was told. And came back faithfully when his days of waiting were no more. So did Robbie, and Eddy O'Neill made him a reporter.

Men find their calling in the oddest ways. When Robbie came to us from the big city of Boston he rejoiced in the cool freedom of quiet, blue pavements where you could run barefooted and clap your hands, startling feeding pigeons from the grain that scattered from the nosebags of farmers' horses. In those days a boy could earn twopence holding a farmer's horse while the owner went into the bank or the post office or the public house. Robbie grew to love the smell of horses and their long, serious heads. Then, above all the methods of transport he had seen across the ocean, nothing equalled the style and colouring of the red wagon. If he hadn't driven the red wagon to ruin, he might never have discovered the magic of Eddy O'Neill's pencil. If he and his father on that day had not been so kind to Shorty Morgan, the boys of the Hill might not have been so ready to oblige him with his first story as a war-correspondent.

Dressed in new tweeds and well-shod, he came to where we sat in council under the ghost of the Big Tree and the ghost of the gallows it had been: the writhing victims of Adam Tait swinging from every branch. To Lanty he said: Here's a proposition. I need something exciting to write about. Something with Go in it. A war-story.

— War, we said.

— Whip fights, he said. The next best thing.

Speaking to the man in his own language, Lanty said: The heat's on.

— You're not scared of the heat.

Which, of course, with his taunting encouragement and with our liking for him, we were not. So, complete with Tall John's razor and police intervention, and several charges in court for breaches of the peace, giving rise to oratory that almost burst Captain Flower's bubbling bloodvessels, the noble game of whip-battle between the

Hill and Brook Street was played for the last time. There are people in the town who still have preserved in wallets or scrapbooks or in boxes of knick-knacks his description of that battle. It was the last piece of writing he did under the tutelage of Eddy O'Neill. After that he moved on to bigger things. Hitler and Hirohito ultimately provided him with better opportunities than we, with the best will in the world, could ever have managed. He was in all sorts of places and survived to write about them. We were proud of him because we had, even Captain Flower aiding, helped him to find his way and provided him with his first battle.

Shorty Morgan, a man now and not much shorter than anybody else, still has the two watches. He was always a great man for keeping things. He has, also, a pair of cufflinks purloined from an elder brother who had them from an Irish-American who was in the milk business, as they called it, in Albany, N.Y. The cufflinks are illustrated with coloured miniatures of the liner on which the milkman crossed the Atlantic for the Eucharistic Congress in Dublin in 1932. For Shorty, still as imaginative as when by night he heard the passing of the ghostly demon coachman, they are, when he shows them off, always an excuse for talking about the life and times and sudden death of Legs Diamond.

A WALK IN THE WHEAT

THREE SWANS FLEW above us, very high and swift for swans, before we turned off the highway. They flew northeast towards the big, islanded, windy trout-lake that fused the borders of three counties. We followed a byroad towards the village in the lost valley. The old man who had been reared in that valley shaded his eyes and looked up at the swans. Looked after them until they were no longer white magic birds but black specks drifting in the haze of a Spring morning. We thought of reeds and water over shore-stones and dirty grey cygnets growing into snowy beauty. He said: In my boyhood here it was a saying that it was a lucky day you saw three swans flying.

We marched down the red byway: the American woman in green slacks and white Aran sweater, the old man and myself.

I love red roads where basic sandstone glows up through the thin surface of tar or, better still, untarred roads in mountain valleys where the rain-puddles are the colour of rich chocolate.

In blue, morning mist this was no midland country of lakes and low green hills. For the lakes were steaming cauldrons and the hills were elevated by haze into floating Gothic palaces the height of the Rocky Mountains. Four miles we had walked from the fishing hotel in the triangular market-town where draughty gusts of Spring wind set the pictures dancing on the walls: where all the photographs in the hotel lounge and dining-room were of a lavish white wedding that had happened in Buenos Aires.

— From these parts, said the old man returning to his native place, they emigrated mostly to the Argentine. Not to New York or Boston or Chicago. There was a reason for that. A famous Irish missionary priest who had gone ahead of them to the pampas. They mingled Spanish and Irish names and blood.

The panelling in the hallway of the hotel had been damaged when a terrified whitehead bullock had invaded the place on the last fair-day. We were surrounded by good, midland grass building beef into red cattle. Behind hedges and orchard trees, chickens sheltered from the ruffling wind.

— There was a man in these parts in my youth, he said, was reputed to own a hen laid three times a day. And one of the three eggs was invariably three-cornered. But I must myself admit that I never saw one of those miraculous eggs.

The gloss of the strengthening sun was on the young hawthorn leaves. Clipped tree-stumps were phosphorescently white. Ash trees, slim as young girls, stood up on their own above the ranked hawthorns.

— My father had green fingers, he said. I'll show to you strangers an avenue of trees he planted.

The old woman with the silvery can in her hand met us just where the narrow road twisted, dipped suddenly, and we had our first sight of the wall and tower of the ancient abbey-ruin. She was tiny, with brown wrinkled face and blue eyes: and the eyes brightened and the face came to life when she saw our guide. She reached out her hand to him. She wore a black shawl with tassels and trimmings, a black skirt, an apron made out of a well-washed potato-sack, a pair of men's boots. She held his hand for a long time. She said: Dermot, you're welcome back to your own place.

— If it was still my own place.

— The ground doesn't change, she said.

The silvery can held goats' milk, and if we stepped with her into her cottage by the side of the road we could share the midmorning tea with herself and her husband. She explained, not to Dermot but to the woman and myself: If you haven't supped tea with goats' milk then you don't know what tea is.

So we went with her to help her carry the milk and, ourselves, to break the morning. Her husband, not quite as old as herself, gillied on the lakes for visiting fishermen, and the rafters under the thatched roof of the cottage were laced with rods and the handles of gaffs and nets. She sang for us, standing with her back to the hearth fire, her hands tightly locked behind her back, her eyes raised but tightly closed, and a young smile on her face. So sweetly, too, she sang a song about the lakes and hills, the valley, the ancient abbey, the monks who once upon a time had chanted and prayed there, the miracles wrought by the patron of the place, the holiness of the last hermit who had lived in the valley: and about a tyrant king who, after the manner of Holofernes, had been tricked and killed by the decent people. The words went haltingly to Tom Moore's melody about the harp that once through Tara's halls. Those words had been written by an old flame of hers who had long since emigrated to the land of the gauchos. When he had been gone for ten years and was showing no sign of returning she married another and tried to forget the song-writer: who afterwards married a half-Spanish woman and died among strangers.

Her husband tapped his pipe on the hob and said: I never did think much of it as a song. There was a young schoolmaster by Granard in the County Longford made a song was twice as good. There was more history in it. And a tune he didn't borrow but made it up out of his own head.

She said, sadly enough, yet still with the sauciness of a young girl: The old tunes were the best.

She put some of the goat's milk in an empty whiskey-bottle and gave it to the green-legged woman. With her blessing hovering about us, and the taste of strong tea flavoured with goats' milk in our mouths, we went down into the valley.

— That song she sang, Dermot said, was a fair resumé of the history of the locality. The people of this place were breastfed on legends and wonders. Miracle springs and miracle mills. Wood that won't burn. Water that won't boil. Water that flows uphill. There now is the wood that won't burn.

Ten yards from the road, in a marshy field, yellow with mayflowers, stood a bare, three-armed thorn bush. We crossed a shaky stone stile and went towards it. Rags and rosary beads hung from the withered arms. A small well, spotted with green scum, nestled down at the twisted roots, and through the shallow, particoloured water we could see coins and holy medals lying on the bottom. Abandoned sticks and crutches decayed with age, and one metal-and-leather leg-brace, were piled to one side.

— Three arms to the bush, he said. For the Father, the Son and the Holy Ghost. The water of the well won't boil. The wood of the bush won't burn.

The woman, sceptical and literary, quoted: Said the wicked, crooked, hawthorn-tree.

— By all accounts the saint wanted it so, he said. It was his holy well.

He had his hat in his hand. He was a big man, still handsome. But the fair locks of youth had gone and his clean, well-shaven chin and shiny, washed baldness, and around his eyes some freckles that lingered from boyhood summers, gave him at times the glow of childish, innocent enthusiasm.

— Did anybody ever try, said the woman. I mean boiling and burning.

— Oh woman, he said, of green shanks and little faith and foreign origins.

Then he covered his head and laughed loudly. He said: Not to my personal knowledge and belief. But the tradition is that anyone who ever tried to boil the water or burn the wood regretted it. And the sick were cured here. Faith made the dry bush blossom.

Faith it was, too, that made the water run uphill and confounded the sceptical miller.

— Look to the right hand now, he said.

We had regained the road.

— That there is the Hermit's Rock. Beyond that rock and the steep hill it stands on, there's one of the loveliest of the lakes of Ireland. And look to the left now.

The width of two fields away and close to the ruined abbey was a shapeless heap of grey stones.

— Over there, the saint built a mill. And no sign of water next or near it. A miller passing the way mocked him. In the legends millers were always mockers.

The water will come, said the Saint. And he blessed the mill and the millstones. And here where we stand by the side of the road the water burst out and flowed past the mill as you see it to this day. It leaves the lake on a lower level. Flows under the earth and under the hermit's rock. Comes back here to the daylight. The story says the mocking miller died of shock.

— You could see his point, she said.

The water fountained up by the roadside, spread out in a weedy shallow pool, then narrowed to make a stream. A man watered a horse in the miracle pool. Geese paddled by the horse's head. Lambs with black noses grazed on the steep slope that went up to the hermit's rock.

— Before God, said Dermot, it's my old friend, the Stone Man. I thought he was dead and gone years ago.

Together the daughter and myself said: Another miracle. A man of stone.

He came towards us, leading the horse. Small, hunched and lame-legged, he splashed through the shallow water, scattering the paddling geese.

— Dermot, he said. I couldn't mistake you. You've come back at last. To see the old places.

— No longer mine, said Dermot. But I've brought a visitor from Dublin. And my daughter.

— So I see. So I see.

The horse grazed the roadside grass. The geese, again at peace, returned to the weedy water. A poet's words came into my head, a lazy description of a Connacht village: Where seven crooked crones are tied all day to the tops of seven listening halfdoors, and nothing to be heard or seen but the drowsy dropping of water and the ganders on the green.

— You're welcome, girl, said the Stone Man. You're also a sort of a wonder. The first woman, I'd say, ever to wear trousers in this valley. Three thousand shaven celibate men once chanted prayers here. They wouldn't have welcomed the likes of you.

— But they might have, she said. As a change from chanting.

We walked through the village of seven houses and a pub, and a small village-green with an old worn stone cross. The place was still asleep. To the right hand the Hermit's Rock towered above us. To the left, across the valley and beyond the ruins of the abbey, was a graceful conical hill, green of grass, gold of furze, topped by a head of stone.

— My hill, Dermot said. If it hadn't been for an aging man in love and a designing young woman. My father's first family were left with nothing.

— I'll walk with you to the summit, said the Stone Man. If you wait till I hand the horse to the servant-boy.

He led the horse down an entry by the side of one of the seven houses.

— He has a name I suppose, she said. A real name.

— He has the name he got at the font. But nobody ever uses it. Old as I am, he's older. He came to this valley, a journeyman stonecutter, when I was sixteen. The year my father married again. The year before he died and the new woman put us out. A local landlord and the parish priest and the Protestant rector paid him to come to restore the abbey. So that the occasional learned visitor could look at it in some comfort. Up to that it was all weeds and dead scaldy jackdaws and stones scattered all over the place. Morning to night he was there like a leprechaun, hammer and chisel tinkling, working by the light of a hurricane lamp in old cloisters that nobody here would go near after dusk. Then he married a woman of the place and stayed here. And was a journeyman no longer. But the jokers said it wasn't the woman he married but the old stones of the abbey.

— Will we walk by the abbey path, the Stone Man said. Or by the church and the schoolhouse?

He had ornamented himself with a grey tailed coat and an ancient bowler. He supported his limp on a varnished blackthorn.

— By the church and the schoolhouse, Dermot said. That's the path I knew best as a boy.

The low, grey, cruciform church had a separate bell tower. To ring the bell you swung on a huge iron wheel. The whitewashed, oblong box of a schoolhouse had narrow, latticed windows.

— My uncle taught there, Dermot said. A tyrant with black sidewhiskers. And more severe on me than on any boy in the valley. He was a cattledealer, too, and thought more of bullocks than of boys. He had a gold watchchain thick as a ship's cable. And a green velveteen waistcoat. He went every week to the cattlemarket in Dublin. Once he came back and by my father's hearth solemnly told us how a young woman. A daring hussy with paint on her face, he said. How she had had the temerity to address him, outside the City Hotel on the northside. Where the cattlelairs were. But, he said, with one glance I froze her to silence. Listening to him I thought sadly of a poor painted Red Indian squaw petrified like Lot's wife. So I asked him, uncle, why did you freeze her with a glance. Dermot, he said, she was a loud woman. Or that was what I thought I heard. Long after I realized he said lewd. But it puzzled me at the time.

— Mayhap she was loud, too, said Greenshanks. Singing. Or swearing. Or playing the guitar.

— Yet I will say this for my uncle. He did his damnedest to fight when my father died. And that woman took the land from us. And threw my brothers and sisters and myself out on the ways of the world.

— Jack Dempsey, said the Stone Man, nor the best counsellor ever took snuff or wore a wig could not fight the sort of marriage agreement they make in this part of Ireland. They could teach lessons to the French.

By a masspath that went under blossoming hawthorn and skirted the edge of a field of young oats we began to ascend. Then, crossing a wooden stile, we were on another narrow road, going up steeply, screening stones loose under our feet. In his boyhood the children used to gather at the foot of the hill and, with cheers, help the horse with the peat-cart, heavy from the bog, to make the grade. His step quickened, his shoulders bent, he was a child among cheering children, digging heel-and-toe in the pebbles, approaching home in the evening. As we ascended we saw more and more of the sights that had remained with him when, faraway in exile, he'd close his eyes and recall beginnings: white crosses in a graveyard above a small lake: the sheen of clipped horses, free and running, manes flying, in the fields: the pebbly way going between red beech hedges: the sun gold on the little lake like a path you could walk on: scrubby, wintry, hillside land beginning to flame with blossoming furze: slopes holy and haunted by the shadows of monk and hermit.

— A tireless wonder to quote both poetry and prose your uncle was.

That was the Stone Man.

— We knew the Readamedaisy by heart, Dermot said. The name of the book as written was *Reading Made Easy*. He had the stonebreakers by the roadside quoting Byron and Burke. Stop, for thy tread is on an empire's dust. It is now seventeen years since I saw the queen of France. And the impeachment of Warren Hastings.

Suddenly the Stone Man is standing up like an orator, asking us to look down from this height on the beauty of his abbey, the square tower, the round columbarium to the left. And, in a voice grating like rusty metal, reciting from the repertoire of the dead schoolmaster: Where the ivy clings to the ruin and the moss to the fallen stones, where the wild ash guards the crumbling gable and the brook goes babbling, where the quiet of ages has settled down on green fields and purple hills, there is the faithfulest memorial of a past that is dead.

Paying no heed to him Dermot strides onward. He opens one half of a creaking iron gate. He says: My father planted that avenue of trees. I told you he was a green-fingered man.

The reverent breathing of the trees, the devotion of a dead man who had digged and planted and loved, for a second time foolishly and late, was with us. Green beech, copper beech, ash coming tardily to leaf, they whispered to us of the man who had helped to give them life. They were, also, his children. Rooted in the ground. Not to be cast out.

— Her one son lives in that bungalow on the slope, he said. He never married. We won't call on him.

I ventured. He's your half-brother.

— He may be. But I'm no brother of his. Half nor whole.

He strode on heavily, leading us between the trees.

— He might have the gall to tell me I was a trespasser. He has the land, legally, that rightfully belongs to us. But it always half-consoled me that he never had the harvest of son or daughter to leave it to. The sheaves in the field wouldn't feel the same in his hands, as in mine. He wouldn't know how ready and willing the ground is to yield. He wouldn't know what these trees are saying.

The road began slightly to descend. Older trees, giant oaks and sycamores, were among the ash and beech his father had planted. From a branch of one of the sycamores a thrush had sung to the good days of his boyhood. Always he had thought, the same brave cock guarding his territory with music. One bird to one tree. A propertied male proud on his own land. That bird would be long gone, his place taken by a younger cock, and another, and another. The trees, the green silence, deepened around us. We were on what had once been a clear cobbled square, now badly weedgrown, in front of a long, low cottage, the old abandoned farmhouse in which he had been born.

— She grew grand, he said, and left the old place to the cattle and hens.

— No, it wasn't that, the Stone Man said. She claimed she smothered living among trees. Some people are like that. So the new house was built up the hillside.

Chickens picked and fluttered and squawked around us. Close to the sagging doorway cattle had softened and muddied the ground. We followed him into the shadowy dung-smelling room that had once been a large kitchen. He had his hat in his hand again. He didn't speak for a long time. The woman took a ballpoint from the bag she carried and wrote her name on one white speck of wall. Then handed me the ballpoint so that I could sign myself beside her.

— Outside there, he said. That garden hedge gone wild. It made a magic circle around my childhood. It spread its leaves and shade over me on mornings like this. I'd peep out through it and see the world. I've seen a lot of the world since then. But nothing as sad to me as the spectacle of this house. This day.

— Things change, dad, the woman said.

— Every rafter in this kitchen had a special name I'd given it. And the polished mantel beam was King of them all.

The woman said again that things change.

— I was born in that bedroom below, he said. And when I was small and in bed, the moon would shine in on me through that door. When I lost the door I lost the moon.

— It's somewhere still, she said.

— And outside in the evening the rocktop of the hill above was a giant's head. Eyes and all. And the green slope was the giant's cloak floating off towards the west.

— We'll go to the summit, the Stone Man said. And study the view. Five counties you can see from the crown of the giant's head.

We could feel his anger, or pain, growing as he led us up to the summit. The Stone Man, to ease the strain, talked of the view we could see, the coloured prospect of five counties and a dozen lakes: and talked of the tyrant of a Dane who had been killed by the decent people. And of the hermit who had lived in the valley. He joked at the woman about her green legs. And about the three thousand celibate men who wouldn't have allowed her into the valley.

— You'd have shattered all the rules of cloisura, he said. Why; women weren't allowed into the saint's mill. It was reckoned to be as holy as any church he ever built.

— It could be, she said, that he was afraid they'd find fault with his baking. If he could bake his own flour that is. Old bachelors never like women near their kitchens.

— Two miles away, said Dermot, there's a place called Hangman's Hollow. A landlord in the eighteenth century had a man hanged there for stealing a loaf of bread.

— The tyrant Dane, said the Stone Man, had a more subtle method. Every year he exacted from every house in his territory an ounce of gold. If he didn't get it he cut off the nose of the defaulter. So they called it Nose Money. But he had a weakness for the girls.

— Green legs, she said.

— History is silent. He demanded that a local chieftain should send him his daughter for divarsion. So she came. And with her twelve beardless youths wearing skirts. And when the poor man was drunk they stuffed him in a barrel and drowned him in a lake.

— If he had been a bible-reading Christian, she said, he'd never have fallen for the old beardless youth trick.

On top of the hill we sat down and drank the goats' milk that the singing woman had given us.

— There's a man walking over there, Greenshanks said.

She pointed across the valley to the slope below the Hermit's Rock. But try as we might we could see nobody.

— The ghost of the last hermit, the Stone Man said. Visible only to a woman who has tasted the magic milk of the white goat. They say he broke his vow in the end. He was a hunting gentleman who gave up the world. And lay in a hole in that rock. With his proctors, as they were called, ranging the country for him. Bringing back corn and eggs, geese, turkeys, hens and sheep. He ate like the quality. It was the chief part of his holiness that he was never to stir out of the cave. But this fatal day he heard the hounds and the horn. Too much for him it proved to be. Off he went on a neighbour's mount. Broke his neck at the first stone wall.

— The man's gone now, she said.

She stood up hurriedly.

— There are ticks in the grass.

White marl fringed the two small lakes at the foot of the hill and shone up at us like silver from underneath the water.

Surveying the carpet of counties Dermot said: My father used to walk a lot around the rock. He said it was holy ground.

— This entire valley is holy, the Stone Man said. Look through the chancel arch of the abbey when the furze blossom is out in all its glory. It's as if you were looking at the light of the heaven.

He led us down by another path so that he could display to us the arches, the cloisters, the cool stones of the love of his heart. We crossed a whole field of clover and yellow pimpernel, then followed a gravelly, slippery goatpath through the furze. The blue air above us was cut by the whinnying sound of flying snipe. Far below, where the stream went on from the saint's mill to join the great lake the swans had flown to, three boys and a dog followed the twisting course of the water. The boys threw sticks and stones. They crossed and recrossed the narrow stream. The dog barked and leaped in the air, plunged in to rescue floating sticks. Their actions had a happiness isolated from time.

— Spring was always a glory in this place, he said.

Then, loudly enough to be heard four fields away, he shouted a verse of a poem: Tomorrow Spring will laugh in many waters, ever the ancient promise she fulfills. Tomorrow she will set the furzebloom burning along my father's hills.

Where the furze ended we crossed a stile, the woman leading. Before us lay a broad flat field bursting with the promise of young wheat.

— Walk round the edge, I called to her. Don't trample the man's crop.

— Sink him to the pit, Dermot roared. Who owns this land?

He went across the field, sinking his heels deeply for purchase and possession. Soft clay spurted up behind him. Tender green shoots lay crushed on his path. With savage steps he wrote out on the land the story of his long-thwarted passion for the lost thing of his own. We followed him, stepping carefully, as if we feared that the stalks might cry out.

That was a late year for the ash. So there were four great ash trees, still bare, but proud and defiantly independent of decoration, on the green in the triangular market-town. Within the square they formed, stood the old collapsing market-house built by an eighteenth-century landlord to resemble a miniature St Paul's. In its cellars, rebels in 1798 had been flogged and otherwise tortured before the dragging-out to death. Or so the Stone Man told us. He had come with us for a farewell night of drink and talk and song.

The rough Spring wind of the morning had died. The pictures no longer danced in draughts on the walls of the hotel's hallway. During the day a carpenter had repaired the damage done by the whitehead bullock. The gentle lady who owned the hotel told us about that white wedding she had attended in Buenos Aires, about the fantastic length of the bride's train. She showed us some sombre religious prints she had brought back with her. Spanish and Irish faces looked at us from the walls of the dining-room.

Then out in the public bar the people were gathered to say welcome to the returned exile and his daughter. A girl in a red dress, without urging or invitation, sang a song about a Donegal beauty called the Rose of Arranmore. There was a great willingness in the people to sing. The Stone Man, elevated, threw his blackthorn and bowler into a corner, roared to the barmaid: Give me, girl, as the tinkers used to say, a glass of Geneva wine and a wisp for the ass.

Then in a voice like the sawing of old branches he sang the song the woman of the goats' milk had sung that morning.

Greenshanks whispered to me: My father loved that hill.

— One tiger to one hill, I said. One singing cockthrush to one sycamore.

We left the crowded bar and walked down the long yard between byres and stables at the back of the hotel. A pig nosed at a cartchain.

There were nettles and abandoned motor-tyres, rusty lengths of corrugated iron, the twitter of evening birds. And slow sparse raindrops. In the bar behind us Dermot had raised his voice and was singing that his boat could lightly float in the teeth of wind and weather and outrace the smartest hooker between Galway and Kinsale.

She said: Since I was a child I always liked him to sing. That was always his favourite song.

She said that he had hurt himself when he hurt the wheat and the ground: And I felt nothing. Nothing at all. Except that it might be cute to have a summer cottage in such a heavenly place. To get away from New York in the heat. That worries me that I felt nothing. That he was a stranger to me.

— He never spoke to me much about this place, she said. As you'd think a father might.

— The subject was too painful. The dispossession. Diaspora.

— He had one funny story, though. About a funeral. And the mourners stopped at a pub and left the coffin and corpse on a stone wall outside. They said, sure God rest him, what would be the point in bringing him in. 'Twould only vex him.

She was laughing and crying.

— But I did see a man walking round the Hermit's Rock. The hunting hermit? Or my grandfather walking on holy ground: Or the shadow of a cloud on the grass? But I saw something that nobody else could see. One woman in a valley with the ghosts of three thousand celibate men. Wasn't it a sign to show that, in spite of them, I belonged to the place?

THE PYTHON

WHEN THE WINE and the after-dinner cognac dies he wakes from the glutton's stupor, sniffs the dark room, knows exactly who has stopped in the place before him. The air-conditioning makes for most of the time like the noises of a Gipsy Moth: then, every four or five minutes, clanks as if a chained man inside were trying to get out. It pumps humid air into an atmosphere already oozing: and odorous. The man who has left that odour behind him has not slept here on his own. Not even in this easygoing hotel do tomcats sign the register on their own. But pets are permissible and somewhere in the world there is a noseless man or woman, or a pair without noses and thinking that a tomcat is a pretty pet.

In the odorous dark he listens to the little man from Paris who says that it is an octopus, so the little man pulls out his knife and opens his eyes, then thinks it's a dream, then thinks that it isn't, that the octopus is reality and is draining him with its suckers: but, no, it is simply the dreadful humid heat: he is sweating, he says, he had gone to sleep about one o'clock, then at two the heat had waked him, he had plunged into a cold bath and back into bed without drying himself and right away the furnace roars again under his skin, and he is sweating again, and he dreams the house is on fire and says that this is more than mere heat, this is a sickness of the atmosphere, the air is in a fever, the air is sweating: and more of the same.

The little man from Paris is writing about humid heat.

At four in the morning the telephone begins to ring, and rings and rings. The crazy woman will just now be leaving the hotel-bar. She calls him from the payphone outside the door of the gents. That woman could clear a bar-counter quicker than the Black Death. But he answers the phone in the end. And will go to her room to get away from the smell of the tomcat. Also: her air-conditioner works. And there may be other reasons. She has long dark glossy hair, and prominent glistening American teeth: and her craziness is not menacing, only gentle and amorous.

When he switches on the light he finds it hard to believe that there is no cat to be seen: yet if a cat may vanish and leave a smile behind it, then another cat may vanish and leave a smell. The book in which the little man from Paris laments about the humid heat lies open on the other, unused, bed. He checks his memory against the text. Not bad, not bad at all: for this clinging, sticky, smelly heat might very well affect a man's memory. But that cold plunge and that crawling back untowelled on to the bed was a bloody bad idea: the little man, a philosopher too, might have killed or crippled himself with rheumatics.

A quick shower now, a quick brisk towelling, helps and cannot harm: go glistening to the gentle crazy woman with the glistening teeth and the glossy hair: and as he combs his hair he thinks that the week that has just passed has been, the papers say, the bloodiest week of this warm season in little old New York. The paper is there on the dressing-table and still saying it: Fiftyeight murders, three young drug-addicts executed on a rooftop, they get a few lines on a backpage: Mafia boss murdered, that makes the front page for Mafia murders are as popular as baseball: and a most poetic policeman says take a poor guy, it's sweltering, he don't have an air-conditioner, he takes a few beers, there's no place to go, he gets mad at something, then all of a sudden it bursts out, he grabs a knife.

The knife is farandaway the most favoured weapon for warm nights.

He does have an air-conditioner. Puff, puff, puff, a wonderful breath of foul air. Clank, clank, clank, jealous Vulcan is trapped in the crater, let me outa here. Dear dark woman with such hair too, I come, I come my heart's delight.

He has never carried a knife.

Or if he had been carrying a knife he would have attacked the python yesterday when the musician draped it around Judith's neck. Young women should not wear pythons around the neck. He recalled then with a shudder a story he had read about an Irish lord who when he was a young man in Oxford kept a python as a pet. He does not trust pythons. He, that is, not the noble lord who was lunatic enough to keep in his lodgings on the High a python fourteen feet long. Tame, he thought. Tame? But didn't like strangers. Nothing is tame that doesn't like strangers. So the landlady's daughter opens the box that the python lives in, and the python coils round and round the landlady's daughter, bruising her to the extent of thirty-five pounds sterling which was big money in the year of the Franco-Prussian war: and the python is banished to the zoo, a proper place for pythons.

All of which he tells the musician who laughs at him and says: Landladies' daughters in Oxford, England, should know better than to poke pythons.

He is not content until Judith and the two girls in her company are away from that python and out of that zany penthouse: all fixed up with blooms and screaming birds like a tropical jungle, and with fish in glass tanks that dance, the fish not the tanks, when the musician plays the piano. A sort of dance: swishing round and round, Boccaccio's seven young ladies and three young gentlemen barefoot in the crystal water and with naked arms engaging in various games. What games? But the piranha fish do not dance. Four of them in a tank which they share with a small black shark, all so dangerous to each other that they leave each other alone. The shark seems to sleep. The piranha deliberately, like the Eleventh Hussars, do not dance. They are small fellows with buck teeth. They stare out through the glass wall and say: If we had you in the Amazon.

Being fair judges of fleshmeat it is to be assumed that they stare hardest at Judith and Marion and Barbara, blooming American belles just turned twenty, fit any morning to play games in Boccaccian streams: not at myself, nor at Murtagh, lean, longjawed sports writer over from Dublin to witness and comment on an ancient Celtic stickball game in a field in the Bronx: nor, by God, at the musician, tough and brown and bald and wrinkled. Even piranha fish may prefer tender meat.

Life is much more liveable in the bar and restaurant on the ground floor. And tolerably cool, too. No puffs, no clanks, but currents of real air reminding me again of Boccaccio in the Italian mornings, and the middle-ages dead and done with, and love and laughter in the air: and cool water fringed by smooth round stones and verdant grasses.

To the three young women Murtagh explains the nature of the stickball game: No, not curling. Hurling. Curling is something you do on ice. Like sliding a flatiron along ice. We don't have enough ice in Ireland. No, this is hurling. And it's not at all like the stickball I saw the Puerto Rican kids play around the corner there in an alley off Seventh. That's a sort of pelota or handball with a broomstick. No, hurling is hurling. Hurling is different. There's an Irish, Gaelic, word for it, but that wouldn't interest you. It goes back into history. It's the most natural thing in the world, for a man to hit a ball with a stick. There's something like it in Japan, I've heard. Though perhaps I'm confusing shinto and shinty. That's what they call it in Scotland. Shinty. Something like hurling. But then the Scots would have borrowed it from us. Great men to borrow, the Scots. Two teams. Fifteen a side. On one pitch, just like American football. The stick's about three feet long with a smooth curving blade. The best ash, cut with skill. The clash of the ash, they say. The ball's the size of two fists clasped. Like that . . .

He shapes the delicate white hands of Marion to resemble the ball. Cute man Murtagh. He is pleased with these young American women to whom last night I introduced him.

— That's the way the game is organized nowadays. Long ago it used to be played by mobs. All the men of one clan or parish against all the men of another clan or parish. And the pitch was unconfined. Over hedges and ditches and bogs they were bound, as the song said. But in the game, nowadays, we have rules and limits. Even in Ireland we have rules and limits. Anyway, you'll see it all in the Bronx. Tipperary vee New York. And what are you all having to drink?

In honour of the heat outside it is mostly cold white wine. Manolo, the Spanish barman, brings the drinks and olives and celery stalks, and impeccable good manners. Piped music, but very mildly, plays a flamenco tune. The musician has stayed aloft, playing to the toucans and the python, and the black shark and the staring piranha.

— Some night, Murtagh says, the piranha will come out and get him. You couldn't feel easy with those brutes about the house. Not a laugh in them from start to finish.

The young ladies from Boccaccio, Pampinea, Fiammetta, Filomena laugh into their cool tinkling drinks. Faraway in the sunny south and in a womens' college he has sat with the three of them and nine hundred and ninety-seven others, in the great dining-hall and over his Hawaiian salad (cherry), reflected that Lord Byron could never stand, or sit, to see a woman eat. That sad-crazy mother of his must have been sloppy over her soup. Or it may just have been that Byron preferred his women otherwise engaged: at falconry, or the careful stitching of samplers, or at the dance, or at playing on the virginals.

— But what, saith the fair Pampinea from Tennessee, did you expect to find in a womens' college if not women.

— A point well made. But knowing from faraway, from the far side of the Atlantic, that a womens' college is full of women, and finding yourself at dinner, one man among a thousand women, are two different things. Not that I object. Now that the first shock is over, I rather like it.

The three young women who have asked him to sit with him at their circular table thank him merrily.

— Sometimes, they say, the chaplain joins us.

— Let us hope we never need a chaplain.

Lord Byron, he reflects again and with increasing wonder, could not have endured to be in that fine, old, southern, circular, timbered dining-hall watching and listening-to one thousand healthy females, hungry and unashamed, by no means walking in beauty like the night. Noble lord and all as he was, one thousand pairs of parents might have had qualms to hear that he was aprowl on the campus and, on faculty row, in possession of his own private lair into which he might entice or drag his prey.

— Belshazzar, from thy banquet turn he says, nor in thy sensual fullness fall.

And has to explain himself at some length. These are serious women. And curious.

Between bites and sups Fiametta talked of St Exupery and Kafka and wonders, God bless the girl's digestion, what effect Schopenauer and Kierkegaard had on Kafka. She was, and is, a thin, intense, freckled girl with spectacles and, in those days, she did most of her study in the reading-room attached to the chapel.

— Because, she said, there is always the crucifix on the wall. You can look at it when you are depressed.

Filomena, who was then plump and writing a paper on American pragmatism, said: There is always tea.

She is trying to slim but she found that strict dieting interfered with her ability to write papers.

Fiammetta said that the chaplain was a devout Calvinist and that one could talk to him about anything except religion. To most questions he returned as answer one and the same question: Cannot we know God.

Filomena said that she had been detailed in the forenoon to cheer up three depressed freshmen. The cause of their depression was not homesickness. But that so far they had had no dates. So she said: Consider, sisters, that somewhere there must be three or thirty young men with the same problem. That cheered them up.

— Hope, she said, there is always hope. Don't I know. Fat girls always know.

That was four to five years away back from this day of the python and hurling and humid heat: and heat or no heat, Murtagh says, duty calls him to the Bronx and we don't have to go with him unless we want to see the hurling. So to hell with the heat and the five of us head for the Gaelic Park in the Bronx.

— Filomena has problems, Fiammetta says. She has a situation. She has three situations. I've asked her to ask you about them. You were once so helpful to me.

This is in the subway to the Bronx: which, the subway, is nothing more nor less than a noisy putrid horror. She shrieks the message into my ear. Her voice has become as thin and shrill as herself. But because of the surrounding noise nobody except myself hears her. Nobody bothers to hear her because of the heat. Murtagh has fallen in love or something with Pampinea. All this is so strange to him. The other day on Lexington Avenue he looked up in boyish wonder and said that never again would he mention Liberty Hall which is Dublin's one skyscraper, lopsided and all of seventeen floors: skies are low, mostly, over the islands. Even the heat is, to Murtagh, a happening. Then to crown it all he has met a genuine belle from Tennessee: Boccaccio himself had never by any crystal Italian stream imagined better. Murtagh whispers into the ear of Pampinea who listens, enchanted, to his brogue. He is as exotic to her as she is to him: and somewhere there may be the prospect of a room with an air-conditioner where they may gather even closer without dissolving into a dew. Filomena is asleep or feigns sleep. Even if she hears, it doesn't matter, for Fiammetta is consulting me, the wiseman, with her permission. What was it that I ever did or said to help Fiammetta? With the heat and the noise I cannot remember: and the situation is, or the situations are, three men, two of them married and all contestants for the hand, by metonymy, of Filomena who, now that she has slimmed, is a mighty attractive proposition.

Next Sunday the pattern at home will be keeping and the young active hurlers the field will be sweeping . . .

It is some time in the eighteenth century and in the prison in the town of Clonmel in the county Tipperary a young man sits and waits to be hanged.

How sad is my fortune and vain my repining, the strong rope of fate for this young neck is twining . . .

And he remembers his home and the boys at the hurling in some sunlit pasture on the lovely sweet banks of the Suir. Who was he? What deed had he done? Who wrote the sad song about him? Burning with enthusiasm to explain the nature of hurling, and much else, to Pampinea, Murtagh sings the old song in the over-crowded cab that carries them, sweating, from the train to the playing-pitch: and far far from green Suirside grass is the rectangle of American scorched earth on which fifteen men from Tipperary, sticks in hand, do battle with fifteen Irish expatriates who, similarly armed, have taken it upon themselves to represent the city of New York. The game itself, and not just its finer points, is lost in clouds of acrid American dust. Every time a hoof or a stick or a ball or a body strikes the earth a spiralling sandstorm, devil of the desert, arises.

But back of the stands and terraces, in bars and in restaurants, several vintages of Irish-America have thrown their hats at the invisible game and are making certain sure that the heat will not dry nor the dust choke their throttles. Joining them, I find that I am among my own and far away from those awe-inspiring moments when the sun catches the tops of the buildings on, say, Seventh and I am shaken into asking myself why did man ever challenge the heavens by building such Babylonian towers.

Out on the pitch the desert devils move here and there. Here in the tents the corks pop and the stout and whiskey flow. The jovial din is only stupendous and, in the middle of it all, two nuns, one young, one old, sit on chairs and confidently shake collection boxes: and Filomena snuggles close and tells me of her three situations, two of them married, one Irish and single and works in a bank, one an airlines' pilot and English, one an American academic, all for one and one for all, and all together in New York on this warm day.

— And to think, she says, that once upon a time I counselled freshmen who were hardup for dates.

To think, indeed. The years and dieting have made her most desirable, and one solution for three situations is to find a fourth that will cancel out the other three. So he turns the topic by talking to her about poetry, about that same convict of Clonmel pining in his prison, and how nobody knows who he was, nor who the poet was who wrote about him in the Irish. Which he quotes mellifluously, and in full, in the cab on the way back to Manhattan. And how the Irish was translated into English in the nineteenth century by a lonely sort of a poet called Jeremiah J. Callanan whose spirit responded to that cry from the past: At my bedfoot decaying my hurlbat is lying, through the boys of the village the goal-ball is flying. My horse 'mong the neighbours neglected may fallow, while I languish in chains in the jail of Cluainmeala.

Which he tells her means Honeymeadow, a lovely name, a handsome town, a lovely river valley, romantic Ireland is not dead and gone but alive and well in the back of a cab in the humid heat in New York: and back in Manolo's Spanish bar and restaurant they are mysteriously alone or together, and Murtagh is somewhere with Pampinea, and Fiammetta has gone somewhere else alone so as to be able to catch an early morning flight to somewhere: and the three situations have been for the moment forgotten about for the poetic sake of the young man pining in the deathcell and sadly remembering his horse and the hurling in green meadows: With the dance of fair maidens the evening they'll hallow, while this heart once so warm will be cold in Cluainmeala.

But during dinner the vision fades and the situations relentlessly return, as later they are expected to do for drink and a discussion.

Her father is an episcopalian clergyman in Detroit.

— But it is not because I feel that life should be sinless. Or can be. Life should be simpler. Or plain simple.

He is prepared to agree. They hold hands across the table. She sips a tiny sip of his wine: then kisses the glass. One, two, three add up to complications. Four is as simple as a May morning. True love is an even number.

— Some things I want to buy, she says, in the supermarket.

So, after dinner, she goes for a while, leaving him gloating like a sultan, and returns with a plastic bag full of the things.

— My studio isn't fifty yards away.

They walk the fifty yards. He carries the plastic bag. It is a long walk in the sweating heat and the things in the bag are surprisingly heavy. Cans grind against each other. Somewhere on Sixth they find a doorway and one of those straight New York stairways. There is no elevator. The studio is on the fifth floor. He grunt and sweats. He fardels bears. Green meadows are forgotten, and crystal streams. Boccaccio was a liar.

She paints. He has already known that. There is something on the easel. An Andy Warhol prospect of a can of Sprite. There are other things on the walls. But even before the door opens he smells them. Not the Andy Warhol nor the things on the walls, but three of the largest cats it has ever been his misfortune to, he was about to think, see. A Manx, near neighbour to a Dublinman, tabby and tiger-striped. An Iranian: long hair sweeping the floor, tail like a living bush. A Thailander: slender as a snake, not sweet as a pawpaw in May nor lovely as a poppy, but mean and snarling behind a black mask. She takes from him the plastic bag. The cans are cans of catfood. He sits and watches while she feeds the jealous brutes on three separate willow-pattern platters and from different cans. She loves them. They love her. There is a camp-bed in the corner. For the cats or Filomena, or all in together this humid weather? She sits on it and they talk, he and Filomena, across a room crowded by cats. The cats stare at him. Could they outstare the musician's piranha fish? After a while Filomena and himself go back to the Spanish bar.

On the way to which he tells her the tale of Big Joe who played the clarinet. In the orchestra in a mammoth cinevariety theatre in Dublin. He was very handsome. He could run like Ronnie Delaney. He had need. He had seven mistresses.

— Knew three of them to talk to and two more by sight.

Because Big Joe was married the most he could manage was to see one of the girls one night each week after the late show. Told each girl he could manage only one night a week because his wife was jealous. Told his wife, to explain about the two hours, that he was having a drink with the boys. Which worked. He possessed man's greatest blessing: a complacent wife. Anyway she had him the rest of the time, when he wasn't playing the clarinet. Satisfactory. All present and correct.

There was one problem. In the interval between the second show and the late show, and when the movie was on the screen, every one of the seven wished to meet Joe somewhere or other for a chat and a drink or a cup of tea. He couldn't have them all in the same place so he, like a general, stationed one here, one there, around the central city, sentries, single spies, redoubts: and ran on foot, the quickest method of transport in crowded places, and sat and sipped and talked and kissed, and so on and on, and then back to the pit to blow the clarinet.

— Joe, I said, rationalize, rationalize. Not the breath of Leviathan could stand the strain.

— And I worried about him.

— What happened? What happened?

She must wash and perfume more than she paints or even makes love: There is no odour of cats.

He tells her that the last time he was back in Ireland he met the man who had played the saxophone in that same pit. And asked him how was Big Joe. And heard: Poor Joe, he went to London and dropped one day running along Shaftesbury Avenue.

— He took on too much territory. Alexander knew when and where to stop. Rationalize, Filomena, rationalize.

But no use in talking to her. She is surrounded, possessed, coiled around by pythons, and perhaps the only man who could be all the world to her would be that odd Egyptian officer mentioned by Thomas Mann whom she read so carefully in college: Weser-ke-bastet, what a bloody name, on imperial duty in the city of Shechem. But known to the Schechemites, wise guys, simply as Beset.

He mentions to her the name of that gentleman. But if in the course of her college reading she had ever noticed the fellow she has long forgotten him.

— What was about him?

— His two passions in life were flowers and cats. The local divinity of his home-town was guess what?

— A cat.

— Bright girl.

— Scarcely a flower.

— A cat-headed goddess called Bastet.

— What a fun idea. I'll paint her.

— Everywhere he went, and morning noon and night, he was surrounded by cats. All colours. All ages. All breeds and sexes. Not only living ones. But mummies. Before whom he placed offerings of mice and milk. And wept as he did so.

— Another fun idea. Could I decorate my studio like that?

He does not remind her that Beset was what used to be called a pansy: and Filomena's nature, it might seem, cries out for more than cats.

— Tarry with me.

She has actually used that word. Tarry.

Perhaps it is that old usages, old words survive in the south. Or is it just remembered from her reading?

— Tarry with me, she says, until they come.

— Tarry with us, he says, for already it is late and a perverted world seeks to blot Thee out of sight by the darkness of its denials.

— What is the man saying?

— That's part of a prayer my mother used to read out loud. At night prayers. With the Rosary. On the first of every month. Consecrating the household once again to the Sacred Heart of Jesus. The reference is to the disciples on the road to Emmaus.

— Wow!

No, it was not Judith here beside him and waiting for her men, it was Fiammetta, Marion, who did most of her study in the reading-room attached to the chapel because the crucifix was on the wall and she could look at it when she was depressed. Judith who was plump and into pragmatism, and who said there was always hope, and that fat girls always knew, is now beautiful and the desired of all or, at any rate, of four men. Correction: three. Four, only for a very brief moment.

— Tarry with us for the drink and the discussion.

— Would I not be, to coin a phrase, *de trop*? Four's company, five's a . . .

— Quorum. Be our chairperson. My master.

— And they knew him in the breaking of the bread.

— Be then my saviour. Marion used to say: Cannot we know God.

— The chaplain used to say.

Her nervous laughter. Three men arrive. All together. He feels that it would be apt if they paralleled the cats: one Manxman, one Persian, one Siamese. But that would be too much to hope for. They are as he heard they would be: two of them married although that doesn't show, one of them Irish which is obvious, one of them quite as obviously English, one of them an American academic: and how would you guess? Not one of them is of any particular interest. That is not just because they have come between himself and Filomena: Judith. No, the cats have already done that, those three cats, that invisible tomcat, that humid heat. Jean-Paul Sartre's octopus, that python.

If there was to have been a discussion my presence has put an end to that. Nothing above or beyond uneasy badinage. What a word. What does it mean? Nothing to do with badminton? Or shuttlecock?

— Hope, she had once said, there is always hope. Fat girls always know.

Fat girls hope that some day they may be slim. For what?

She leaves us for a while to go to the loo. It is the Irishman who says: Gentlemen, let us settle this. Once and for all.

No pistols, no swords are to be seen.

Carefully he takes from his wallet a small airmail envelope with green, white and gold trimmings. The Irish Republic. He shakes it. It rattles. He says: This envelope that you see in my hand contains three quarters. One of them is marked with a cross.

To me he says: Sir, as an impartial member of the audience inspect this envelope and the coins therein to see that there is no deception. It contains three quarters, coins peculiar to the United States of America, one of them marked with a cross clearly cut. When you have made your inspection and assured yourself of my veracity and bona fides, kindly pass the bag along, keep it moving, look, inspect, satisfy yourselves that all is fair and square, ladies and gentlemen, in for a penny in for a pound, come in your bare feet, go home in a Studebaker . . .

All is fair and square. The coins are restored, the envelope rattled, and he who finds the cross takes the woman. The Englishman finds the cross. They shake hands all round. And also with me. Fair field and no favour. The Englishman buys a round of drinks. All smiling, yet perhaps nervous, she returns from the loo. My advice or chairmanship is never needed. Later on the Englishman takes her by the elbow and gently leads her away. Quite uncomplainingly she goes: insofar as I can tell. Snarling cats stand there to prevent me from doing anything about it. A drink with the losers, perhaps myself a loser. A friendly goodnight.

That was all yesterday and late last night and now it is four in the morning, and the phone rings and rings, and the daft dark woman with the glistening teeth will be waiting, air-conditioner working: no cats.

I come, I come my heart's delight.

What do I mourn for? Lost innocence? Lost opportunity? The crowded condition of the world? The fury and the mire of human veins?

In the penthouse the python sleeps and the piranha stare into the darkness.

SECONDARY TOP

WE COME UP from the river and watch him playing darts with young fellows in the alcove off the public bar in the fishing-hotel. Young fellows are tolerated there: just about. Darts and rings and baby-billiards, but no juke-box. A side-door opens to what has once been the stable-yard so that the fishermen won't be disturbed by through traffic. We sit where we can see and consider him. An atracap of a man with tight trousers, too small even for his small legs. He hasn't, the poor devil, the least idea of who we are. Or who I am. He could have seen Dale's picture in the papers. Or listened to him at an annual conference. Or passed him on the street in Dublin. Or observed him playing golf at Lahinch, the tough old bastard. Or heard about the way he forever jingles loose change in both pockets of his plus-fours. Plus-fours, anyway, have lived long enough or died long enough ago to be unusual. But the heart of the atracap is with the noisy boys. His eyes are on the dart-board. He notices nothing else.

— I am the Martian Marksman, he screams in fake falsetto.

And dances upon his little feet and scores a bullseye.

— I am the Black Wizard of Blue Mountain.

Stepping high he goes round and round the green baize of the baby-billiards. Bent double and moaning low, the half-dozen boys follow him.

— He plays darts with the boys, I say.

— An unnecessary comment, young man.

Dale jingles, but only in one pocket. He has a glass in his right hand. He says: With the girls too. Darts.

— I'm O'Driscoll the rover, the little man says in a startlingly profound baritone. That's me. Fineen O'Driscoll the rover, Fineen O'Driscoll the free.

He darts and, to applause, has another bull's eye. He is popular among the boys. He dances from one little foot-full of turned-up toes to another and chants, really chants: I am the Seawolf. I am Blackbeard Teach. I am old bold Henry Morgan. I am Captain Blood. I am the fastest gun in the West.

— In this secondary top, old Dale jingles, do they do everything through Irish.

He seldom or never now comes out of headquarters and has to be enlightened on details.

— Everything, I tell him. Every single thing.

Although, under the circumstances, it may be conduct unbecoming inspectors of the Department we laugh right heartily: and next morning study the girls the Seawolf plays darts with. Which is easy because the back or business entrance to the secondary school is right across the sleepy street from the fishing-hotel. Not exactly a complete secondary school but the smaller establishment we call a secondary top. The toddlers and under-twelves go in by the front door which looks down over lawns and flowerbeds to the river widening out into the lake.

The first letter of complaint had come to the Department from Worried Mother, no other identification. She had heard rumours and she had suspicions. No hard facts, no fingerprints. The letter was filed away but not forgotten. When Worried Mother wrote again she signed her name and had three other worried mothers to support her. Still no hard facts. No little girl had talked. There was a slight suggestion that the mothers were thinking of the law and that if the fathers knew and also worried, the remedy might overstep the law. Like tar and feathers. Then there was a scrawled letter from the parish priest to say that he was too old and his two curates too young to handle such a case.

— The church is done, Dale said. Ecumenism. Truckling to Protestants. Guitars on the high altar. In the old days the parish priest's blackthorn would have settled the case in five minutes. But I'll be glad to go with you, young man. You'll need a guide, counsellor and friend. Bloody maniac poking at the little girls. And I'll fish that river again. Fished it before you were born. With the long

Castle Connell rod that you won't see the like of nowadays. Spliced with waxend made up of many strands of shoemaker's thread spun together by hand. The line running through the rings. Soak the cast in the pool . . .

He jingled, and rambled on for a long time about the way gentlemen fished before glass-fibre or Japan were heard of.

— I'll show you fishing, young man. We'll combine pleasure with our painful duty. Also the rods will be a sort of disguise. Incogniti.

Incogniti here we sit, girl-watching from the bay-window of the residents' lounge on the first floor. Green skirts, bare knees, green jerseys, white open-necked shirts: mostly. Some daring spirits have their own styles.

— They say, I say, that you're in trouble when you begin to look at your daughter's schoolfriends.

— Worse trouble if you begin to look at your grand-daughter's schoolfriends.

That jolts me a bit. He has a name for being a puritan. He says: They eat a lot of toffee.

A sweet little redhead, thirteen or so, goes by, cheeks swollen by an iced lolly, the stick of the lolly standing out white and stiff. Does the manikin hold their lollies while they suck?

— Atracap's a funny word, Dale says.

For our man has come into view, alone amid the lightsome throng, wearing, startingly, a flat black Mexican hat, taking short steps, carrying a bundle of books.

Dale says: Texas Jack.

For no reason that I can think of: and, anyway, I am meditating on that word atracap. Never, I tell Dale, did I find it in any dictionary.

— For the good reason, young man, that it's not there to be found. A rural corruption of apricot, I'd say, and meaning something like arc or arcan which Father Dineen's dictionary will tell you means a chest or a coffer, or the last little pig in a litter. Or a dwarf. Or a lizard. Or a diminutive creature of any kind.

— Or simply an ark. As in Noah. How about acrobat?

— Or if you spell it eeayarcee, the heavenly arch or vault. Or a rainbow. Or water. Or honey. Or, as an adjective, bloody or blood-red.

— Like the poet, Whitman, Father Dineen contained multitudes.

— Or knew that our native language did.

We are talking pedantic nonsense because we feel, uneasily, that it's a mean thing to come sneaking up and spying on the little man. We have our orders. Fair enough. The Department is the Department. What else? But still!

Inside the building the warning bell sounds: five minutes to go. The flow of green girls strengthens, is blocked for a minute or two at the narrow doorway to form a green living pool. Shrill voices rising. Laughter. A teacher, or two or three or four, patiently, pressing through. Our quarry has vanished. Where did he get that hat? Old Dale says that in the cowboys and Injuns he read when he was a boy, Texas Jack always wore a flat black hat. He stands up. He steps forward into the bay of the window. He says two or three times: They came like swallows and like swallows went.

He tells me that he is moved to tears by all those light voices, by all that innocence. But he weeps no tear: and because we know what we know, or suspect what we have been led to suspect, the girls, twelve to seventeen, don't seem like that to me at all. Not all of them: several of them, by heaven, very well developed indeed. But how, merely by sight and a distant prospect at that, are we to know which of the young ladies are involved. Look now at that beauty: an Italianate sort of a girl, dark glossy hair blowing in the wind, shining back at the sun, turning and turning her head like a tennis umpire. No, that simile's trivial. Like an exotic bird that would spring and fly. Then thoughtfully, solemnly, with her left hand pushing her hair back, smoothing her forehead. She is also an original: she wears a red cardigan and levis. But she is by no means old enough to be a teacher. Dale says: Pitiful to think of them all growing up to be harridans, scolds, barges.

So touching, I think, the way they fold their arms over growing breasts: a discovery, an embarrassment, something to hide. Or protect. Look at that one now, stepping stoutly forward, schoolbag like knapsack on shoulders, spectacles, a sullen face, tails of hair in her eyes, the heavy green skirt clinging and making a valley, a coom, a gougane, up and up the coom until the mountain splits and the stream comes down from the sacred source. Old Dale and myself may not see eye to eye on these matters so I keep my poetic thoughts to myself and say tentatively: Such a leprechaun of a man to be engaged in such astronomical deeds.

— Atracap, he says.

And jingles.

But so far, he reminds me, we have no proof of anything. It may be merely gossip. Nasty matrons. With dirty minds. Who may have some other reason for disliking him. We must get some reliable information.

Going the other way along the street are three young women in blue jerseys and skirts, white shirts, precise blue neckties. They're a bit older than any we saw in the flight of swallows, now all gone through the gateway. Their age, difference in direction and slight difference in style puzzles Dale. He doesn't notice that they're blue and not green. The old walrus is colour-blind.

— In a place in England, he tells me as we go out into the morning, two young ones got up a charge against a teacher. A popular fellow. Handsome. Thirteen years of age. The young ladies, as you may guess, not the teacher.

Dale would be a striking figure to meet in the early morning in Paris, France, or London, England, or New York, N.Y. On the main street of a small town in the West of Ireland he is a wonder to behold and a problem to walk with. He attracts attention: six feet three, shining high-domed bald head, strong bright roughcast pebble-dashed tweeds, no plus-fours this morning, just normal trousers, but even at that. And the walrus moustache, and the bright yellow-brogued feet stamping to shake the earth, and the jingling in the pockets: the sheep are coming home in Greece, hark the bells on every hill. The walrus moustache: red, gone grey at the tips, not yet drooping. When the scholar and poet, Douglas Hyde, was President of Ireland, his secretary, a Mr Dunphy, up there in the Phoenix Park, wrote a book about the office of the presidency and was known as the Keeper of the Great Seal because Douglas Hyde had a Dale moustache, or Dale, here stamping like a warhorse beside me, has a

Hyde moustache. He confuses me. He talks down to me: from his altitude, from his experience, down to my five feet nine, dark suit gone a little shiny, dark featureless hair combed straight back. Everyone in the town, if anyone of them ever was anywhere, must recognize him. The management of the school will as soon as they see him: he need scarcely identify himself. Anyway he was here before, fishing that river, and over the years he can't have changed much except for the worse. Incognito my backside. But, as he explains to me, it's not that we're here. It's what we're here for. That's the incognito, young man.

The town stirs sleepily around us. Towns like this don't rise early in the morning.

— The trouble began when the young English ladies heard that the teacher was plotting matrimony. To a grown woman. The girls followed him around. Not only the two who made the claims. But the whole school. Like the children after the Pied Piper. One of the two kept a diary full of fantasy.

— Three in a bed and all, I say.

That's to irritate him. Anyone can read the Sunday newspapers. All human life is there. Or even the *Daily Telegraph*.

— He must have had something, I say.

— He had, young man. He had a lot of trouble. One of them had the gall to ask him why had he got to get married. Women can be demons, you know. Big or little. Worse even than little boys. That sensible English poet said he never liked children. Even when he was a child. Read the Sunday newspapers, young man. Not *The Times* or the *Observer*. All opinions and no news. But the other papers.

It is one of the many aggravating things about him that he constantly repeats your own opinions and statements to you, without copyright acknowledgement. There are people like that. From me he heard about the poet who didn't like children. That also is the sort of thing that, rightly or wrongly, I am always saying about the Sunday papers.

Searching for that reliable information we are on our way to the parish priest. For even after the advent of the twenty-third John, the Venetian joker who put the whole establishment on a skater-board, the parish priest in Ireland may still be the man, and the master of morals. But this one isn't where he should be: in the parochial house at a mahogany table as wide as Wembley stadium, and eating his breakfast of bacon, egg and sausage. The table's there, fair enough. We can see it from where we stand in the wide linoleumed hallway. It's in there in the dining-room where it should be, and the door is open. But the dining-room, the hallway and the table have about them a desolate and abandoned air. Even though the place smells most diligently of polish and the table shines and glimmers. The housekeeper says: He's in his office.

— Tell him we're here, young woman.

Dale shows a card.

— His office is below, sir. Down in the town. I'll phone him and say you're here.

She picks up the telephone from a hall-table. From the first landing on the stairway a clock chimes ten. Most solemnly. Against the booms she speaks her message. She is most noticeably a young woman, early twenties, brunette, excellently formed. Dale is so astounded that he jingles with a new fury. As I said he hasn't been out of cold storage for a long time: and only the river and the lake it flows into drew him out. He has expected the door to be opened by the traditional dragon, over canonical or any desirable age. She tells us, lisping a little, rising on her toes to look up into Dale's face, that her master, if not her man, has a delegation with him below: that he can't come up but, perhaps, we could come down. Dale stops jingling. Is the Department being lightly treated? To steady himself he massages his high dome with both hands. She lisps and politely smiles us out. The door closes behind us. We stand for a while looking down on the town.

— We may only hope, he says, that she's a nun in disguise.

— Incognita, Mr Dale, I say.

And with some slight satisfaction.

From the high hill the house stands on there is a splendid view of the town: the big eighteenth-century mansion that became the convent and the school, the lawns sloping down to the river, the beechwood through which, after leaving the lawns, the river disappears and reappears. Beyond the beechwood the morning glitter of the lake. The avenue going back down to the town goes round and round the conical hill.

— A sacerdos, I say, seated on a high mountain.

Dale snorts.

The parish priest tells us that he got rid of them before we came in. He says: It was excellent or lucky that you went to the wrong place first. I never no more use the parochial house for bidnis. I'd sell it if the bish would allow me. It would make a better hotel than the one you're staying in. But it doesn't seem fair to ask my parishioners to walk up that dangerous hill if they want to see me. It wouldn't be good for the hearts of the old. Unless they could drive or be driven. And the young would do it on autocycles. A danger to themselves and everybody else. The young actually do come to see me. Mr Dale you're welcome.

He also welcomes me. And by name. He did say bish. And bidnis. He may have been for a while on the American mission. As they may still call it. To the heathen. But even that may be no longer necessary when every boy from an Irish bog can make singing or something noises like any boy from Memphis. He has met us in a narrow hallway opening off the main street and beside a butcher shop. His office is on the first floor above the shop. We go up a stairway narrower than the passage.

— I'm not a king or God himself that people should have to go up a high hill to see me.

— Or, Dale says, up a high hill not to see you.

— Sorry about that.

Since he seems a little in awe of Dale, and may be talking fast to reassure himself, I mumble that no harm was done, that the climbing exercise was better than jogging. Dale jingles menacingly: How did you know we were in the hotel? And our names?

— Eyes and ears. It's a small town. Like also, I was expecting you. So was the delegation I got rid of before you could get here. The three afflicted mothers. Not so much afflicted as ready to rend the poor fellow limb from limb. These young ones are a menace. The kittens entice you in. The tigresses pounce.

To demonstrate a pounce he opens the door of his office with a whoosh. No jingles from Dale. Which indicates that he is momentarily off-balance, malfunctioning. He stoops to enter. The sergeant is there waiting for us: and a lot more that's odd in a priest's cell or office or sanctum or what-you-will. The odour is of oil, but not of chrism. Through the one of the two windows that is open comes the sound of a male baritone, a good one, proclaiming that the moon hath raised her lamp above: then the sounds of chopping and what may well be the sharpening of the knife on the steel. In high summer the window would be, pray God, barred and bolted or closed with gauze against the butcher's bluebottles.

The sergeant sits on what, because of its position between the desk and the closed window, has to be the priest's chair: a faded cane with wobbly legs. For it creaks pitiably as he stands up and reaches out a strong hand to Dale and myself. With the other hand he steadies and gentles the restive chair. A big, obviously jovial man who carries his uniform with splendour, stripes shining like the distant lakewater in the morning. He says: Mr Dale, they tell me you have the rods with you. We met a while ago on Lough Derg, Dromineer, for the mayfly.

So Dale tells him that his intelligence service is working well. But he is gratified, laughs happily for the first time since he left Dublin. We help him with the laughter. In various keys. And sit down on an assortment of seats: the priest on an upturned wooden box, Dale in a well-preserved oaken desk-chair that stands apart in a corner, myself on an abbreviated bench on part of which somebody has placed a folded newspaper, almost certainly to prevent the backsides of trousers from sticking to the greasy surface. Dale says: You're interested in machinery.

The sergeant explains: Motorbike, Mr Dale. His reverence here thinks the clergy shouldn't go in cars. The new Church, Pope John, you know.

The bits of the bike are all over the place: cleaning, confession, is in process.

— When I was in the States, the priest says, I read a New Zealand poet who wrote oh wouldn't you laugh at the top of your voice if ever it came to pass that Christ went by in a big Rolls Royce and the bishop went on his ass. That changed my outlook.

I venture: The road to Damascus.

Dale jingles: and glowers across at me as if I had stolen his thunder. But sometime in the future he'll tell the story and claim my remark as his own. He says that we were expecting to meet an older man: and, sure as God, this is not the man who wrote to the Department to say that he was too old and his curates too young to handle such a case. This is a live-wire of a man somewhere in his forties. He wears a sailor's gansey or polo-necked sweater: clerical black, though. He is small. His hands move all the time. His dark, tousled, curly hair is oily but still straggles down over his forehead. Deep-brown eyes burn out at us from behind thick spectacles, rimmed also in clerical black. What has come over Rome and the bishops and where did they get him? A name, perhaps, for building churches.

— My predecessor, he says. Gone to glory. Full of years and merits. He wrote to you three months ago.

The sergeant tells us that the first thing is that the law, if it can help it, doesn't want to have anything to do with this business.

— Nor, says the priest, does the Church. Much.

— And I'll tell you why, says the sergeant.

— Playing doctors, says the priest.

— Will we ever forget it, says the sergeant.

They must have rehearsed that bit. At any moment they may rise and go up and down, singing, soft-footing, on the littered floor, like Byng Hope and Bob Crosby.

— It was in all the papers, says the sergeant. The shame of the locality. The world was pointing the finger at us. We don't want that again.

We wait. Neither of us have in any papers, Sunday or Monday or any other day, ever read a damned thing about this place. The singing down below has changed to: I come, I come my heart's delight.

And there is the demented scream of a disordered mincing machine.

— The long and the short of it is, Dale says, that they're passing the buck to the Department.

— Buck is correct. The Department. That's us.

— No. We are but delegates. Lords lieutenant. Viceroys. The Department is the king.

And later: Young man, that was a deplorable pun.

We have finished the soup and the sole, and are finishing the white, and breathing before the meat, and allowing the red to breathe. It can be said for him that he sees to it that we lunch and dine like viceroys. He picks his teeth. He repeats: Viceroys.

Then to my amazement and, possibly, also to the amazement of the few people in the hotel dining-room, he stands up, raises his right hand and proclaims: Upon the king! Let us our lives, our souls, our debts, our careful wives, our children and our sins lay on the king! We must bear all.

And sits down and bellows with laughter: and I am somewhat shocked even to suspect that an oldtimer like Dale could seem in any way to mock the Department: and in the presence of a subordinate. But he has been in an odd mood ever since the motorcycle priest told him that he, Dale, had been a close friend of the priest's father: and that discovery had come at the end of the sergeant's solemn narration of the scandal that had rocked the town, and, unseen by either of us, reached the newspapers.

— We'd never have moved, the sergeant said, if two of the little blackguards hadn't attacked a married woman. Five months' pregnant. In broad daylight. In the middle of the convent meadow. There's a public footpath, you see, across the meadow from the bottom of the marketyard to the Mullinagowan Road. A rightaway. From time immemorial. And even then we shouldn't have moved. Publicity's the worst possible thing. If somebody, not the guards, had just taken the brats aside and beaten their backsides sore. But we had a Super then who was all for law. And we can't even beat backsides to settle this one. And whose backside? His or theirs?

The historic right-of-way had only been the proximate cause of the outrage and attempted assault: frustrated by the screams of an aged nun who was watching from a convent window.

— No. Two families under one roof. Always a risky thing. Cousins. Sort of. In and out through each other. You couldn't count them. Male and female. It began with tickling and what they called playing doctors. And after a while you wouldn't know who was up to what. Or with whom, as the rhyme says.

The sergeant wrinkled and wiped his brow and was genuinely embarrassed: perhaps not so much at what had happened as at where it had happened: in his jurisdiction. Two of the boys, he said, real cousins, legitimate as the Four Courts, were thirteen and fourteen. They called the tune, made up the games. Anyway they were thirteen and fourteen when they got too big for their boots and attacked the woman. The capers were going on for twelve months and nobody any the wiser. Strange thing was that once it was well started the girls took over.

— Not so strange.

That was Dale. Jingling. But slowly. Meditatively: A case in the Sunday papers a few weeks ago. A fifteen-year-old spent a night with an Arab student. In a most respectable English city. So far so good. But the next night she was back for more, bringing her eleven-year-old friend with her. Broke into the fellow's flat where he was with two other students. Students, indeed. And there they all were, happy, until the police came. The police inspector said: They obviously went with the intention of receiving attention.

He had stolen the story from me and it was necessary to fight back: In the same paper it said that in Saudi Arabia nine men were beheaded for murder and sexual offences, three for rape, three for sexual assault, and three for having sex during the holy month of Ramadan.

— Ram is right, said the sergeant. The Arabs may have the answer. Beg your pardon, father.

Father, laughing heartily, did not seem in the least offended.

— And outside the courthouse, the sergeant said.

He was speaking only to Dale. Courtesy? Respect for rank?

— Outside the courthouse, on the day the case was heard, three of the worst of them were there in white socks and skipping ropes and butterfly ribbons in their pigtails. Skipping and playing hopball. The defence put them up to it.

— That, said the priest, was the picture that made the Sunday papers. Our image.

— One, two, three O'Leary, said the sergeant. Ten O'Leary catch

138

the ball. A rhyme, he explained, the children used to sing, hopping the ball.

After that there was a long silence. Except for the singing and the slashing from the shop below. The song now was: *Funiculi, Funicula*.

— He has a fine voice, Dale said.

He stood up. He said: We'll do what we can. And as quick and quietly as we can.

The priest thanked him: I've looked forward to meeting you, Mr Dale. My father used to talk a lot about you.

— Who was your father?

A name was mentioned. And recognized. With emotion.

— He went to the States, Dale said. A good man. He died there. God rest him.

— I was born there. When he died my mother brought me back here to go to school. A chaplain in the navy for a bit. Small men get on well in the navy. They don't hit their heads so often. But I was seasick most of the time. You couldn't get me into a ship now for love of God or man.

— Or women, I said.

Uproarious laughter.

By that time we were down the narrow stairs and out again into the street.

A pert, redcheeked face and a fluffy white scarf and a shoulderbag. Followed by a little mouth simultaneously pouting and trying to suck the last drop out of an orange. Three steps behind the orangesucker that unusual Italianate girl with the cardigan, patterned fairisle today though, and the levis. Never may I know why she dresses differently. No, she looks too adult, too self-controlled to be part of any group, even, by heavens, of a hockey-team: there are certain women who always walk alone: she would be more than a match for the little man, homunculus with a beard and a flat black hat, now dancing and dartplaying down below in the alcove off the public bar and giving himself, with bright imagination indeed, comic names. School is over early for this day. Dale is off somewhere with the parish priest, sentimentalizing about the priest's father or something: and his absence is an ease and a chance to read, and to study the girls emerging, and to speculate. There's a girl with a sort of German helmet hairstyle, a fringe, the classically-proud pale face of a king's mistress, courtesan, made beautiful by the painter's sycophancy and skill: but real and alive out there in the crowd at the side-gate. A man might easily be tempted. Or set to thinking. She carries a brown leather violin case. Above green stockings her bare knees seem very large. Perhaps later on in life knees may slim or lessen of their own accord. There's a blonde with fine thoughtful features walking arm-in-arm with a tall, pimply, darkhaired, bespectacled girl who, cool as a breeze, produces cigarette-case and lighter, and lights up, with a skill that any schoolboy of the thirties might have envied. Arm-in-arm again, they proceed, a fragrant cloud above them.

But most of them favour the chewing of toffee, or the chewing of something: most unlikely that it could be tobacco twist. Perhaps the way of it is that he has fallen for the odour of toffee on dew-fresh lips. Where the bee sucks there suck I. Or down in the house of the funeral, the wakehouse with the mourners all assembled and rejoicing, I first put eolas, knowledge, on my brownhaired girl: her cheeks were like the roses and her little mouth like the brown sugar: there was sweetness on the tips of the branches and honeycombs at the roots of the bushes, and the fish in the waves were leaping with pleasure because she was alive. That's my memory of a song I heard an old woman sing in Donegal Irish and a poet I know who heard the song at the same time improvised a sort of New Orleans rhythm: Honey with the mouth like brown sugar.

Repeated over and over to the stamping of feet and clapping of hands: Honey with the mouth like brown sugar.

How tall they are. Vitamins. Orange juice. Young people in the States get taller and taller. Perhaps our laws should take that into account. And they learn so much so soon: magazines, discotheques, television programmes that would have set our greatgrand-mothers running out of the room. Or would they? Mysteries, mysteries, mysteries, masks in green jerseys and skirts and blazers: except for that daughter of Italy in levis and patterned fairisle cardigan: all bound for homes where so far they have kept their secrets, those of them who have secrets to keep.

One last straggler: a sideways look, long dark hair, white stockings, long loose green coat. Honey with the mouth. And the fish in the wave are leaping with pleasure because she is alive: and two of the blue young women, one with vivid red hair, cross the street and disappear from my view. Into this building, perhaps. Now that the parade is over I'll descend to the public bar and find better company than my own thoughts: or Dale who tomorrow, God be praised, goes to the lake with the sergeant. Even in a place like this there must be somebody.

There is, too. There is Fineen O'Driscoll the Rover, Fineen O'Driscoll the free, as straight as the mast of his galley, as strong as a wave of the sea. His name is not O'Driscoll: his mother's name was. We have made a study of his papers, his record, up to the moment faultless. Up to what they call, here and there in Munster, this little weakness. To what might, in any other part of the world, be regarded as a sign of strength. He is a dab hand at the darts. With the boys or with the girls. With no effort in the world and with, in succession, an underhand and an overhand, he notches two triples. The enthusiasm of the boys shows that they really like him. He hops on his two little feet. He wears those boxer's coloured boots that have ruined the walk-style of half the world. He chants: I'm Fineen O'Driscoll the Rover, Fineen O'Driscoll the free.

He teaches while he plays: The O'Driscolls of the southwest were famous sea-rovers. Or pirates the Saxons would have called them. As if their own greatest hero at the time wasn't the greatest pirate who ever sailed a ship. What was his name, Jimmy?

A sallow-faced boy who could be the brother of the girl in the cardigan and levis answers: Drake, sir. Drake he's in his hammock and a thousand miles away.

The features and colouring don't suit so well on a boy.

— Correct, Jimmy. Sometime you should see his statue on Plymouth Hoe. It's alive. He played bowls, though. Not darts. Do you know why he went on playing? Even when the Spaniards were in sight.

— No, sir.

— Tide. The tide, man. He couldn't get out until the tide rose. But we had our own pirates. Who was the greatest of them all?

141

— Granuaile O'Malley of Westport, sir. Grania of the Ships.

— True, Jimmy. A queen among men. But a tough woman. Too tough for any of you.

He picks up the darts that the inferior aims of two boys have scattered broadcast. He says: Fineen isn't frightening. There's a great ballad about Fineen. An old castle towers o'er the billows that thunder by Cleena's green land, and there dwelt as gallant a rover as ever grasped hilt in the hand. Eight stately towers of the waters lie anchored in Baltimore Bay . . .

Is this the way he talks to the girls?

— Does that remind you of anything, Tommy?

— The other poem, sir. The sack of Baltimore. About the Barbary corsairs kidnapping the Cork people. She only smiled, O'Driscoll's child, she thought of Baltimore.

— Nifty, Tommy. You are the flower of the flock. You will be a writer someday.

He scores a bull's eye. He doffs that odd hat to mop his brow. This mannikin is good for these boys. Wisdom and learning and poetry at the dartboard.

Without the hat he is different, thoughtful, melancholy, a lonely little frightened man, good for the boys and hiding in their company. But what about the girls and what do the boys know about the girls and Fineen the Rover? Ah well, screw the girls I was unfortunately about to think. Yet sitting here spying I feel like a . . . What? A spy, and how does it feel to be a spy? It depends, it depends, as the strong farmer said about his prize bull's pizzle. So to Gehenna with the whole pathetic business and let Dale, the old departmental windbag, do his own moral dirty work. This is not why my sainted parents sent me to college. Carry my drink to the far end of the bar. Sit with my back to the wall that separates the bar from the entrance hall and reception. Look around for company: and hope to find it. Virtue is its own reward but no man would refuse a few fringe benefits.

It is the east and Juliet is the sun. It is the blue girl with the red hair. She enters through door on my left, walks the length of the bar, and what a walk, exits by door at far end. Beyond that there's a narrow hallway and, perhaps, a powder-room. No youthful whinnies or whistles or snickers. The presence of the master? Or the over-whelming style of the girl? The master speaketh not. But the boy who might be the brother of the Italianate girl is a cool cookie and also, perhaps, inured to beauty, and ventures: Miss Moynihan, may we go with you?

Briefly she pauses, swivels, smiles, snaps her fingers, says: Follow on, boys, follow on.

And leaves an awed silence behind her and an air warm and crimsoned with things unspoken, the game for a few moments forgotten, the master meditating, his hat in one hand, a few darts in the other: myself turning my glass in my hand and looking into its depths and suspecting that away down there something may be made manifest, a sunken city, a mermaid, anything. The barman, polishing glasses, taps one of them on the counter and when I raise my head he winks and smiles and clicks his tongue as you would to a horse, and I raise my glass to him and to all the memories of all the queens that ever were. We are brothers akin, guesting awhile in the rooms of a beautiful inn.

The jet-trail of her perfume is still in the air when she is back. For the sake of good manners my eyes are cast down as she advances, *oculis dimissis, omnia videns*, as the Jesuit said about the pensive nun, devout and pure: and what I do see just across my table is her blue skirt, cunningly filled. The blue girls, I know, work in the bank: and God be thanked that I am not like Dale, the old walrus, colour-blind: and thanked again because association with the bank-girls can't leave a man on the windy side of the law. She speaks to me by name. She says: There's a small private bar behind reception. Where you might be more comfortable.

So, like the gentleman that I am, I take her word for it and go with her. To find that she told me no lie, and to meet the other girl in a discreet little pine-panelled room with fire in the grate, hunting-prints on the walls and, in a glass-case in the corner, the biggest pike that ever against his will came out of the lake. The other girl is dark and quiet and coy. They are engaged at sausages and toast and tea. Nothing coy about this redheaded woman: because for God's sake let us sit upon our rumps and forget about girls, greenwood that smokes and weeps, Elvis Presley yahooing I'm a redblooded fellow and I can't help thinking of girls, girls, girls, good enough for the likes of Elvis or Fineen: and let's talk about women, the something dame rejoicing and crackling in the flame.

More to the dark girl than to me she says: We might as well be blunt.

Waiting seems to be in order. So I read from the hunting-prints that Aiken etched and Sutherland aquatinted. The dark girl says that this room is used mostly by lawyers from the courthouse. Nothing very blunt about that. Continue to wait. There are no lawyers visible. Miss Moynihan says: It isn't their day. So the place is quiet. That's why we enticed you in.

— Am I in danger?

Laughter.

— We can talk, she says.

— We can tell you, says the dark girl.

— Tell me what?

But, Ireland being Ireland, I know. They know my name and status, they know my business, they know more about it than I do or Dale does, half the town must know and be at this moment passing the glad tidings on to the other half: and the quicker Dale and myself and Fineen are up and away the better. No scandal, the sergeant said. No bobbysoxers playing hopball at the Courthouse steps. No pictures in the papers.

— We watched Mr Dale and yourself watching him playing darts with the boys.

— We didn't see you watching us watching him.

No point in pretending ignorance. Had they also watched us at the first-floor window watching the little, not so little girls, and not exactly thanking God for them. But no. She demonstrates. In the wall behind one elongated hunting-print there's a peephole from which the affairs of the public bar and the alcove are visible.

— He's a good little fellow, she says. He's happy with the boys. But he's afraid of women.

— Not according to report.

— I mean women.

— They know that, the dark girl says. So they surrounded him. They're a ring of little demons. They make jokes about him.

144

— He's afraid of women, Miss Moynihan repeats. Grown women. And who are we to say that we blame him. We work with ten of them. And the young ones can be worse. Or every bit as bad. Or not so well able to hide it. They'd giggle at the separating of the sheep and the goats. Then he drifted into it gradually. Through teaching, you know, holding their hands when they draw a map.

The dark girl says: Geography, how are you? Tell what you know about the River Ganges. The river Ganges in this way resembles the river Shannon. He teaches geography and history.

— Where, I ask, did he get that hat.

— Amateur acting, the dark girl says. He's very good at that. As you might imagine. He wore that hat in Blood Wedding and liked it and wouldn't surrender it.

Through a hatch beside the peephole I order another drink. They abandon tea for vodka, just one, and back to the bank, and no odour, and no one the wiser. They come in here often at this time. Marie is engaged to a solicitor but he's away today.

— The talk of those girls, she says. Shameless. One of them I hear shouting to another, shouting, the town and the reverend mother could have heard every word. Shouting can you keep a secret, cross my heart and hope to die, Mary Sherlock in the fifth has had her monthlies. We didn't talk like that in our time.

— Marie, can you remember that far back?

Laughter.

Angela says: The curse has come upon me cried the Lady of Shalott.

— Angela, you're shocking Mr . . .

Again I'm mentioned by surname.

— My name, I say, is Larry.

— The night, says Angela, before Larry was stretched.

Laughter from all three of us.

— What the little man needs, Marie says, is a good gentle woman to mother him.

— Somebody just like me, Angela says.

Marie crows like a rooster. Then she says: They talk about him to each other. Naturally. Women do talk. And especially little women. I've heard them. One of them said, you know that litle redhead,

Mona something, she said he's a funny little man, he'd cry for anything, like a baby, he'd make you tired looking at him crying: and the other said why does he cry and she got her answer, he cries if you don't, then he cries if you do. That, as sure as God, I overheard here one day in the powder-room, two of them slipping in to smoke where they had no right in the world to be.

— Did they talk to anyone else?

Miss Moynihan enlightens me: One of them did. To me. For a reason. You may not believe it. Love. She fell in love. And jealousy. He was giving too much attention to her best friend.

With mock profundity Marie says: Eternal triangle. Too many strings to his bow. Getting his lines crossed. He's a good fisherman and should know better.

To my horror the two of them laugh quite merrily. Well: not absolutely to my horror. The wrong, or whatever it is, may be mixed.

— Which reminds me, says Angela. There are worse things afoot.

— The mothers, I say. The law.

— The fathers, Marie says. Lynch law.

— Word gets around, Angela says. Tarring and feathering. I heard it mentioned. And the cat of ninetails.

— And worse, Marie says, I heard suggested.

Angela nibbles the last fragment of sausage and sips the last sip of vodka. She hums. But our good times all are gone and I'm bound for moving on.

And I cap the quotation: I'll look for you if I'm ever back this way.

Then back to the bank with them and back with me to my balcony, *id est*, that window on the first floor: to watch the street and the convent gate and to wait for Dale. To hear that he and the sergeant have made all their plans for a day on the lake, and Fineen the Rover to go with them. So all I know I keep to myself, for the present, let old Dale have his swink to him reserved: and I telephone the bank the next morning and make my own plans for better things and thrills than the hooking of harmless fish.

Suddenly I am surrounded by girls, little women, no longer in school uniform, no longer chewing, no longer smoking as they step daintily along, the clothes have changed them, this could be a dream, if I try

146

to escape they surround me they seem to be everywhere, grave Alice and laughing Allegra and Edith with golden hair. They wear skimpy jackets, all colours, and flimsy jeans, more like pyjamas, all colours, and perfumes and hairstyles. They smile and speak politely as they pass along the corridor, Dale holding the door for them, a most impressive figure. A school-party on a trip to Dublin: and the last in the line that Italianate girl, brown eyes studying Dale gravely, even sparing a glance for his curate.

— Pygmy women, Dale says.

As we relax into our own compartment.

— Not so pygmy. Anyway pygmies, I hear, have some odd customs.

— Yet, he says, that parade should help you to realize how a man might wobble, waver, go astray. Might even be inclined to forget that the law, not nature, makes a difference between seventeen and fifteen. You were yourself talking about vitamins and orange juice. And those tall American teenagers.

To Dale, back in his plus-fours and monstrous as anyone may imagine, my mind and heart, if not my eyes and ears, are closed, are back in a lakeside wood with Angela, are leaping forward to meeting her again when she comes to Dublin. People meet, the mountains never. Fineen the Rover, pointing darts with the boys, weeping over the girls, has brought us to that meeting the mountains may never enjoy. Sunlit landscape drifts happily past. Ireland has never been so beautiful. Dale talks on from the top of a faraway mountain. As futile as Jehovah. As ignorant. Fineen is the fellow who has made things happen.

— But the Department, Dale says, might make some of it up in expenses. That is if the Department wasn't aware that it was so doing. Did you ever hear the story of the Bad Linnane's hat?

That may well be the only one of Dale's stories that I have never heard.

Then he says oddly: He's lucky. He has neither wife nor family. Neither chick nor child, he said. It was necessary to query that. Should the phrase not be check nor child?

The western mountains fall away behind. We cross the big river. In the lull at Athlone we can hear the girls singing.

— His father and mother died young, Dale says. An aunt somewhere is the only relative. He's free to run. He won't be missed. The sergeant didn't intrude. A discreet, considerate man.

Then, after a pause: A good wrist and a great man for the Red Butcher.

— The sergeant?

— No. Fineen, as you call him. The Red Butcher is a fly. I'm not so sure he's right in that. On that water. But it worked. And he knows every ripple by name. No man with an eye and wrist like that should be confined.

— Worried Mother would be overjoyed to hear you.

Flat fields and dark bogland slumber all around us. With the renewed rattle of the train, we can no longer hear the girls singing.

— He ties his own flies. He has very nimble fingers.

— Daresay he has. At the darts too.

— Young man?

But, oddly again, he laughs.

— Texas Jack, as I prefer to call him. Canada's the place for him. Or Oregon. The Far West. Great rushing rivers. I fished some of them. The Rogue river. Zane Grey, you know.

A brief pause at a small halt to allow a westbound train to proceed. No sound of singing. What are they up to now?

— Texas Jack. Fineen the Rover. He's three men or more. The Martian marksman. The Black Wizard of Blue Mountain.

— The cat among the pigeons.

— Advised him to work only at university level and to pray to St Joseph every night to keep him from screwing the freshmen.

Astounded I am. Has he picked up that one from associating with the motorbike padre, heaven's angel?

— He hadn't his fare, you see. But without knowing, or anonst to itself, the Department might make up to me some of the money. That's the Irish i ngan fhios do. Without his being aware of it. In the north, English-speakers in rural places used to corrupt it to anonst. They were, in fact, speaking Irish anonst to themselves.

— I know.

— That's why I was thinking of the Bad Linnane's hat.

No invitation will he get to bore me with another story but he's in

148

the mood for it, needs neither invitation nor encouragement: In my days there were two brothers on the reporting staff of a certain Dublin newspaper, the Good Linnane, the Bad Linnane, both good men, gentlemen, but one was a strict sober disciplined man, the other a humorous fellow, God's good company in a bar or on a journey.

A pause. A long stare. At me. Two girls pass along the corridor, one a chubby, freckled, bespectacled redhead. They smile at us. He waves a hand.

— He was reporting, the Bad that is, an open-air political meeting when a scuffle began. His hat was knocked off and trampled in the mud. And at the end of the week he added to his expenses, item one hat, and the cashier told him that it was no part of the policy of that paper to provide its reporters with hats: and at the end of the next week said, with a sneer, no hat this week and the humorous man said it's there but you don't see it.

— The invisible hat.

— It became proverbial. Invisible like the Bad Linnane's hat. So the Department may never know the good it helped to do.

— You astound me.

He really does. How all along we have misjudged this man.

— I thought I might. You're young yet, he says. And easily astounded.

In the corridor six more young ladies file past, demurely, on some private business.

— He'll make out all right in Canada. We're all entitled to one mistake.

— One?

The redhead and her companion, still smiling, go back the way they came. He waves again.

— Throw no stones, he says. Throw no stones.

Two of the six returning, meet another two. There is some giggling in the corridor. The city is not far away. Giggling, that is, from three of them. The fourth is that daughter of Italy. Or could it be Egypt? She doesn't giggle.

— There was a young one when I was a boy, Dale says. Something like that sallow girl. The same eyes. My first love. Made an assault on her one day. Went wild. Wrestled with her for a long time.

The girls have moved on. He stands up and looks out the window. He goes, jingle, jangle, jingle.

— Crazy with curiosity I was. Nothing much transpired. Fortunately. She cried a lot. But she never told. She was twelve. I fourteen. I might have made the newspapers.

— Few of us haven't some secret, I say.

The corridor is crowded with laughing girls, a sudden rush from the stairway, a sudden raid from the hall, such an old moustache as he is might be a match for you all.

— Young man, I'm not hearing confessions.

— Father Abraham, you're not getting any.

— But how did we miss it, he says. How did we miss that picture in the papers? Three girls in pigtails and skipping ropes and playing hopball before the Courthouse.

Still wondering we walk the platform. Marshalled by two teachers, female, a crocodile of young ladies goes before us.

A LETTER TO PEACHTREE

ALWAYS I PREFER not to begin a sentence with an I, so I'm beginning this sentence and letter with the word Always. Which can be a beautiful or a terrible word, all depending on where you are, how you feel, who you are with, what you are doing, or what is being done to you. Days may not be bright always and I'll be loving you always. That last bit I really do mean, you, over there, soaking in the Atlantan sun on Peachtree.

Do you know that there was an Irish poet and novelist, a decent man who, as they would say over here, never laid his hand on a woman, and who tore up his mss. and died a Christian Brother, and who wrote a lovesong to say that he loved his love in the morning, he loved his love at noon, he loved his love in the morning for she like the morn was fair. He loved his love in the morning, he loved his love at noon, for She was bright as the Lord of Light yet mild as Autumn's moon. He loved his love in the morning, he loved his love at Even. Her smile's soft play was like the ray that lights the western heaven. He loved her when the Sun was high. He loved her when He rose. But best of all when evening's sigh was murmuring at its close.

Clear, godamned clear that he knew nothing about it. How could he keep it up, always?

Howandever, as Patrick Lagan says, here we are on this crowded train, the cameraman called Conall, and Patrick and Brendan and Niall and myself, and this plump girl in jodhpurs, well, and a red sweater as well, and good horsey boots to walk about in. And a mob of people, a jampacked train, dozens standing in the corridors, and going towards the wide open spaces of the Curragh of Kildare where the great horses run. There's a man with a melodeon sitting on the seat in the john, merely because he has nowhere else to sit, his big, square-toed boots nonchalantly over the threshold, the melodeon tacit, the man sucking an orange. Jodhpurs leans her right shoulder, her round cheeks flushed, against my necktie spreading like the Shannon between Limerick and the sea, the tie you gave me when I took off for Ireland, a tie wide, I say, as the Shannon, a basic blue and green and, floating on that, slices of orange, a bloodred cherry and a branch of blossoming dogwood. Some tie. The tie that binds us.

This all about Jodhpurs I tell you not to make you jealous but to explain to you how crowded the train is and to give you a general idea of the style and spirit of the journey. Conall the cameraman has asked Jodhpurs to pose against my tie, your tie. She has been on the train with some friends on the way to the races. But when she sees Conall she drops out and joins us. She has the hots for Conall. He is quite a guy. Italianate handsome, dark wavy hair, quick gestures, good tweeds, and style, and as tough as a hawser and, to add the little dusting of pimento, a slight stutter, only noticeable when he's sober. But good-humoured and talking all the time.

Now let me tell you something.

My grandmother came from Ballintubber in the county of Mayo. She had the old belief about how it was ill-luck to meet a redheaded woman on the way to market. Jodhpurs is sure as hell redheaded. But howabout, for added value, a redheaded man, big as Carnera, dressed in rustcoloured chainmail tweed, whose too-tight trousers betray him and burst wide-open between the legs when he is strap-hanging in this crowded train? What would you do on an occasion like that? Walk the other way? Look the other way? As any lady would or should.

One little railway-station, two, three, four little railway-stations whip by, then wide-rolling, green spaces with racing-stables, a silhouetted water-tower, a line of exercising horses. Conall says that over there in the national stud by Kildare town he once did a set of pictures of a famous stallion, and he, the stallion, was the smallest thing you ever saw, everywhere and every way no bigger than a pony, Conall says, and says that he, Conall, was himself better hung and I'm prepared to take his word for it. But he is clearly meditating on the goodness of God to the big man who burst. Who has had to borrow a mac from somebody to cover his glory, or his shame. Which it just about does. He is a very big man. Seems to me that that earthquake or revelation, or whatever, just about sets the tone for all that is to follow. Conall puts his curse on crowded trains and on the sharp corners of the leather case he carries his camera in, and says that if there isn't a fight at the play tonight his time will have gone astray. Because of the crowd on the train he missed a proper, or improper, shot of the red man who burst: at the actual instant of bursting, that is. But he knows the red man and the red man's two comrades. Three army officers, out of uniform for a day at the races. The big red man has not, say the other two, been out of uniform, except when in bed, for years. So they have almost forcibly fitted him, or stuffed him into that tweed which, under strain, has not proved a perfect fit from Brooks Brothers.

Then the crowd leaves us at the railway halt, one platform and a tin hut, out on the great plain of Kildare: and off with them all to the races. Conall, who already has had some drink taken, must have sucked it out of the air, no jug visible at any time since Dublin, sings after the racegoers that the cheeks of his Nelly are jolting like jelly as she joggles along up to Bellewstown hill. Which Lagan assures me is a bit of a ballad about another race-meeting somewhere to the north. He promises Jodhpurs, whose cheeks, fore and aft, are firm and by no means jolting like jelly, that he will sing it for her later on. He's a good man to sing a ballad or quote a poem. She latches on to us, and to hell with the races, and we are elsewhere bound, and not to any market.

But how did we all come to be on that there train when the red man was unseamed from the nave to chaps? Listen!

The previous evening, a lovely May evening, Dublin looking almost like one of those elegant eighteenth-century prints, I walked over the Liffey at O'Connell Bridge, then along Eden Quay and for once, the name seemed apt: and into the Abbey bar to meet Patrick Lagan, a man I've mentioned in previous letters. Like, when I went to Brinsley MacNamara to talk to him about his novels and my dissertation, he passed me on to Patrick Lagan. He said that Lagan had more of his books than he had himself, all autographed by me, I mean all autographed by Brinsley. He said that Lagan knew more about his books than he himself did. Curious thing, he said. Brinsley begins many statements with those two words: Curious thing.

Life seems to him almost always absurd and he may well be right about that. He even made a collection of some of his short stories and called it: *Some Curious People*.

Along Eden Quay, then, and left round the corner at the Sailors' Home, and past the burned-out shell of the old Abbey Theatre. Which has recently gone up in smoke taking all sorts of legends and memories with it. With Brinsley I walked through the rubble, a big man, Brinsley, once a great walker by the river Boyne, but now moving slowly, arthritic feet, and leaning on a stick, and remembering and remembering many curious people.

But the Abbey Bar, round yet another corner, still survives, and Lagan was there in all his glory and a few of his friends with him. There was a lawyer and a professor of history, and a bank-manager, who is also a music critic and who plays the organ in a church, and two actors from the Abbey Theatre, and two reporters from the paper Lagan works on, and one cameraman from same: a mixed and merry throng. And Brinsley, dominating all in physical size and mental dignity, and being treated by all with the respect which is only his due.

Curious thing, he says, how landscape, buildings, environment, physical surroundings can affect the character of people. Take, for instance, your average Dublin workingman. A rough type. A man with a young family, he goes out to the pub in the evening. He drinks a pint, two pints, three, four, five, six, perhaps ten pints. He's a noisy fellow. He sings. He talks loud. He argues. He may even quarrel. He staggers, singing, home to the bosom of his family, in tenement apartment or corporation house, goes to bed quietly and, soundly, sleeps it off. But down in the so soft midlands of Meath and Westmeath, where I come from, things are different. The heavy heifers graze quietly, and the bullocks, all beef to the ankles. The deep rivers flow quietly. Your average workingman there is a bachelor. Living most likely with his maiden aunt, and in a labourer's cottage. In the quiet, green evening he cycles six or so miles into the village of Delvin for a drink. He drinks quietly. One pint, two, three, anything up to ten or more. In the dusk he cycles quietly home and murders his maiden aunt with a hatchet.

Curious thing, environment. Curious thing.

The name of Conall, the cameraman, is also Lagan, but no relation to Patrick. Patrick says that Patrick was a saint but that Conall Cearnach was a murderous bloody buff out of the mythologies before Christ. There's a poem about the fellow, Lagan says, you'll hear it from me sometime, as I feel we will, he's a helluva man to quote poetry. In a booming base barreltone that would put Ariel to sleep.

Then, when I tell Conall that I am over here from Harvard to write about Brinsley's novel, *The Valley of the Squinting Windows*, about village and small town hatreds, and in relation to Sinclair Lewis and the main street of Gopher Prairie . . .

How are you over there on Peachtree Street in sunny Atlanta? Think of me in the Margaret Mitchell museum.

And in relation to Edgar Lee Masters and all the tombstones on the Spoon River, and Sherwood Anderson away out there in Winesburg, Ohio, and a Scotsman called George Douglas Brown and his House with the Green Shutters, about whom and which Brinsley has put me wise, and about all the dead life of small places . . .

Well, then, Conall Cearnach he says to me, but, man, you have to come with us to where we are going. You'll be missing copy if you don't. This is going to be it.

At this stage Brinsley leaves us but only briefly and only to travel as far as the john and back again. We are sitting in a nook or corner of the bar. The door of the john is right in there. For the reason that his feet give him some discomfort Brinsley doesn't stand up rightaway but slithers, sitting, right up to the door of the locus. Niall of the Nine Hostages, ancient Irish King, and Brendan the Navigator, ancient Irish saint, who sailed an open boat all the way almost to Peachtree, who are sitting between Brinsley and the holy door, stand respectfully out of his way. Then he stands up finally to his most majestic height.

Curious thing, he says. This reminds me of the only good parody I ever heard on the style of John Millington Synge. It was the work of that great player, J. M. Kerrigan, and it began like this. Was it on your feet you came this way, man of the roads? No, 'twas not, but on my arse surely, woman of the house. As in the Shadow of the Glen.

Then with an amazing agility for a man so big, he dives into the john and we laugh at the joke and respectfully hold our conversation until he returns. When Conall tells me that there is this company of travelling players and that, in this country town, they are planning to put on in the parochial hall this play, says Conall, by a French jailbird about a Roman Catholic cardinal taking off his clothes in a kip. Or worse still, says Conall, about two women, a madame and a hoor, (anglice: whore), disrobing or disvesting or devestmentizing a peacock of a cardinal, and think of that, for fun, in an Irish country town. So the parish priest naturally, or supernaturally, prohibits the use of the parochial hall and, having done so, takes off for the Eucharistic Congress in Antananarivo, or somewheres east of Suez. He didn't have to read that play to know it was no go, and the players have booked another, non-sectarian hall and are going ahead and, Conall says, the man who owns that hall must fear not God nor regard the parish priest, and must be so rich and powerful that he needn't give a fuck about King, Kaiser or cardinal.

But there is this organization called Maria Duce, like the Mother of God up there with Mussolini, which will picket the hall to keep the clothes on the cardinal, and a riot is confidently expected, says Conall, and if you want to see what life is like in an Irish country-town, man, you gotta be there.

Conall lowers his voice.

Even Brinsley himself at his worst and wildest, he says, never thought of that one. A cardinal in a kip. In the buff.

For kip, here read brothel. Not kip as in England where it may mean merely a place to sleep in.

So here we are on the train, Patrick and Conall and his camera, and myself, and Brendan and Niall and Jodhpurs: and the world and his mother are off to the races: and, somewhere ahead, a red cardinal is roosting and waiting to be depilated: and the priest of the parish is awa, like the deil with the tailor in Robert Burns, to Antananarivo: and Patrick is singing that on the broad road we dash on, rank, beauty and fashion, it Banagher bangs by the table of war. From the couch of the quality down to the jollity, bouncing along on an old lowbacked car. Though straw cushions are placed, two foot thick at the laste, its concussive motion to mollify, still, the cheeks of my Nelly are jolting like jelly as she joggles along up to Bellewstown hill.

Onwards and upwards. The play's the thing.

Eighty miles from Dublin town.

The poet Cowper points out, as I would have you know, that not rural sights alone but rural sounds exhilarate the spirit and restore the tone of languid nature, that ten thousand warblers cheer the day and one the livelong night.

He means the nightingale. I reckon.

What lies ahead of us is not going to be exactly like that.

The gallant lady who leads the strolling players holds back the raising of the curtain for our arrival. But with the best or the worst intentions in the world, or with no godamned niggering intentions whatsoever, we succeed in being late and the play is well advanced when we get there. We have been delayed in the bar in one of the town's two hotels. Not drinking has detained us but a sudden attack of love, or something, not on me, already, as you know, wounded and possessed, but on Conall the fickle, the flaky, the volatile, the twotimer of all time, who wouldn't even curb his bronc until Jodhpurs had gone for a moment and what else to the powder-room. No, just one look over the bar-rail at the barmaid and he was hogtied, and said so out loud, very very loud. Like I love my love in the ginmill, I love her in the lounge. A mighty handsome brunette she is.

Jodhpurs, though, takes it all mighty cool. She is by no means in love with Conall, just lust, and she tells me that he does this everywhere and all the time, and Lagan intones like a monk of Solesmes: O'er Slieve Few with noiseless trampling through the heavy, drifted snow, Bealcú, Connachia's champion, in his chariot tracks the foe: and, anon, far-off discerneth in the mountain hollow white, Slinger Keth and Conall Cearnach mingling hand-to-hand in fight.

Prophetic?

Wait and see.

That's the beginning of the poem about the ancient hero or whatever.

Lagan explains in considerable detail that Slieve Few is a mountain in the heroic north, and in the mythologies. A few notes I make. Research? You never can tell.

For Connachia read Connacht.

Conall is now behind the bar. He went over it, not through it. He's a pretty agile guy. His arm is around the barmaid's waist. She is laughing most merrily. Nobody by now in the place except the four of us. For Brendan and Niall have really gone ahead to the theatre. But when Conall had first attempted to go over the top, Lagan and myself decided it might be wiser to stick around and keep a snaffle, Lagan said spancell, on him. That may be not all that easy.

Jodhpurs, I may tell you, has the same surname as myself. Except that she spells it differently. Carney, not Karney. So much I found out by standing beside her when she was filling in the hotel register. Waiting my turn I was. With the register.

We are now at last in the theatre. Or in the substitute hall. Which is by no means in the most elegant part of the town. There are no praying pickets. Conall is outraged. No pickets, no picture.

Perhaps they have prayed and picketed and departed before we got here. But no. Later we are to hear that they were never there. Also flown to Antananarivo?

To get to the hall we go through a dark entryway. Seventeenth century at the least. Footpads? Stilettos? Christopher Marlowe? No. Bludgeons? Newgate calendar? No. Nothing but bad lighting and potholed ground underfoot. Easy here to sprain an ankle. We are in an ancient market-place, long ago forsaken by markets and by everything and everybody else. A hideyhole for Art? A last refuge for strolling players? Then up a covered and creaking wooden stairway that climbs the wall, then down four shaky wooden steps and here we are, and where is the kip and where is the cardinal?

But there is no kip. There is no cardinal at the moment to be seen.

Conall, as is his custom, has got it wrong. Or so Lagan later booms.

What we are looking at is a weeping broad in a long, black dress, kneeling down before a roaring Franciscan friar. Or a fellow roaring, and wearing what might be a Franciscan habit except that it's so badly battered from strolling with the players that it's hard to tell. He could be Guy Fawkes or Johnny Appleseed or Planters' Peanuts or the man who broke the bank at Monte Carlo. But whoever or whatever he is, he sure as hell is giving that broad hell. Boy, is he giving her hell. What I mean is, he is telling her in considerable detail where she will find herself if she doesn't mend her ways and get smart, and get real smart and give up that old wop trick of screwing her brother. If you can tell by a slight protuberance she seems to be in the family way by her brother.

Curious thing, Brinsley is later to say, but there was always a soupçon of that in the midlands where I come from. John Ford, not the man who makes the cowboys, seems to have been much possessed by the idea. As T. S. Eliot said Webster was by death. Curious fellow, Ford. And Webster. And Eliot.

Brinsley met Eliot when Eliot was round the corner from the Abbey Bar to give a lecture in the Abbey Theatre that was. My research proceeds. Curious thing.

But listen to the friar as the broad is listening or pretending to listen.

He is telling her about a black and hollow vault where day is never seen, where shines no sun but flaming horror of consuming fires, a lightless sulphur choked with smoky fogs in an infected darkness: and in that place dwell many thousand thousand sundry sorts of never-dying deaths, and damned souls roar without pity, gluttons are fed with toads and adders, and burning oil poured down the drunkard's throat, and the usurer is forced to sip whole draughts of molten gold, and the murderer is forever stabbed yet never can he die, and the wanton lies on racks of burning steel.

Watch it, chick, watch it.

The friar also wises her up about lawless sheets and secret incests. About which, we may reckon, she knows more than he does. And tells her that when she parks her ass in that black and gloomy vault she will wish that each kiss her brother gave her had been a dagger's point.

Jasus Christ, says Conall, this is worse than any sermon I ever heard at any mission. What was the parish priest beefing about? He couldn't do better himself.

He says all that out quite aloud and several people hush him up, and the friar thinks they mean him and gets rattled, and, to my high delight, the incestuous broad giggles. For her it is mighty obvious that hell hath no furies.

To you, down there on Peachtree, a mission would be a sort of a tent-meeting, hellfire a-plenty, the Baptist tabernacle in Marietta, yeah Lord Amen, and washed, when the time is ripe, in the blood of the Lamb or the Chatahoochie river. What has the Good Lawd done for you, as the preacher roared and pointed by mistake at the harelipped, hunchbacked cripple, and the harelipped, hunchbacked cripple, in so far as his cleft palate would allow him to articulate, whistled back that the Good Lawd damn near roont me.

Then when the curtain creaks down to separate the scenes, something has to separate them, and the lights come up in the body of the house, Conall stands up to take pictures and to make a speech.

Jesus and Amen!

We are, *in tempore opportuno*, to find out that the valiant woman, far and from the furthest coasts, who leads the strolling players was so annoyed with the parish-priest that she cancelled the kip and the cardinal for something in which, when most of the cast has been massacred, another cardinal and the Pope get any loot that's left.

For we're off to Anarivo in the morning.

Then and thereafter Conall has bad luck with his photographs. For why? He keeps dropping the camera. The audience love it. Light relief. Charlie Chaplin. The audience need it. Some of them know Conall very well. He has been around. They cheer when he drops the camera. But in a mild, friendly, appreciative sort of way and not so as to disturb the players. Overmuch.

Conall's speech begins by thanking the audience on behalf of the valiant woman and the strolling players. Then he thanks the players and the woman on behalf of the audience. Then he sits down where his seat is not, or a place to put it. He has a standing ovation for that one. Then Brendan and Niall and Jodhpurs persuade him into a corner at the back of the hall and hold him there, good old Jodhpurs, and the curtain creaks up again, it sure as God creaks, and here we are back in Renaissance Parma and nothing worse going on than incest and multiple murder.

Not one picture all night long did Conall capture.

Up on the stage, Grimaldi, a Roman gentleman, has just knocked somebody off, the wrong person, as it so happens, or, at any rate, not the person he means to knock off. The cardinal, when the matter is drawn to his attention by the citizens of Parma, is inclined to take a lenient view. For why? See text. The cardinal, in brief, argues that Grimaldi is no common man even if he is somewhat inclined to first-degree homicide. Grimaldi is nobly born and of the blood of princes and he, the cardinal, has received Grimaldi into the protection of the Holy Father.

Hip, hip hurrah, cries Conall, for the Holy Father. Send Grimaldi to the Eucharistic Congress.

There are some murmurs but more laughs among the audience. Stands to reason they're the laughing rather than the murmuring sort of audience. Otherwise they wouldn't be here.

Then Soranzo who is a nobleman, who wishes to marry Annabella and who thinks he has all the boys in line, is raising his glass which he has filled from the weighty bowl (see text), to Giovanni who is screwing Annabella, but not just then and there, who is, as I may have already explained, Giovanni's sister, and Soranzo, in all innocence or something, is saying: Here, Brother Grimaldi, here's to you, your turn comes next though now a bachelor.

Then to Annabella Soranzo says: Cheer up, my love.

Conall repeats that, and shouts something that sounds like: Tighten up there, M'Chesney.

Lagan basebarrelltones: Gag him, for God's sake.

And the house is hilarious.

Then enter Hippolita, masked, followed by several ladies in white robes, also masked and bearing garlands of willow. Music offstage. They do a dance. Not the Charleston, you may safely speculate. Soranzo says: Thanks, lovely virgins.

Conall says: How do you know.

The house rocks.

You see the joke, such as it may be, is that Soranzo has been having it off with Hippolita and now wishes to jettison cargo, and she, knowing this, is out to waste him but, before she can do so, Vasquez, a low type and no nobleman, slips her the old trick of the poisoned cup, and the friar, wise guy, says, fairly enough, that he fears the event, that a marriage is seldom good when the bride banquet so begins in blood. He sure is the greatest living authority on hell and matrimony.

Curious thing.

Read the rest of it for yourself.

Enter Soranzo, unbraced, and dragging in Annabella, and calling out: Come strumpet, famous whore.

Conall: Give the girl a break. She'll come on her own.

Soranzo: Wilt thou confess and I will spare thy life?

Annabella: My life. I will not buy my life so dear.

Soranzo: I will not slack my vengeance.

Conall: They're not getting on. There's a rift in the flute.

Soranzo: Had'st thou been virtuous, fair, wicked woman.

Conall: Thou can'st not have everything.

Soranzo: My reason tells me now that 'tis as common to err in frailty as to be a woman. Go to your chamber.

Conall: Politeness is all. Carry the chamber to her, sir.

Conall seems to know his Shakespeare.

Curious thing.

Three pictures are taken.

Not by Conall Cearnach of whom, the original warrior I mean, more hereafter. But by Brendan the Navigator who proves to be a good man in a crisis. He is a blond block of a man in a brown, serge suit. He is a Fingallian. That means that he comes from the north of the County Dublin, or Fingal, the land of the fairhaired foreigners where, Lagan assures me, some of the old farmhouses still preserve the high, pointed, Scandinavian gables, a style brought in there a thousand or so years ago by sea-rovers who settled.

One picture Brendan takes of Giovanni entering from left with his sister's heart impaled on a dagger, and dripping. A red sponge, I'd say, soaked, for additional effect, in some reasonably-inexpensive red wine.

All hearts that love should be like that. Mayhap, they are.

One picture he takes when the banditti rush in and the stage is strewn with corpses, and Vasquez, I told you he was a low type, tells the banditti that the way to deal with an old dame called Putana, whose name's a clue to character, is to carry her closely into the coalhouse and, instantly, put out her eyes and, if she should be so unappreciative as to scream, to slit her nose for laughs.

Exeunt banditti with Putana.

And that's about the next best thing to the riot that didn't arise.

The survivors are the cardinal, and Richardetto, a supposed physician, and Donado, a citizen of Parma, and Vasquez, the villain, who rejoices that a Spaniard can, in vengeance, outgo an Italian. Giovanni has just cashed in his chips. So the cardinal wisely advises those who are still able to stand up, that they should take up those slaughtered bodies and see them buried: and as for the gold and jewels, or whatsoever, since they are confiscate to the canons of the church, he, the cardinal, or we, as he calls himself, will seize them all for the Pope's proper use.

Conall: To pay for the . . .

But Jodhpurs has put her strong hand over his mouth.

Hautboys.

Sennet sounded.

Curtain.

The third picture Brendan takes is of the valiant lady making her curtain speech, and all the players, to the relief and felicity of all of us, resurrected and reunited. She thanks the audience. She thanks the gentlemen of the press. She thanks Conall personally and as Conall Lagan and not, as Patrick says she should have done, as Conall Carnage. To loud applause. Even I am astounded. Ireland is a more wonderful place than I ever thought it could be. Later I find out that Conall and the valiant woman are firm friends, that she even loves Conall as a mother might love a wayward son. Also I find out that to make absolutely certain of a good house, she took no money at the door: and that the picketers did not bother their ass picketing because the priest was far awa, far awa, and the weather was raining.

Up to that moment none of us have noticed or mentioned the weather.

And the next act opens back in the bar in the hotel.

The night is in full swing.

We return to our festivity and do our best to put the corpses of Parma out of our thoughts. We manage to do so.

To tell you the whole truth as I have promised always to do, well to tell as much of the whole truth as a lady should hear or wish to hear, we sit drinking, slowly, sipping, no gulping, spilling or slobbering, and the talk is good. We sit for several hours after official closing time and in the learned company of two uniformed police-officers and two detectives in plain clothes. One of the detectives has been among the audience and thinks the play the funniest thing he ever laid eyes or ears on since he saw Jimmy O'Dea, a famous comedian, in the Olympia theatre in Dublin when he, the detective, was in training in the Phoenix Park.

Jasus, the detective keeps saying, I tought dey'd never stop. And de lad coming in wit her heart on a breadknife. I could have taken me oat 'twas a pig's kidney. And Himself dere was de best part of de play.

The detective comes from a fairly widespread part of Ireland where they have problems with a certain dipthong.

By Himself he means Conall whose constancy and endurance is astounding, for talking and dancing and singing and telling the women he loves them: Jodhpurs in one breath, the barmaid in the next, with a few words to spare for any woman in the place, under or over sixty. He sits with us for a space. Then he is up at the bar or behind the bar and occasionally kissing the barmaid who objects, but mildly. To much general laughter. He is, believe it or not, most courteous. He knows *tout le monde* and it knows and likes him, and I do notice that he seldom renews his drink, and I wonder is it booze that sets him going or is he just that way by nature. Outgoing. Extrovert. You could say all that again. He can dance. He can sing. He does both at intervals. He even wears a wedding ring. He uses all his talents to the full.

We may be forced, Lagan says, to hogtie Conall as his namesake, Conall Cearnach, was hogtied by Bealcú, or Houndmouth, from Ballina, the champion of Connacht before Christ was in it. Not that Christ ever had much influence in certain parts of Connacht.

Nothing I know can stop Lagan. He will boom and drone on now until the sergeant and the guard and the two men in plain clothes, and anybody else who cares to listen, will know all about the wounding and healing of the ancient hero. But, hell, what am I here for? Research is research. And where is my notebook?

Lagan explains to the plain-clothes men and the guard that when Bealcú urges his charger and, ergo, his chariot across the snow to the place where he has seen the two warriors in combat, Slinger Keth lies dead and Conall Cearnach, wounded, lies at point to die. The guard and the plain-clothes men show every evidence of interest. The sergeant is up to something else. He has the ear of Brendan, the Viking sea-rover or the sanctified navigator, what you will. He, the sergeant, is saying slowly, spacing out the words carefully: Soap . . . necktie . . . chocolates . . . cigarettes . . . pipe and tobacco-pouch . . . book or book token . . . shaving-cream or aftershave . . . socks . . . record or record-player . . . pen . . . handkerchiefs . . .

Or rather he is reading those mystic words out of the newspaper that employs Lagan, Conall, Brendan and Niall. He asks Brendan what he thinks of all that. Brendan says: Aunt Miriam is a very good friend of mine. And a most considerate and efficient colleague.

This is extremely curious. Niall is, for the moment, at the far end of the bar, engaged at conversation with some friends he has encountered.

Lagan says: Put jockstrap on the list. For Conall over there.

Seems Lagan can narrate to four men and simultaneously listen to a fifth. There is much general laughter at mention of the jockstrap. Over at the bar, but on this side of it, Conall has one arm around the barmaid and the other around Jodhpurs. All seem happy. Am I losing contact? Events mingle and move too fast for me. It is a long way from here to Spoon River.

But aside from all that: When Houndmouth sees Cearnach flat on his ass on the snow he proceeds to badmouth him. Calling him a ravening wolf of Ulster which is where Conall, hereinafter to be known as Cearnach, comes from. Who answers: Taunts are for reviling women.

That's pretty good.

— Hush up, he says, to Bealcú, and finish me off.

But no, Bealcú will not have it noised abroad that it took two Connachtmen to knock off one Ulsterman. His game is to bring Cearnach home with him to Ballina or wherever, to have him patched up by the Connacht medicos and then, for the glory of Bealcú, and whatever gods may be in Connacht, to kill him in single combat. So Bealcú binds Cearnach in five-fold fetters, which is what Lagan thinks we should do with our Conall, then heaves him up or has him heaved up on the chariot, to be somewhat cheesed when he tries to lift the Ulsterman's war-mace.

What a weight it was to raise!

Brendan interrupts, reading out aloud from the newspaper. This is what he reads: The girl in the picture is playing with her white mice. Do you have a pet mouse? If so what colour is it? Do you like mice? If not, write and say why. Could you write a poem about a mouse? Try.

— Christ of Almighty, says Lagan. What are you all up to?

And the sergeant says that his sixteen-year-old daughter is a magician all-out at the painting and drawing, and can turn out a poem should be printed.

Brendan explains. Mostly or totally for my benefit. The others know all about Aunt Miriam. Which is the name of the mythical lady who edits the page from which the sergeant and Brendan have been reading: Aunt Miriam's Campfire Club.

The sergeant's daughter and a slew (sluagh, in the Irish) of her schoolfriends wish to join. Brendan says that he will look after all that. He reads further to explain to me about that odd list of objects: Choosing birthday presents for fathers, uncles or older brothers can sometimes be quite difficult. So what about carrying out a birthday survey? Ask your father, brother, uncle, teacher or any man over twenty-fiveish to put the birthday presents on this list in order of their choice. Bring your completed list into class next week. Check the answers and count up in class how many men put socks or soap . . .

Or de jockstraps, says one of de plain-clothes men.

Let joy be unconfined.

It is early in de morning. Am I losing my diptongs?

Brendan later admits, blushingly, that Aunt Miriam is his beloved wife. That is not true. Aunt Miriam, in fact, is a somewhat eccentric and retired clergyman. That is supposed to be a wellkept secret. But

Brendan writes down the names and addresses of the sergeant's daughter and all her friends. He says that he will see to it that Aunt Miriam's secretary, who doesn't exist, will send to each and every one of those young enthusiasts the Campfire Crest, a sort of badge. He promises that the letters they write to Aunt Miriam will be printed in the paper. And the poetical works of the sergeant's daughter. All this, for sure, he looks after when back in Dublin. But the entente he sets up between us and the sergeant is to prove real precious some hours later when Brendan and Niall are on the road, by automobile, to Limerick city where they have something else to report. Or on which to report. Even in Ireland, English is English.

Action stations!

The clock strikes three.

Jodhpurs says she will hit the hay. A challenging thought. The barmaid has vanished. Brendan and Niall have taken the road for Limerick city. Conall and Lagan and myself would seem to be the only living people left. One of those corrugated things has been pulled down and the bar is closed. Lagan and myself set sail for the bottom of the main stairway. But is that good enough for Conall? No, no, by no means no. He says that he wants one more drink. But he is a lot more sober than he pretends to be and he has something else, as you may imagine, in his calculating mind. We try to reason with him. To talk him into calling it a night, or a day. No use, no use. Down a long corridor that leads towards the back of the building he sees, and so do we, a light burning. That, it may appear, is where the barmaid has found covert. So hitching his wagon to that star, Conall Carnage steams (block that metaphor), down the corridor and through the heavy-drifted snow, and thunders on the door of the room of the light as if he owned the world, and barges in, and finds . . .

Two young clergymen drinking-up. The curates, or assistants, or lootenants of the parish. The mice relaxing while the tomcat is farawa, farawa in Antananarivo. One of them turns angry-nasty. Through embarrassment, it may be, at being found out. Tells Conall, and in a clear shrill voice, that this is a private room. The barmaid is nowhere to be seen. So Conall demands to know what in heaven, or hell, two clerics are doing drinking-up and being merry in a private room in a public house at three o'clock in the morning. And why are they not at home writing sermons and banning plays as any zealous sacerdotes should be. Cleric Number Two asks him, politely enough, to leave. Then Lagan grabs Conall and begins to urge him out and Lagan, although an anti-clerical of the old style, apologizes to the polite priest, explaining that Conall has a drop too many taken. Out of nowhere the proprietress appears, a tough sort of a lady in late middle-age. She exhorts Conall to have some respect for the cloth. From halfways up the stairs Conall intones: Bless me, fathers, for I have sinned.

Lagan chants, but only so as to be heard by Conall and myself: *Dies irae, dies illa, solvet saeclum in favilla* . . .

We propel Conall as far as and into his room. That day, we reckon, has been called a day.

So Bealcú urges charger and chariot westward through the borders of Breffny. Bearing with him the corpse of Keth the Slinger and the wounded and captive Cearnach. They come to a place called Moy Slaught where the ancient Irish used to worship a pretty formidable idol called Crom Cruach. He was a hunk of stone or something and his twelve apostles, twelve lesser hunks, sat round him in a ring. Along came Jones, meaning St Patrick, and thumps old Crom with his Bachall Íosa, or the staff of Christ, and Crom bears forever the mark of the bachall, and the earth swallows the twelve lesser idols: and, just at that moment in Lagan's narration, all hell breaks loose in the street outside the hotel.

Lagan and myself are sharing a room. Where Jodhpurs has vanished to, we do not know. Jealousy, at last, may have driven that tolerant girl to roost in some faraway place. The hotel is a corner house. Our room is right on the corner and right above the main door. On which door Crom Cruach and his sub-gods twelve seem at this moment to be beating. Where, cries Lagan, is the staff of Jesus.

He looks out one of our two windows but the angle is awkward and he can see nothing. The beating at the door lessens. Then ceases. But there is a frenzy and a babel of voices. Then the door of our room opens and the sergeant steps in. And says most modestly: Mr Lagan, as the eldest member here present of the press-party, could you please come down and put a tether on this young fellow before he wrecks the town.

For Carnage is off on the warpath again, with or without benefit of chariot. Meantime, back at the ranch, Cearnach has been unceremoniously dumped on the fairgreen of Moy Slaught where he is getting a poor press from all the widows he, in happier times, has made in the West of Ireland.

And Bealcú says: Let Lee, the leech, be brought.

And Lee, the gentlefaced, is brought from his plot of healing herbs. Like Lagan walking down the stairs to see what healing he can bring to Conall Carnage in the hall below. Followed, at a safe distance, by myself and the sergeant who gives me a brief breakdown on what has caused the brouhaha. Seems Conall made down again to the door of the lighted room. To find it locked and bolted. To Carnage that presented no problem. He bangs on the door and roars out that he wants somebody to hear his confession. Lest he die in sin. Then comes a-running the lady of the house and with her a big guy she has somewhere drafted so as to throw Conall out. This big guy is a mighty-big big guy. So he pushes our Conall back as far as the main hall where Conall, who is nifty, steps backwards up two rungs of the stairs, so as to gain purchase, and throws a hard, roundhouse swing at the big guy, who is also nifty. And ducks. And Conall knocks down the lady, and the lady screams bloody murder, and the big guy and the clerics just about manage to heave Conall out the front door and lock it, and Conall goes to work with fists and feet, raising holy hell on the oak, three inches thick, and ringing the bell, and roaring Bless me, fathers, for I have sinned, and lights going on and children crying all over the town as if, says the sergeant, Jesus had come again, and the lady phones the fuzz, and here we are again, happy as can be, and Jodhpurs, neat girl, and one of the plain-clothes men are holding Conall, and Lagan is saying that Conall is a good kid, and the lady is shouting that he's a pup, a pup, a pup.

Lagan shows himself to be some diplomat. M. de Norpois. Hit the Guermantes trail. The matronly presence of Aunt Miriam is still there to aid him. He and the sergeant mutter together in one corner. Conall calms down. Jodhpurs is good for him. Like Hector in Homer she is well known as a tamer of horses. Then Lagan and the sergeant come to this arrangement. That Conall will go for the night to the calaboose with the lawmen. For no way in hell will the lady have him for the night in her hotel. What, she says, will my husband say when he comes home and hears that I was assaulted under my own roof. What, says Lagan, will the parish priest say when he comes home from wherever in heaven he is and I tell him that his two curates were drinking in your office at three o'clock in the morning.

Détente.

The lady screams that rightaway she wants to prefer charges. The Sergeant, gently but firmly, says that she must wait until the next day or, to be exact, daylight of the same day. She screams again that Conall's swipe has smashed her spectacles. For corroboration, the big guy has already gathered up the fragments, *colligite fragmenta ne pereant*, into a brown paper-bag. Evidence? Or second-class relics? Jodhpurs, gallant girl, offers to go with Conall. To burn on his pyre. But Conall, like a hero going into transportation, kisses her farewell, several times, advises her to catch a few hours sleep, she may need them: that the night to come, and still so far ahead, is yet another night. The lady of the house is about to have a fit. So the big guy leads her away. The clerics have vanished. Up the chimney? Then Conall marches off, taking the lead with the sergeant, the plain-clothes man bringing up the rear. But halfways across the street, the plain-clothes man stops, shakes hands with Conall and goes off another way. Home to his bed and his wife, if he has one. Conall marches on, under escort, to his lonely prison cell. Or so I sadly and foolishly think.

Carnage now lies in the hoosegow. Cearnach lies under the care of Lee the Leech. Who, gentlefaced as he is, still strikes a hard bargain with the victorious and vengeful Bealcú. Has Lee, like the sergeant, a soft, melancholy voice and a moustache that droops as if the humid heat had gotten to it?

— Do you know what he said to me, Lagan says.

Not Lee the Leech, but the sergeant.

When the two of them, Lagan and the sergeant, were muttering in the corner.

— He said to me, Lagan says, that if the lad never did worse than knock that damsel down, he won't do much wrong in the world. She would skin a flea. (For the price of its hide: a native colloquialism.) 'Tis well known, says the sergeant, that she adulterates the whiskey. Anyway, the lad never hit her.

No direct hit. The wind of his passing, like that of a godamned archangel, simply flattened her.

— Anyway, the sergeant said. The lad struck out in self-defence. And missed. The only bruise would be on her backside where she sat down with a thump. He that cares to feel that way may find it.

— But keep an eye on things here, the sergeant said. You and the Yank. And I'll watch the young fellow. We want no trouble. Nor capers in the courtroom. We're overworked as it is. And that's the true.

Then Jodhpurs kisses us goodnight.

And that's the true, as the sergeant says.

And we rest our weary heads. And somewhere in gardens, and on the fringe of the town, and all over Ireland, the birds are beginning to sing.

— Curious thing, Brinsley says to me through my tumbling half-sleep.

— Curious thing. Georgia is famous for peaches. Or that's what the Irish Christian Brothers told me.

Once I had told him that there was a dame on Peachtree Street, Atlanta, Georgia. Meaning you. Well aware I am that there are many and various dames on Peachtree.

He capped my statement by telling me that there was once, he had heard or read, a dame in Belmont, richly left, and she was fair . . .

Then he went on about the peaches.

Seems there is or was a geography compiled by an Irish Christian Brother for use in schools run by the Irish Christian Brothers. It lists or listed the chief products of various places. Inchicore, a portion of Dublin, has rolling-stock. Georgia has peaches.

It is the dawn. The summer dark, the poet said, is but the dawn of day. That's Lagan quoting. He is up and shaving at the handbasin.

No rooms with bath here. Rise up, he says, and do begin the day's adorning. He is a healthy man. He needs no cure. He tells me that Lee the Leech says that healing is with God's permission, health for life's enjoyment made. My American head is a purple glow and my belly full of the linnet's wings: and Lee the Leech agrees to heal Cearnach but insists that when the healing is perfected there shall be a fair fight and no favour, and that if Conall is triumphant he is to have safe conduct back to the Fews, his native part of Ulster. Also: that while the healing is in process no man shall steal through fences to work the patient mischief or surprise. He demands an oath on the matter: to Crom the God, to the sun, to the wind.

Lagan pulls open the heavy window-curtains and the sun comes through with a scream.

All quiet on the street outside. The good folk here do not arise betimes.

What healing is there for my hapless head?

My eyes I close and see viscous, bubbling peaches.

What healing for Carnage in his dungeon drear?

Lee the Leech has unlocked Cearnach's fetters.

Valiantly I face the razor.

— Curious thing, Brinsley says, Plato never bothered his barney about anachronisms. Curious thing.

But I swear by God and Abraham Lincoln, and by the body of Pocahontas, lovely as a poppy, sweet as a pawpaw in May, he is there in the dining-room and leathering-in (as Jodhpurs says), to his breakfast when she, me and Lagan get downstairs to the dining-room. He? Who? Brinsley? Plato? Bealcú? Lee the Leech? Conall Cearnach? Crom the God? No, but our own dear Conall Carnage for it is he. Eating egg and bacon and sausage and black pudding and drinking black coffee by the bucket. And eating butter, putting it into his mouth in great globs. Lubrication, he tells me. Oil the wheels. And the big end. Never did I see the like. Almost threw up to watch him. The lady of the house hovers in the background. Out of arm's reach and the swing of the sea. Amazed me that they served him anything. But he's a hell of a hard man to resist. Jodhpurs is all joy.

Growing boys need food, she says. She glows. She is, I blush to say it, looking ahead to the night ahead.

Then while Carnage roisters and we nibble he tells us about the night or the remnants of a night just passed. Seems he never had it so good. Here is what happened. Conall and the sergeant walked back to the barracks. Who should be there but the second plain-clothes man (as in Shakespeare), and the garda or guard who had been drinking with us earlier in the night. Conall asked if they were going to lock him up and they said no way. Then another garda appeared with a tray and teapot and bread and jam. Everybody was, as Conall put it, fierce polite. Then the lot went home except Conall and one man or guard or garda, or what-in-the-hell, who was on night-duty. Who placed six chairs in strategic positions. Then produced a spring and a mattress which he balanced on the chairs. Then the all-night man said hop in and the two of them, and the town and the cattle in the fields and the birds in the bushes, slept until the sergeant came in at dawn, and with a bottle of wine from faraway Oporto. There were drinks and handshaking all round and that was that. Curious thing. Curious country, Ireland.

The healing of Conall Cearnach is, by now, well under way. He is still on his bed or on the scratcher (a Dublin usage), and he heaves thereon, Lagan quotes, as on reef of rock the ocean wildly tosses. Don't quite get that. The bed, the ocean, should be tossing, not Cearnach, the Rock. And the sons of Bealcú are worried. What is Lee the Leech up to? How fares the Ulsterman, the man from the Fews? So from a distance the sons of Bealcú spy, as best as they can, on the medical treatment. The patient no longer tosses on the bed nor does the bed toss under him. Now he is up and about even if he is pallid as a winding-sheet. Swear I do to Edgar Allen Poe that I do not know, nor could wildly guess at the pallidity of a winding-sheet.

Now Cearnach is out of his chamber. This isle of is full of chambers.

Cearnach is walking on his feet. What else?

We have paid our bill to the barmaid who is doubling in reception and who has the giggles. She giggles beautifully. All over. She kisses Carnage a fond farewell. The lady of the house is not there to be seen. Nor to see. We walk on our feet, all four of us, on eight feet, through the town to the other of the two hotels. It is an ancient and historic town. And looks the part. But I have a hunch that we have become part of the history. For the people on the pleasant side-walks are peeping at us and trying to pretend that they are not peeping. As are the sons of Bealcú peeping away out west, not in Kansas, but on the fair green of Moy Slaught. To see Cearnach, a ghastly figure, on his javelin propped he goes. But day follows day and Cearnach convalesces and convalesces, and with herbs and healing balsams he burgeons like a sere oak under summer showers and dew, and the sons of Bealcú are fearful for the future of their father.

Or the Dazee, as Carnage puts it.

Another Dublin usage.

Carnage is beginning to show some interest in the story of the healing of his namesake.

We have reached the other hotel. A mighty handsome place. But it is now bright morning and, after last night and all that happened where we were, even a roominghouse on Ponce de Leon, which flows into and out of the street of the Peachtrees, as you know, could be a mighty handsome place.

The valiant woman is here, having her morning gin, and some of her players around her. She is a widow. Her husband, who was a playwright, had a long enmity with Brinsley who is, also, a playwright. But valiantly she did her best to keep the peace between them. She tells me a lot. Research, research, research. The hardships of strolling players in rural Ireland. The money she is losing. Seán O'Casey, she tells me, is a cantankerous bastard when it comes to giving permission to anyone to put on his plays in Ireland. He wants money, for God's sake, money. Ah well. To make him madder still the Maria Mussolini Duce people picketed a play of his in the Gaiety in Dublin, and the Sinn Féiners, long ago, nearly wrecked the old Abbey over *The Plough and the Stars*, and one old nut of a theatregoer roared at O'Casey that there were no prostitutes in Dublin, and O'Casey said, mildly, in return, that he had been accosted three times on his way to the theatre and the old nut cracked back that if there were prostitutes in Dublin it was the British army put them there.

— Good on the army, Carnage says.

Lagan hushes him up.

But all that about O'Casey is history. Away back in the 1920s. Return to the here and now.

We have one hell of a lunch. The valiant lady pays.

Then honking in the street and shouting at the door come Niall and Brendan, all bright and glittering in the lunchtime air, and all the way from Limerick city, and all ready to drive you all back to Dublin town.

They have had their own adventures.

For on the way to Limerick city they rested for a while in a roadside tavern. Not a roadhouse. Just an Irish pub, open day and night and to hell with the law. Niall had driven that far. And in the tavern they got to talking with this elderly farmer who lived back in the boondocks in mountains called the Silvermines. He sang songs. He hobbled on a stick. So kindhearted Brendan reckoned that the old-timer was too old and too hirpled (an Ulster usage) to walk home. Off with the three of them, and a bottle of whiskey, through a network of mountain roads to a shack where Senex lived alone. Brendan uncorked the whiskey. Senex produced three cracked and yellowing mugs. Out with Niall to the henhouse to rob the nests. Shall it be my lot, he thought, in the screeching and fluttering dark, to be beaten to death by the wings of hens in a cró, or hutment, on the slopes of the Silvermine mountains. Then out of all the eggs he could find he made, he says, the world's biggest-ever bloody omelette, chopped it into three fair halves, and they ate the lot and drank the whiskey, and Senex staggered safely to bed and, with Brendan the Navigator at the wheel, the pair of them set out to try to escape from the mountains. Which does not prove to be all that easy. For the dustroads go round and round about to find the town of Roundabout that makes the world go round. Nor is an overdose of whiskey the best navigational aid. In the chill dawn, with Brendan asleep and Niall at the wheel, they stumble on Limerick city which is beautiful, as everybody knows, the river Shannon, full of fish, beside that city flows: and Niall, shaking Brendan awake, says where is Hanratty's hotel, and Brendan sings out: You find Hanratty's. I discovered Limerick.

Then they find the hotel and are no sooner asleep than the phone rings from the Dublin office to say that it has heard that a pressman has assaulted a woman during or after the performance of the banned play, and would somebody please tell the other end of the phone what in hell is going on down there.

Enter now the garda of the previous night.

Not into Limerick city but into that handsome hotel in which we are washing down our lunch. Seems the lady of the other hotel has called the Dublin office to report the disorderly behaviour of two cameramen, Patrick Lagan and John Karney, meaning me. Now I have become a cameraman and a knockerdown of ladies. She has threatened legal action. The old blackmail — settle-out-of-court trick. The office disowns both of us. Lagan is on holidays and I was never there, and even Conall Carnage is under semi-suspension for some previous misdemeanour and, anyway, he hasn't been mentioned. So Lagan calls the lady and says that if she wants legal action or counteraction she is more than welcome any time, and that those two young clergymen would sure smile to be subpoenaed, and about the hell there would be to pay when the boss gets back from Antananarivo.

Enter the sergeant.

To approve of Lagan's diplomacy, or whatever. To bid us godspeed and a safe journey, and to say that things will surely settle if we see Carnage safely back to Dublin.

Exeunt omnes.

One little town. Two little towns. Three little towns.

No stops, Niall says, until we're safe in Dublin. Or, at any rate, as far as Roche's of Rathcoole.

Meaning a famous singing public-house about twenty-five miles from the city centre. The public-house does not sing. Only the people in it. Well, they try. A master of ceremonies at the piano. Ladies and gentlemen, one voice only, please. And the saddest man in the house stands up and wails: Caan, I forget you, when every night reminds me . . .

Well you know that I cannot forget you. Accept this letter in lieu of vows.

Anyway, Lagan is quoting: Forbaid was a master-slinger. Maev, when in her bath she sank, felt the presence of his finger from the further Shannon bank . . .

— That guy, says Carnage, had a mighty, long finger.

Jodhpurs smacks him. But gently. She is sitting on his knee. It is a small auto. We are six people. We are counted, Brendan says, like the elephants, after they are washed, at bedtime in Duffy's circus.

Lagan annotates his quotation. Research.

Conall Cearnach, do you follow me, had killed Aleel, the last husband of Maev, queen of Connacht. Aleel and Maev started a war when they quarrelled in their bed because he had a bull and she hadn't.

— So, Carnage says, that we don't have to be professors or literary editors to know what that was about.

Again Jodhpurs smacks him. Then they kiss. Niall who is at the wheel says that somebody or something is rocking the boat.

Then, after the killing of Aleel, Maev retires to an island on Lough Ree in the river Shannon. Once a day and at dawn she takes her bath in a springwell on that island. Vain woman, she thinks there isn't a peeper in Ireland dare peep on a queen. But Forbaid of Ulster has long sight as well as a long finger, and spots her from afar, and comes in the dusk secretly to the well and, with a linen thread, measures the distance back to the far shore. Then he stretches the thread on the ground, in a safe and secret place, plants a wooden fence-pole at each end of it, puts an apple atop of one pole, stands at the other, practises with his sling or handbow until he can take the apple ten times out of ten. Then one fine morning he stands where the river Shannon's flowing and the three-leaved shamrock grows and, across the wide water, where my heart is I am going to my native Irish rose, he clobbers the queen between the eyes with a two-pound rock, and she falls into the well, and that is the end of a queen who was longer in the bidnis than Queen Victoria: and the moment that I meet her with a hug an' kiss I'll greet her, for there's not a colleen (cáilín), sweeter where the river Shannon flows.

— Smart guy, Carnage says. But he hadn't much to peep at. She must have been a hundred if she was a day.

More smacks and kisses. Niall heaves to. Threatens irons for mutiny. Jodhpurs kisses back of Niall's neck. On we go.

Then more kisses, did I stop them when a million seemed so few? That was Lagan. Courtesy of Mr Browning.

Wait for it, Carnage says

Then we get the entire spiel about Oh, Galuppi, Baldassaro, this is very hard to find, I can scarcely misconceive you it would prove me deaf and blind, but although I take your meaning 'tis with such a heavy mind . . .

And much more of the same.

That's Lagan's party piece. Or one of them.

We know now, Carnage says, who broke up the party in Fitzwilliam Square.

Much laughter. For the benefit of the visitor Lagan explains: It is, John, one of the many afflictions of my life to have the same surname as our dear friend, Carnage. Here and now happily restored to us, through my, shall we say, diplomacy, and the friendship of the sergeant. Although, if the case had gone to court, even the most humane District Justice would have felt compelled to give him six months without the option. For last night's performance and, furthermore, for his previous record. That gold ring he so proudly wears. Consider it.

Carnage raises and swivels an elegant right hand. The ring glows.

That ring is by no means his ring, Lagan informs me. He is not married. Do not think it. Not a woman in Ireland would have him. In wedded bliss, that is. No, that ring belongs to a lady with whom he is, shall we say, familiar. Who received it from her husband. From whom she is now sundered.

Life, life, says Carnage.

And twists the ring on his finger.

Who to support herself, Lagan says, ventures out occasionally on the scented and sacred sidewalks of Dublin.

We all, says Jodhpurs, have to do our best. Poor Maryanne.

Jodhpurs has a lot of heart.

So Carnage has a friend, Lagan explains. Odd as it may seem, he still has friends. This friend lives in an apartment in Fitzwilliam Square. A select area. And invites Carnage and Maryanne to a party.

Invitation instantly accepted. Conall Carnage is hell for parties. And two or three or four, accounts and authorities differ as in Edward Scribble Gibbon, two or three or four cabloads arrive somewhat noisily in the elegant Square, Carnage and Maryanne, and some of Maryanne's business colleagues, and some of their friends, and create such immortal havoc that the gardai or the guards or the guards or the police or the coppers or the bobbies or the peelers or the fuzz or the pigs or the gendarmes or the effing Royal Irish Constabulary or whatever in hell you visiting American scholar, or embryo scholar, may care so to describe them, are called by the startled and highly-respectable neighbours, and the unfortunate man is evicted from his apartment in Fitzwilliam Square . . .

With more kisses, who could stop them, Jodhpurs is keeping Carnage quiet.

Does that sentence, or does it not, need a question mark. This one does????

Niall is singing about the sash his father wore.

Brendan, his voyaging o'er, is asleep.

The green countryside flows past.

And the great and much-appreciated joke, Lagan says, was that the news went round the town that I was the Lagan responsible.

More green countryside. Beautifully sunlit. One more small town.

How lucky, Lagan says, was Conall Cearnach to live so long ago.

But the sons of Bealcú are on the warpath and one of them reminds the other of the method by which Forbaid, the masterslinger, had fingered Maev, the Queen. Every morning from afar they watch Cearnach grow stronger and they fear for their father, and watch Cearnach coming at dawn to the fountain or wellmargin to drink: while Cearnach is thinking, in the words of the poet, how a noble virgin, by a like green fountain's brink, heard his own pure vows one morning, faraway and long ago, all his heart to home was turning and the tears began to flow . . .

Jodhpurs likes that bit.

Not many pure vows, she says, do I hear. Nor Maryanne, in the course of her career.

So Lagan explains that Cearnach is thinking, while he weeps, of the wife and the weans (children, to you), back home in Ulster in Dunseverick's windy tower. Then up he leaps in a fit, runs round like a whirlwind, swings the war-mace, hurls the spear, and Bealcú, also peeping, but from another point of vantage and unseen by his sons, has the crap frightened out of him.

Cearnach, Carnage opines, has had his morning gin-and-tonic. There must be good stuff in that there fountain. Mayo poteen? Mountain dew? Georgia Moon Cawn whiskey?

Which may be more-or-less what Bealcú thinks. Not in relation to booze but about a god who, Bealcú thinks, may be in the fountain and to whom Cearnach prays, and Bealcú reckons he might just sneak in and, himself, mention the matter to the god.

But what about his vow, cries Jodhpurs. His vow to Crom Cruach and the sun and the wind.

She seems to know more about the story than a man might imagine.

She and Carnage are cheek-to-cheek.

Even if not dancing.

Has she tamed him?

Briefly we pause at Roche's of Rathcoole. Just long enough to hear six times on the jukebox one of Niall's favourite songs. Idaho, Idaho, I lost her and I found her at the Idaho State Fair, he broke twenty broncos and one grizzly bear, but she broke one cowpoke at the Idaho State Fair, Idaho, Idaho . . .

Once in my life I passed, by Greyhound, through Boise, Idaho.

No singing customers are present in Roche's of Rathcoole. It is too early in the evening.

Caan I forget you . . .

No questionmark here needed.

But this is not Dunseverick's windy tower. No, we are back somewhere in the environs of Dublin and we are in a tower, one of four, and one of them at each corner of an ancient castle. For Lagan, Patrick, has been invited to a party in this tower. A friend of his rents it. Just the one tower. He is a prominent painter, this friend. We get there about midnight. There is a tree in the courtyard that was planted there more than five hundred years ago. At Lagan's suggestion Carnage tears off a bit of the bark and some leaves to send to you. They are safely in a small box and I will bear them with me across the broad Atlantic. There is a tradition that Edmund Spenser ate his first meal in Ireland in this castle. As for myself I ate there what, but for the grace of God, might have been my last meal on earth: the ghost of the poet, perhaps, looking over my shoulder and babbling of a goodly bosom like a strawberry bed, a breast like lilies e'er their leaves be shed, and all her body rising like a stayre, and you know the rest of it, and I love my love in the morning, I love my love at noon . . .

Poor fellow. No wonder he entered the Christian Brothers. Not Spenser. But that other gentle poet.

But speaking of ghosts, this castle is haunted by a peculiar shade. Or by peculiar footsteps that are heard going up the winding stairs. But never coming down. Steps only. No person. No wraith.

Carnage says: Don't blame me.

The Castle has other associations which I will enumerate when I see you. And a pleasant seat which I was unable to see. For it is now past midnight. We enter the great hall. Not of the castle. But we enter a pretty commodious room halfways up the tower. To see a fine throng, glasses in hands. And to be welcomed. And to see a distinguished-looking, elderly, moustachioed gentleman trying to climb the wall. Uttering foul oaths the while. Seems that he has been attempting to climb the wall for several hours. Nor is he alone at that caper. Several of the guests are having a go. A hop, step and jump across the room. Then a roar and a run and a leap at the wall. Does not make sense at first. Then it dawns on me. The aim of the game is to leap higher than the door, turn round in mid-air and end up seated on the wide lintel shelf. Solid oak. Only one guest succeeds. A small man with a Chaplinesque moustache. A painter. Or, also, a circus acrobat. He is rewarded by a bottle of champagne. Which he drinks while sitting on the shelf.

Lacking the long finger of Forbaid, the master-slinger I stay safely on the carpet. For the wear and tear of the journey to renaissance Parma and back is beginning to tell, and all I want to do is to lie down.

So up with me, up the haunted, twisting stairway, up two more floors, the furore dying away below me. No rough men-at-arms do I meet, cross-gartered to the knees or shod in iron. No footfalls do I hear but mine own. A small room I find and, joy of joys, a bed. On which, fully clothed, I collapse with a crash. Then down below in the Hall of Pandemonium, Carnage becomes aware of my absence and is worried. Believe it or not, but Carnage is a real human being. He begins searching all over for me. He runs downstairs and looks all around. All around the grounds and in the pouring rain. Checking all the cars. Climbing the ancient tree. Then, systematically, he begins to search the tower from the ground up. Where, at the end of an hour, he, inevitably, finds me. Shakes me awake to find out if I am still alive. Puts a pillow under my head. Tucks blankets around me. All the while assuring me that I should come downstairs and have another drink to help me to sleep. He is very concerned about me. He says that he mainly worries because I seem so tall, blond, thin and innocent, and mild-mannered, that I can only come to harm among the rougher Irish. Even the women are hard, he assures me, and you have got to be tough to stand up to them. He is taking care of me all the time, talking to me like a worried father to a not-too-bright, not-too-strong son. He is twenty-one. As you know I am twenty-five and have survived even the army.

At four in the morning I arise to begin the day's adorning. Still slightly stupefied. Go down the haunted stairway. My host gives me coffee and sandwiches and tells me that I should write not about Brinsley but about Joyce. He is actually a relation. Not of Brinsley. But of Joyce.

So in honour of James Joyce we go for a morning swim off the Bull Wall where Stephen Dedalus walked and saw the wading girl and cried out heavenly god and all the rest of it. Research, research! Oh, the delights of a dawn plunge in the nude in the dirty water of Dublin Bay. Jodhpurs and all, or Jodhpurs without her jodhpurs. My eyes I modestly avert. Credit that if you can. She swims well. Not Dedalus himself, when he walked into that epiphany, ever saw the like. So strip I do and clamber down the rocks. Brendan, who has more sense, stays clothed and warm and holds my spectacles for me. The water is colder than ice and about as comfortable as broken glass.

But it almost restores us to sobriety. We splash around there for thirty minutes or so and nobody, praise the Lord and hand me down my bible, is cramped or drowned. Then we sit on the rocks and watch the day coming up over Dublin city, and over the bay, and over Clontarf where Brian Boru bate the Danes, the dacent people, Lagan had said, without whom there never would have been a Dublin. For Brian, Lagan had argued, was a wild man from Limerick or thereabouts, as bad as or worse than Carnage or Bealcú . . .

Now Lagan has gone. For unlike the rest of us he has a home and a family to attend to, and Jodhpurs tells to the end the tale of the killing of Bealcú, another sore case of mistaken identity. She has read the poem, or has had it read to her, at school. Seems hard to believe that a strong broad like Jodhpurs ever went to school or to anywhere except the racing-stables. But Carnage says she was very bright at school, prizes and scholarships, and still is, and in all sort of places and ways, and can hold her own in talk on such topics even with the learned Lagan himself who is, says Carnage, as you have noticed, a sound man, and he will have my suspension lifted, he has the decency, he has the influence and he doesn't really mind being mistaken for me, it gives him stories to tell, and you may have noticed that he has a weakness for telling stories.

It is now the intention of Carnage to finally (Lagan would violently object to the split infinitive but since he's not here to hear me I'll split it wider still), get in the sack with Jodhpurs, when she will be once again divested of her jodhpurs, and Jodhpurs is raising no objection. As for me, I walk alone because to tell you the truth I am lonely, I don't mind being lonely when my heart tells me you're lonely too . . .

Then Karnage who is Kind, forgive that one, says come home with him to his apartment, he has a spare room and Maryanne is not, at the moment, in it, and he wants me to sleep for eight hours while he and Jodhpurs do what they have to do, and he loves his love in the morning and all the way to noon. So he hits the gas and speeds back towards Dublin city. Only the three of us left. The roads are wet and slippery. They almost always are in Ireland. We turn a corner. We approach a bridge. We go into a spin, an all-out spin. To you I pray. We ram the brick wall of the bridge. It rams us. Karnage is thrown out of the Kar. The front windshield kisses me, my only kiss since I left Atlanta. But it holds up under the strain and Jodhpurs gets the reins, the wheel, and tames the horse and all is almost well. What I sustain, you may be glad to hear, is, merely a stunned elbow, a bruised black-and-white forearm and a cut finger. They will be perfect again when I get to Peachtree.

We are now somewhere on the outskirts of Dublin city. It is very early on a Sunday morning and nobody to be seen and, to top it all, it begins once again to pour rain. We try to push the car over off the road into a vacant lot. But the front right fender is crushed into the tyre and will not allow the wheel to move. We pull, we push, we grunt, we strain. No deal. Well, we make twenty-five yards but that gets us nowhere except into the middle of the road. But, God a mercy, along comes a big milk-truck, ties a rope to the battered bumper or fender, drags the wreck into the vacant lot. The rain continues. We start to walk downtown. The truck is going the other way. Another truck. Going my way. Offers us a ride. Do we accept? You're goddamn right we do. And gratefully settle back. To travel half a block when Truck Number Two cranks out. Oh Gawd! We walk on. The rain continues.

In the north of Dublin city there stands a small hotel. More than one, but one will do. It's not the Ritz nor the Savoy but the door is open and the coffee hot and strong. Karnage has left his Kamera in the Kastle. Now we krack. Karnage and I. Not Jodhpurs. She pours the koffee. We sit in the lounge. Just the three of us. But when Karnage talks to me I hear instead the booming voice of Lagan. Not imagination. Really, the booming voice of Lagan. He sings about the sash my father wore. He sings in Irish about a maiden in Donegal whose cheeks were like the roses and her little mouth like brown sugar. Honey with the mouth like brown sugar. A good beat for a black combo. He recites about dear Pádraic of the wise and seacold eyes, so loveable, so courteous and so noble, the very West was in his soft replies. But Lagan is nowhere to be seen. He says that free speech shivered on the pikes of Macedonia and later on the swords of Rome. He says Love that had robbed us of immortal things, and I rise to protest, but he is not there.

This is ghastly and I tell Karnage who says that, Good God, he hears him too.

We search the lounge. But he is nowhere to be found. Nobody anywhere to be seen except an unconcerned and bored female clerk. We pay for our coffee. We depart.

In the spare room of Karnage I lie down and try to sleep, remembering Thee, oh Peachtree. But rightaway the room is full of voices and above them all the voice of Lagan intoning that by Douglas Bridge he met a man who lived adjacent to Strabane before the English hung him high for riding with O'Hanlon.

Then up I leap up and dress, and tiptoe, almost running, out of the house to walk, in a daze, the awakening streets and find a restaurant, and eggs and coffee. Then I go to my lodgings.

I might not have bothered to tiptoe. Karnage later tells me that when he has done the gentleman by Jodhpurs they sleep, off and on, for thirty-six hours. You may have noticed that I have just broken one of my rules.

Stretched out again on a bed and sleeping, I suppose, I have this strange dream. This poem I have written and I am reciting it to a group of Roman citizens. It ends like this: A wooden sagging is in my shoulders and wood is dogma to an infidel.

Those words I take from my dream exactly as dreamt. No meaning. No connection with anything. But in my dream they made sense. Houseman said that each man travails with a skeleton. Lagan had been booming about Wenlock Edge and the wood in trouble and then 'twas the Roman now 'tis I. Perhaps I was trying to say that each man carries within himself a cross, the shoulders the crossbar, the spine the upright.

Damned if I know. Or care.

Time passes.

We are back in the Abbey, the bar not the theatre. A lawyer, or professor of history, a bank-manager who is also a music-critic and who plays the organ in a church, two actors from the theatre, and Niall and Brendan and Karnage and Lagan. No Jodhpurs. No Maryanne. Maryanne I am never to meet. But Brinsley honours us by his entrance. Huge, stately, brown overcoat, wide-brimmed hat. Leaning on stick.

Karnage has confiscated your, or my, necktie of many colours which he is wearing with wild ostentation. Cleverly he conceals the coloured body or expanse of it under a modest pullover, then whips it out like a lightning flash to startle and dazzle each and every newcomer. Lagan says that he and Karnage will wear your necktie, week about, so that they will never forget me nor the voyage to Parma. I am touched. (For a second time I have broken one of my rules.) Leaving that resplendent necktie with them I know that as long as it lasts, and the material is strong and well-chosen, I will be remembered and spoken of in the land of my forefathers.

And Lagan has used his influence and Karnage is no longer suspended.

They go off to work together.

Times passes.

Curious thing, Brinsley says to me, but there are young fellows who say about me that I belong to a past time. I don't mean a pastime. But a previous period in history. But there is no time that is absolutely past, and little time in the present, it passes so quickly and, for all you or I or anybody knows, there may be no time in the future. Only eternity, we have been told. A most dismal idea. Imagine listening to (he mentions a well-known name), and God help and preserve him and lead him to a better and happier way of life, but imagine listening to him forever. So here's to the young fellows who think they know more than their elders. The total sum or aggregate or whatever you call it of knowledge, or whatever, in the human brain is always about the same. You might as well listen to your elders. You'll end up like them and nothing much accomplished. Lagan, though, is different. He raises his cap, mentally, to men older than himself. He admits that we have been here first and he knows that he is on the way to join us. Curious thing.

Time passes.

But whatever exactly did happen to Bealcú who broke his vows to the god, to the sun, to the wind. The poem I will read to you when I meet you, as arranged, in Washington D.C. My vows I have kept and will keep. All of the forty-one verses of four lines each I will read to you when you have the leisure to listen.

Conall Cearnach is safely back in Ulster.

Time passes.

If anybody in time to come ever reads this letter, found in a tin box in a hole in the ground on Kennesaw mountain, it may be said that it is merely a zany folktale from an island that once was, way out in the eastern sea. All parish priests and all that. And drink. Well, there are a lot of parish priests in Ireland and there is an amount of drink consumed. Apart from a curious crowd called the Pioneers. Not a damn thing to do with Dan'l Boone and the New River that runs west where so many rivers run east.

Here I give you a genuine slice, or bottle, of old Ireland, as I ate, or drank, it.

There may yet be worse things than parish priests in store for the new Ireland.

Time passes.

My money from home has arrived.

To Lagan I owe ten pounds. Not that he would remind me. In an envelope I fold the notes, and leave them, no message enclosed, at the counter in the front-office of his office. Way back behind, the machines are rattling for the morning paper.

Farewells I abhor.

So from the far shore of the Liffey I salute his lighted window and walk home to pack.

Peachtree, here I come.

By way of Cork city and Cobb and a liner over the wide Atlantic.

Look for my ghost on Eden Quay. Round the corner from the Sailors' Home ...   .

Benedict Kiely

NOTHING HAPPENS IN CARMINCROSS

Benedict Kiely's latest novel tells the story of a journey to his childhood home undertaken by Mervyn Kavanagh, a man in middle age who has been living and teaching in America. The wedding of a favourite niece takes him travelling back across the Atlantic and Ireland to Carmincross, the small town in Ulster where he was born. As he journeys towards this family celebration he repeatedly encounters people and events from his own and his country's past, while the constant flow of news of contemporary acts of terrorism and counter-terrorism invades his consciousness more and more insistently. Somewhere, it seems, the past and the present are bound to collide . . . .

'Even readers who know of Mr Kiely's comic gift from his previous novels may find it hard to see much scope for comedy in such material. Yet the first thing to say about *Nothing Happens in Carmincross* is that it is often brilliantly funny . . .'
John Gross *The New York Times*

'Written with zest and grace, humour and irony in a style that is totally individual . . . It must be read by everyone interested in Irish writing and the peculiar tragedy of the Irish situation.'
Kevin Casey *Irish Times*

'Richly, grimly funny . . . At its best this is a remarkable study of a man struggling to come to terms with the country he thought he'd left behind him and with his own complicity in the troubles.'
Margaret Walters *The Observer*

'I have been waiting for a novel as full of rage about contemporary Ireland as this one. And this is the book I have been waiting for.'
Frank Delaney *BBC World Service*

'[A] dark and compellingly troubled meditation on our contemporary situation. Read it.'
Terence Brown *Sunday Independent*

Jeremy Leland

BLUFF

Conor de Burgh is in retreat from life on his remote farm in County Clare to escape from his deep sense of guilt for his girlfriend's death in a plane crash. Here he has been raising livestock, is trying unsuccessfully to form a relationship with one of the Riordan daughters who are his neighbours, and is experimenting with a pair of wings with which he plans to take to the air like a bird.

His solitude is invaded by a number of women, each like yet unlike the others, who could all be the same person: Maggie McSweeny, a lawyer from Belfast, in hiding from sectarian squabbles; Dorothy Benson, a visitor from Australia; Josephine Grant, a terrorist hunted by the police; Inika Van Winken, a Dutch tourist; Nel Farrell, an investigative journalist on a Dublin newspaper, and, finally, Rachel Martin.

Conor, bemused, baffled and aroused, attempts to sort out the traumas of his past life in relating to these women who may be one or all; and in doing so has to come to terms with the real world he inhabits.

Maeve Kelly

NECESSARY TREASONS

When Eve Gleeson joins the women's movement in Limerick, she finds it is a largely disregarded concern. Young, naïve but grimly independent, she begins to work for a battered wives' refuge, and her increasing anger and pain at women's lot – especially among the ill-educated poor – is matched only by her growing frustration at the movement's limited resources and support.

Set against this is her relationship with Hugh. Twenty years her senior, he clearly sees in Eve the chaste and tender bride he has always wanted, and is baffled by her more 'modern' side and her growing resentment. To complicate things there are also his four possessive sisters and lonely ancestral home; and the attractions of unthinking, rigid matronhood begin to dwindle considerably while what Hugh calls Eve's 'hobby' becomes an issue of central importance.

'Maeve Kelly writes with a kind of bitter elegance ... Her descriptions of modern Limerick with its shoddy affluence and its comfortable contempt for 'social' issues are vivid and accurate.'

The Listener

'Ms Kelly's insights ... are shrewd, her style incisive ... A fine, provocative first novel from a writer already noted for her sharply individual short stories.'

Sunday Independent

Methuen Modern Fiction

While every effort is made to keep prices low, it is sometimes necessary to increase prices at short notice. Methuen Paperbacks reserves the right to show new retail prices on covers which may differ from those previously advertised in the text or elsewhere.

The prices shown below were correct at the time of going to press.

☐	413 52310 1	**Silence Among the Weapons**	John Arden	£2.50
☐	413 52890 1	**Collected Short Stories**	Bertolt Brecht	£3.95
☐	413 53090 6	**Scenes From Provincial Life**	William Cooper	£2.95
☐	413 59970 1	**The Complete Stories**	Noël Coward	£4.50
☐	413 54660 8	**Londoners**	Maureen Duffy	£2.95
☐	413 41620 8	**Genesis**	Eduardo Galeano	£3.95
☐	413 42400 6	**Slow Homecoming**	Peter Handke	£3.95
☐	413 42250 X	**Mr Norris Changes Trains**	Christopher Isherwood	£3.50
☐	413 59630 3	**A Single Man**	Christopher Isherwood	£3.50
☐	413 56110 0	**Prater Violet**	Christopher Isherwood	£2.50
☐	413 41590 2	**Nothing Happens in Carmincross**	Benedict Kiely	£3.50
☐	413 58920 X	**The German Lesson**	Siegfried Lenz	£3.95
☐	413 60230 3	**Non-Combatants and Others**	Rose Macaulay	£3.95
☐	413 54210 6	**Entry Into Jerusalem**	Stanley Middleton	£2.95
☐	413 59230 8	**Linden Hills**	Gloria Naylor	£3.95
☐	413 55230 6	**The Wild Girl**	Michèle Roberts	£2.95
☐	413 57890 9	**Betsey Brown**	Ntozake Shange	£3.50
☐	413 51970 8	**Sassafrass, Cypress & Indigo**	Ntozake Shange	£2.95
☐	413 53360 3	**The Erl-King**	Michel Tournier	£4.50
☐	413 57600 0	**Gemini**	Michel Tournier	£4.50
☐	413 14710 X	**The Women's Decameron**	Julia Voznesenskaya	£3.95
☐	413 59720 2	**Revolutionary Road**	Richard Yates	£4.50

All these books are available at your bookshop or newsagent, or can be ordered direct from the publisher. Just tick the titles you want and fill in the form below.

Methuen Paperbacks, Cash Sales Department, PO Box 11, Falmouth, Cornwall TR10 109EN.

Please send cheque or postal order, no currency, for purchase price quoted and allow the following for postage and packing:

UK	60p for the first book, 25p for the second book and 15p for each additional book ordered to a maximum charge of £1.90.
BFPO and Eire	60p for the first book, 25p for the second book and 15p for each next seven books, thereafter 9p per book.
Overseas Customers	£1.25 for the first book, 75p for the second book and 28p for each subsequent title ordered.

NAME (Block Letters) ....

ADDRESS..

....